I0739811

The Dew of Heaven

ANGELO PARATICO

Cactus Moon Publications

The Dew of Heaven

Copyright © 2016 by Angelo Paratico

All rights reserved. No part of this book may be reproduced or transmitted in any form or by any means without written permission of the author.

The characters and events in this novel are not a creation of the author's imagination. What likeness they may bear to persons or events, living or dead, present or past, is a likeness to reality.

Cactus Moon Publications, LLC
1305 W 7th. St
Tempe, AZ 85281
www.cactusmoonpublishing.com
info@cactusmoonpublishing.com

Creative Editor: Melissa Rupp
www.revisionsandedits.com

Cover Design: M. Carrigee

ISBN: 978-0-9975363-3-1

Prior works penned by Angelo Paratico

Poetry

Rendiconto Giovanile

Fiction

The Karma Killers

Black Hole

Ben

Non-Fiction

Storia di Castano Primo (with Alessandro Miramonti & Armando Torno).

Un Manuale Per Uomini Superiori (Confucius' Lun Yu)

Nuptialia

Writing First (with other authors)

Nero. An Exemplary Life (A translation from Latin of Girolamo Cardano's Neronis Encomium)

Five Centuries of Italians in Hong Kong and Macau 1513-2013 (with Gianni Criveller).

The Angel of the Lepers (a film jointly directed with Ciriaco Offeddu).

Leonardo Da Vinci. A Chinese Scholar Lost in Renaissance Italy.

Facts

In 1921 the capital of Mongolia, Urga, was taken by a White Russian-Mongolian army led by Baron Roman von Ungern-Sternberg. He freed the Bogd Khan from the Manjusri lamasery, after murdering most of the Chinese garrison in the process. A vicious pogrom of the resident Jewish community ensued; a native of Graz, Austria, Ungern-Sternberg shared several traits with his fellow countryman Adolf Hitler. He became known as the Mad Baron, and his men believed he was the reincarnation of Jamsaran, the Tibetan god of war.

In reaction to the actions of the anti-Bolshevik Ungern-Sternberg, some units of the Soviet Army invaded Mongolia, capturing Urga on July 6, 1921. The Mad Baron was executed on September 15, 1921 and after the death of the Bogd Khan on April 17, 1924, the invaders took over the territory and held it until 1990.

Ironically, it is because of the Mad Baron's intervention and the subsequent Soviet invasion that modern Mongolia is not a part of the People's Republic of China.

Stalin's henchmen razed lamaseries, burned libraries, shot thousands of lamas, smashed precious artworks and sacred relics; it was then that Genghis Khan's spiritual banner, known as the Khara Sulde - a steel trident with silver rings carrying the black mane of his war horse - disappeared from the Shankh lamasery of Ovorkhangai Aimag in central Mongolia, never to be seen again.

Part I

Behold, thy dwelling shall be the fatness of the earth, and of the dew of heaven from above.
Genesis XXVII, 39

Hong Kong Island:
Friday, September 2, 2011

Three old men were sitting in a flat on the twelfth floor of a crumbling building in Hollywood Road in the western part of the island of Hong Kong.

One of them, Ferdinand Montecorvo, nicknamed Mogul, closed the book he was reading aloud and fell silent as the clock on the wall ticked louder. The men were surrounded by shelves loaded with books and magazines, on top of which were several blue and white porcelain jars. Old posters of opera performances by Maria Callas with wording in Italian and English were pinned to the wall. Noon was approaching and on the RTH3 radio program's Morning Brew they were playing the songs of Anita Mui.

"You were damn right, Mogul. The diary of your father is quite something. Where did you find it?" Fatty Ng asked, clearing his voice.

"He gave it to me before dying," answered Mogul, "and since then I have kept it in a safe box."

"That's how your father met your mother. I would never have guessed. . ."

"This is not the most exciting chapter, I can assure you," added Mogul warily. He looked imposing, tall and with a bald head, like a Buddhist lama's. His tanned skin was crisscrossed by a fine web of wrinkles extending over his face and neck.

"Then why don't you carry on with the reading?" demanded Fatty sourly, repositioning his buttocks on the chair.

"This chapter is the only part which your profane ears can take," smirked Mogul, switching from English into Cantonese.

"Why, don't you trust us?" The other old man, Richard Chan, spoke with an unusually sharp voice. He was a man who did not mince words - one of the old commanders of the

14K, as the Hong Kong Mafia is known, and a master in the art of Chinese shadow boxing. He was over ninety years old but strong and lean like a bamboo cane.

"This is something going beyond trust," commented Mogul.

"Is it really that big?" Richard pressed on, rather sardonic.

"Bigger than you may imagine, bigger than all of us put together, a sort of Holy Grail, so to speak. . ."

"Holy Grail, eh? Some more tea, Mogul?" Fatty asked politely, playing the host, for the place where they were sitting was his home.

Mogul slowly pushed his cup forward on the marble top of the table. A gecko came out from behind the closet and ran along the wall, hiding under an oil painting representing a fiery-looking Turandot singing in front of Beijing's Forbidden City. Mogul stared vacantly at the wall and added, "I should talk to my grandson Marco first, and to my son Aldo."

"So even Aldo ignores all this? And what about Marco? Is he coming up here from Italy?"

"Yes, Marco will get here soon, even if he still believes I died before his birth."

"Ah, that grave in Happy Valley?" demanded Fatty, with a broad smile.

"Yes, that one."

"How old is Marco?" asked Richard, without lifting his eyes.

"Twenty-six."

After a few seconds in silence, searching for the right words, Mogul added, "Marco doesn't know the family history, for he grew up with his mother. He works for a bank in Italy."

"Pure like a lotus flower," said Richard, with a smack of his tongue.

"Right, but you know all the details of my story, Richard."

"Almost all, apparently," Richard said and looking straight into his eyes added, "I still cannot understand why you have given us only a part of the story. What are you hiding?"

Wanting to take a breath and break the mounting tension, Mogul stood up and went to the window. He opened it and let inside a waft of wind, but the air was overheated by the asphalt below, which was exposed to the sun. Only a small silvery strip of sea was visible through those decrepit buildings facing Kowloon. Down there, right over Possession Street, the British had planted their flag after having landed in 1841 and taken control of the island of Hong Kong.

The friendly voice of Phil Whelan coming from the radio announced a new Anita Mui song, this time in Mandarin instead of English, called *The Sheep that Fell in Love with the Wolf.* They listened intently, moved by the emotions radiating from her vocal performance, and felt their old hearts beating with passion for the Hong Kong that they had known but that had since vanished, like the singer who had died eight years before. It was midday, ghosts' time for ancient Romans, when all objects lose their shadows.

"I still feel that you are not treating us as real friends, Mogul," remarked Fatty, with lingering bitterness in his voice, and then he added, after an angry frown, "How could you treat us like this? This is like *coitus interruptus!*"

Mogul thought about it for a few seconds, but, still unconvinced, put his black book with gold letters stamped on the spine into his canvas bag and phoned the driver to pick him up. Richard did the same, and after exchanging a few words, they went down in the small lift, leaving Fatty behind. He closed the window and, when he was sure of being alone, placed a call.

"Yes, hey, Monsignor! Mogul has the book as you thought, and it should be about Mongolia. I'll call Beijing, they will be happy."

"First, we must get it!"

"Fine, then I'll be waiting for your instructions," Fatty said with a condescending tone.

"Indeed, they will be forthcoming."

"Mogul refuses to let us read more than a chapter but I am going to see his son, Aldo. I may try to arrange a business deal for him."

"Good. But we should be ready for murder this time if we want to stay on top of this game, if you know what I mean..."

Fatty put down the receiver and lightened off his ass. He pulled the fan's chain to stop it and went to give water to his two songbirds chirping in the next room.

II
Hong Kong Island:
Thursday, September 8, 2011, 8:00 p.m.

Aldo and Fatty met at the bar at the Foreign Correspondents Club on Lower Albert Road, a place close to Lan Kwai Fong. For decades, Fatty had been a journalist for newspapers and magazines, always in charge of the China desk. He was close to his seventy-fifth birthday and had a round, polished face, large belly, and white, abundant hair cropped short.

Because it was a hot day he was sporting a flashy Hawaiian shirt printed with coral-colored flowers, sneakers, and short chino pants. Even though he was improperly dressed for the club, sneakers were not tolerated there - the waiter made an exception with a wink and let him inside.

Aldo, Mogul's son, was working as a fund manager with his own office, in association with a large American investment company. After studying at Harvard, he had worked in New York and then returned to Hong Kong four years previously, where, with his father's money and the right connections, he had been able to start his own practice. He was tall, close to thirty-seven years, half European and half Chinese, with sleek hair and dark, bright eyes. To people who were not particularly close to him he gave the impression of being humorless and ambitious, the type of investment executive to whom wise and simple men would not lend a dollar, but who was otherwise capable of raising billions from scores of faceless fools.

That day he was wearing a dark Armani shirt, gray linen trousers, and handmade brownish shoes which were as shiny as mirrors. To Fatty, his actions were similar to Robert Kissel, an American who had held the same job and had been murdered in Hong Kong eight years earlier by his wife;

Fatty had known him fairly well since they had both been members of the same club in Clearwater Bay.

Same profession, same mold, Fatty disdainfully thought on seeing Aldo enter the main bar and stopped to watch him, standing close to the bronze bust of Richard Hughes, a maverick Australian reporter and writer who appeared as a character in some of the books by John le Carré and Ian Fleming.

After an aperitif, they decided to discuss their business later and since it was dinnertime, they walked down to the Sevva Lounge on the twenty-fifth floor of Prince's Building, on Chater Road. The panorama view was perhaps the restaurant's best asset, overlooking Statue Square, the pulsating heart of Victoria.

Fatty, old and shabby as he was, appeared incongruous among the many elegant and testosterone-charged young men who were filling the terrace. Since he did not give a damn about it, they were feeling uncomfortable and out of place - not him.

They ordered fried chicken with a bowl of jasmine-scented white rice and washed it down with red wine.

Fatty asked, "So, Aldo, how is Mogul?"

"He's still in Macau, waiting for his grandson, Marco, coming from Milan, he's pinning great hopes on him."

"Yes, he mentioned it the other day. Great guy, possibly. Are you perhaps a bit jealous?" asked Fatty with a laugh.

"Me? Why should I be? I have other things to concern me."

Touché! Fatty thought. *I was right. He is jealous, afraid of losing his influence over Mogul and being sidelined.*

A sudden rush of wind swept the terrace, sending napkins and nuts onto the floor and the waiters rushing to help rearrange the tables. Aldo poured some Chianti and said, "Now, getting down to business, I have to thank you, Fatty, for this great chance you are offering us."

"No need to thank me, it is exactly what they are looking for. When I can help friends to connect I am always at the ready. My Chinese friends need to invest in something more solid than swaps and futures if you know what I mean. Your Mongolian mining project seems to be a perfect alternative," Fatty answered, looking askance.

"And what do you think about the terms proposed by our firm, do they look favorable to you?"

"Not an expert; however, in Shanghai they seem favorably impressed by the idea," he said warily, "So they may sign a contract with you in the coming days, as I am under the impression they got the all clear from high above. That's all I know."

"Very well, then."

"Hey, Fatty, how are you?" A man with an appearance of nerves and agility was walking toward them.

"Hello, Alex," said Fatty, standing up to greet him. "Alex, may I introduce you to Aldo Montecorvo, the son of a friend. Alex is a famous barrister in Hong Kong, you may have heard of him."

"Far too generous," said Alex.

"Well, you defended Nancy Kissel, so you can't deny fame. I was thinking about her a while ago."

"Yes, but that story ended badly for our client," he said and added, looking slightly embarrassed, "At least the retrial was not our doing," and after exchanging a few more words about his last trip to Thailand, he moved away.

"Nancy Kissel's case?" inquired Aldo, looking puzzled. "What was that?"

"That was a *cause célèbre* here. You were still in the United States and missed it. The protagonists were an American couple - very rich and very spoiled - successful people with three wonderful children. They lived at Parkview, in Tai Tam, in a luxurious apartment. Are you certain that you haven't heard anything?" asked Fatty.

"No. Why should I?"

"Two books were published on this story and it appears they'll be shooting a movie. They were high-flyers, if such a thing truly exists, and yet in November 2003 she killed him, smashing his skull after lacing his milkshake with a powerful cocktail of sleeping pills. Then she wrapped his body in a carpet and hid it in a storage room. Once discovered she was arrested, tried, and sentenced to life imprisonment. During the trial the local newspapers published all the filthy details of their daily ménage. . .you know how exciting it is for salary-men to peep from the keyhole of the door into the bedroom of the rich and powerful . . . that sort of thing. She told the jury he was beating her, sodomizing her, yes, buggery - stuff that is becoming a common occurrence in the pornographic world, but back then, few spoke about it - and cocaine. With all the boredom of daily life, the easy money of an investment banker with few moral scruples and a strong sexual appetite. . . All Hong Kong was smitten, mesmerized, we were following that trial like zombies."

"Is she still here, in prison?" Aldo asked, a bit afraid of being put in the same category as Robert Kissel.

"She obtained a retrial on the basis that public opinion, driven by the media, was against her. She was portrayed as a sort of killer with eyes of ice, but in fact, she was only a wretched woman who felt lost and lonely."

"This does not constitute a justification for killing a man! What about the retrial?" Aldo asked.

"I believe that keeping her locked up for life will not change anything, the man she killed cannot be resurrected. Only Jesus can do that sort of thing and she has already paid a heavy price," said Fatty. "Women are like roses, you ought to take care of them, give them water every day, admire and worship them, put them under the sun. If left alone, they wither. She did not want to stay in Hong Kong, but he, Robert Kissel, received an offer from Merrill Lynch which

- as people say - could not be refused. He decided to leave Goldman Sachs and scrap his plan to return to the United States. About the retrial - in March this year the sentence was confirmed - she ought to spend the rest of her life behind bars in Hong Kong."

"Wrapping him in a carpet, what kind of plan was that? Impossible to get away with that!" commented Aldo.

"Spot on! You see, that was the plan of a desperate woman," Fatty said. "They had seen a movie together, *Unfaithful*, with Diane Lane and Richard Gere. Have you watched it? A fine example of how an adulterous relationship can destroy the lives of two ordinary people. A woman, with whom Nancy identified, who was bored with her life, had sex with another man. Many young people here are like them. They have little morality, no grand ideals, no inner beauty, no time to raise their heads to watch the tops of buildings, no time to smell the fragrances of a Sunday morning at sunrise. This is why we had so much interest in this criminal case, apart from the sex which is always a great attraction. They were talking about us. We had been murdered, and we were the murderers. Do you know Auden's famous poem about Hong Kong?"

"Afraid I don't have much time for poetry with my work," said Aldo, a bit wearied by Fatty's tirade.

But Fatty recited it anyway like a consummate actor, "Only the servants enter unexpected; their silence has a fresh dramatic use: Here in the East, the bankers have erected a worthy temple to the Comic Muse."

"Ah, the Comic Muse! Okay, got your point," concluded Aldo and, hurriedly changing the subject of their conversation, said, "Now, let's go have some fun!"

They drank the last of their red wine, went down to the street in the lift, and walked uphill towards Lan Kwai Fong. There, they briefly lingered in front of Milan Station, a small shop which sold bags. Even though it was closed,

Fatty admired a large Gucci bag in the shop window. Then they ascended a steep staircase until they reached Wyndham Street. Young men and women mixed in the middle of the road, divided into knots.

"There it is, at number sixty. Dragon-I. We should reach the podium; it's hidden behind the bamboo scaffolding," indicated Aldo, pointing upwards.

They took a short escalator up to a spacious terrace built like the deck of a ship with wide cages that contained live birds. They were challenged by two muscular guards who, with stern facial expressions, kept watch at the entrance of the bar. They had low foreheads and haircuts typical of the soldiers in the People's Liberation Army.

"Restricted entry, sorry mate!" warned one of them, lifting his arm.

"My name's Aldo. Is the boss in?"

The two stepped aside with a wary smile.

"Cool place!" exclaimed Fatty. "Never been here before, it looks good for young people like you."

The lounge bar was immersed in a red light coming from hanging lanterns. Two attractive girls entered after them, perhaps models judging from their height and deportment, walking arm in arm, like sisters.

"Mogul told me that you are well read in Italian opera and ancient Chinese history. Is it really so?" Aldo asked.

"I read and I listen. That's all. Yes, I love books but we should be careful. Books can liberate but can also kill," Fatty said, with a cynical smile.

"Kill?" Aldo asked, looking puzzled.

"Yes, and I could give you some practical examples if you want." Fatty was getting increasingly sarcastic. "The first example that comes to my mind is this - three years ago, Law Chi-wah, a local writer, editor, and Kung Fu master, died buried under his library. His crushed and decomposing body was found ten days later. It was indeed a sad loss for the literary community and another homicide committed by books. . . that time in complicity with gravity."

"Ah, I took you seriously, but you just wanted to pull my leg. . . that was just an accident!"

"Might be so but poor Law Chi-wah is really dead, because death is real."

"Hey, who drinks alone, dies alone!" Someone behind them had spoken in English. Fatty and Aldo turned to see the two girls who entered after them. They had silently moved behind their backs, playing on surprise, standing there and snickering at their little joke.

III
Hong Kong Island:
Thursday, September 8, 2011, 11:30 p.m.

"Please, do sit down," Aldo invited them to their table, pointing to two empty chairs. They gladly accepted. A waiter quickly put two more crystal glasses down and poured champagne for them.

They were wearing Japanese-style make-up on their faces, with a white base made of ground pearl, giving them a cadaverous look in accordance with the traditional Japanese fascination with necrophilia. Their long garments appeared a cross between Chinese tradition and Western high fashion, made of silk embroidered with golden threads. A thigh-high slit on the left side of their skirts gave them a glamorous look. These kinds of dresses were called *quipao* and had been forbidden in communist China because they were considered too bourgeois and provocative.

"Hey, stay cool, boys, we are not chickens!" said one of them, laughing, lifting her glass for a toast.

"Beautiful women are never chickens but always birds of paradise," noted Fatty dryly.

"I like that comparison, Betty. We mustn't forget it!" said one of the girls whose companion agreed, comically shaking her head. They looked a bit high. Then the music played again, harsh and metallic.

"Can you dance?" asked one of the girls.

They shook their heads.

"Oh, no man can dance anymore!"

"What's your name?"

"I'm Matilda; she's Betty. And you?"

"Fatty and Aldo."

"Have you had your dinner?" Matilda asked, getting half-serious.

"Yes, we have, and you?"

"We haven't, would you take us for a bowl of spaghetti? If you can't dance, what's the point of staying? If you came here to pick up nice girls, well, mission accomplished. You couldn't hope for two better chicks."

"They have a point," admitted Aldo, smiling and looking at Fatty. "We could go to Isola at the IFC. . . Do you want a bowl of noodles or a dish of spaghetti?"

"Oh, better Italian spaghetti. I know Isola, Pino is a friend, let's go there."

"It's midnight. Let me call Gianni, the chef, and I will ask him to keep the kitchen open for us," said Aldo, placing a call with his mobile phone. Gianni was no longer working there, he was told. Paolo from Gaia had temporarily stepped in and he promised to wait.

They paid the bill and descended onto Wyndham Street, passing in front of the old police station. On Hollywood Road, they went up to the escalator and used a side path to get across the Central Market to Connaught Road, then entered the International Finance Center. On the third floor was the Italian restaurant, with a terrace facing Kowloon and the tallest building in Hong Kong, the ICC tower, which was blazing with lights.

Only two tables were still occupied, and the waiters were preparing the restaurant for next day's lunch. Paolo welcomed his late guests and then hurriedly took their orders.

"A bottle of 1997 Banfi's Brunello of Montalcino and two dishes of spaghetti for our friends," Aldo ordered.

Two generous portions of pasta topped with tomato sauce arrived in five minutes and the two girls helped themselves. They had been starving but became very cheerful after toasting with wine and, not yet satiated, ordering two large slices of tiramisu.

"Now, my dear girls, could you tell us who sent you?" Fatty asked point-blank, staring into Matilda's eyes.

At first she pretended not to understand what he was saying but her laughter vanished at once.

"What do you mean?" she asked, "nobody sent us. You grabbed us, remember, or are you drunk already? It all began at Dragon-I a while ago. . ."

Fatty could not be fended off easily and persisted, "You grabbed us, not the other way around. Our meeting was no coincidence. Who sent you? Ken ilgeku nokur?" demanded Fatty, speaking Mongol.

Aldo was bewildered by the turn of the events, unable to understand what was happening.

"Are you crazy? Who do you think you are?" Matilda shot back, angry and feigning surprise.

"I am someone who knows what he's saying, and who is not as stupid as you may have thought."

"I think you are more stupid than you think, trust me, old man!" Matilda said with a cold laugh, while Betty bowed down her head. They weren't euphoric anymore, pretending to be drunk while in fact being quite sober.

Fatty suddenly seized Matilda's left arm, twisting it slightly up and revealing a small tattoo - a black trident over a sort of crown which had been engraved close to her armpit.

"I may be stupid, as you say, but explain to me this tattoo. Here, is it not a Sulde?"

Furious at being so roughly treated, Matilda wriggled herself free from his hand and jumped to her feet. She backtracked three steps, enraged like a wolf and baring her white teeth, and she yelled back at him, "I am covered in tattoos, you piece of shit! Do you want to see?"

She turned and picked up the edges of her *quipao*, pulling it up above her waist. She had no underpants and bared her nude buttocks; each side tattooed with a dragon. These mythological monsters, so dear to the Chinese people, were facing one another with angry looks. They had three claws per limb, a feature typical of the dragons which had symbolized imperial power during the reign of Kublai Khan, when Mongolia had enslaved China. The beasts were using their tails to stay balanced while swirling inside a powerful vortex and fighting for the possession of the flaming pearl of wisdom. This mystical pearl - which they were constantly hunting - would have been positioned somewhere in the proximity of the girl's vagina, as it was in that direction that these beasts were fixing their predatory eyes.

A waiter, walking a few steps away, was transformed into a statue of salt, staring at that living work of art with wide eyes. Aldo was also stunned by the freakish show. Masterly moving the muscles of her buttocks, Matilda enlivened the two beasts, which were seen moving their claws, alive and trying to grasp the elusive sacred jewel.

Full of disdain, she turned, dropping the edges of her dress and screaming at Fatty, "See that? And I have other tattoos. Let's go, Betty, these two impotent assholes don't qualify for our company. All lions at the circus but outside. . ."

Before making their dramatic exit, Matilda turned once more and shouted, "Kobegun noqai!"

"What was all that, and what was that foreign speech?" demanded a pale Aldo, slowly recovering from his amazement.

"Well, this is Hong Kong, Aldo. You spent too much of your time abroad. Hong Kong is a place apparently ruled by the law but we should rather say, by the laws," cryptically answered Fatty. He turned to the statue of salt, asked for the bill, and added, "Mongol, she was speaking Mongol. She called us 'sons of a dog'."

"Mongol, but weren't they Chinese? And what about that strange tattoo? Not the one on her ass but the one under her armpit?"

"No, they are not Chinese; can't you distinguish faces after so many years kicking around here? They are

Mongols, two Mongol Amazons." Fatty carried on with the explanation, "That tattoo is a *trisula*, that's what it's called in Sanskrit. Do you know what it is? Well, it has several names but generally it is known as *tug* or *bunchuk*. It is a trident with suspended mane hairs of a horse. The trident is the symbol of Shiva, the god of creation, protection, and destruction. When the dark mane of a horse is tied under it, it represents war. Mongols believe that when a chieftain dies, his soul resides in there. In that case, they called it *Sulde*, the soul. I published a paper on this subject many years ago, that's why I am so well prepared and I know a bit about these things."

"But what did those two Mongol Amazons want from us?"

"I don't know but I believe it was no coincidence they approached us. They had been following us since we came down from the Sevva. I saw them reflected in the window of that shop selling bags. But let's go home now, we need some sleep."

"Let's call a taxi. We'll meet again in the coming days to finalize our deal."

"Not my business, Aldo, you may go on talking with my Shanghainese friends without me. I am not in finance, I am in history and Italian opera, as you know," said Fatty, standing up and looking wearied.

IV
Macau: Friday, September 9, 2011, 11:00 a.m.

Zorig, the Mongol servant of Mogul, picked up the phone in Mogul's palatial villa on Macau's Praia Grande. He was in charge of security there and also helped as a driver.

"Ehi, Zorig."

"Who might be there?"

"Me, who else? You shithead!"

"Oh, yes, Fatty, now I recognize your voice. Just wanted to be sure, eh, eh. . ."

"Good boy, Zorig. Now you are sure. I need your help."

The burly Mongol sneered, "I knew you would need Zorig soon enough."

Zorig was a stout and burly man with very pronounced Mongol traits which made him look like a caricature of the cruel archetypical Mongol warrior with vicious eyes and strangler's hands. To some he resembled Odd-job, the actor who threw his hat with lethal effect in the James Bond movie *Goldfinger*.

"The work will be difficult this time."

"Well, try Zorig!"

"You told me that you know the combination of Mogul's safe box, right?"

"Yes, I do. But I don't want to steal from Mogul. . ."

"Hey, don't be so cocky with me, should we speak of your affairs with your little girls?"

"I thought we were friends," Zorig gulped, "but fine then, I will do it just once."

"Good, open the safe and take out a black book. It is written by hand in English. Take it to your friend Hippolytus at the Church of Saint Augustine; he will pass it to the Monsignor. He must read it. Then he will give it back to you. Do you see? Not stealing, just borrowing."

Zorig, somehow relieved, put down the receiver and silently moved into the sitting room. He knew the safe was under an old oil painting, but what he was not supposed to know was the combination. Still, since he had seen Mogul turning the wheels so many times he had memorized the code.

There was a large safe box, about a meter in diameter, in which the black book lay on top of a large yellow silk box which Zorig had never seen before; intrigued, he opened the lid and in it he saw, right there, Genghis Khan's Sulde. Three steel blades shone in the light of the morning, with symbols lightly engraved on them: the moon on the right and the sun on the left. The black manes under it were well combed and inserted in a depressed side, complete with the two silver rings tightening them. Zorig put it down and dropped to his knees, praying in Mongol. Still bewildered, he stood up, keeping his head bowed as a mark of respect, and closed the door of the safe, hanging the painting back on the wall.

Shaking with emotion, Zorig put the book in the paper bag of a famous cake shop of Macau and went out to where his car was parked.

The Church of Saint Augustine was not far away, right in front of the Dom Pedro V Theater. It was built in the sixteenth century and partially rebuilt later following a kind of messy Neoclassical style, with Tuscan columns near the entrance and strange Corinthian ones on the edges of the façade.

Zorig walked in, wary of that ghostly place. The colors inside the church were impressive: the ceiling was blue and the walls yellow and white. He crossed the nave towards the altar, where a famous statue of Christ as the Lord of Passion was lodged. The bloodied prophet was painfully carrying the Cross up to Golgotha.

Zorig was feeling troubled there. People in Macau spoke of the ghost of a young girl carrying her baby and the severed arm of a man. Mogul had told him the disquieting story and Zorig, being superstitious, believed the ghost sightings were real.

"The ghost's name is known," remembered Zorig worriedly, *"as Maria de Moura Vasconcelos."* And on the right side of the apsis was a granite headstone with the name engraved on it.

Mogul had told him that her body was interred there together with her infant daughter and an arm of her husband. Zorig remembered well Mogul's story, which had impressed him greatly. A pedophiliac love story that blossomed in 1706 between a frigate captain, Don Antonio Albuquerque Coelho, and a seven-year-old girl.

The child was a rich orphan in the care of her grandmother. The twenty-four-year-old captain, later a governor of Timor and Goa, fell in love with the pretty child and her money. But he had a competitor for the child's affection: Don Henrique de Noronha, who set up a trap to kill him. However, Don Henrique's men bungled the ambush, managing only to wound Coelho's arm, which was then amputated. Four years after their first meeting - casting aside the hostility of the girl's grandmother - they were husband and wife. Two years later, a baby girl named Agnes was born, only to die after a few days. In 1714, she delivered another baby, a boy who survived, but the young mother died shortly thereafter of an infection. They were buried together - Maria, Agnes, and Coelho's severed arm.

Zorig, because of his own personal sexual preferences, rather like those of Don Antonio Albuquerque Coelho, thought their love story was wonderful, but he wondered whether, if her ghost was returning, old scores hadn't been properly settled.

"I was expecting you, Zorig!" A feminine voice spoke in the dim light filtering from the apse window. Zorig jumped and felt his heart pounding in his chest.

"Father Hippolytus?" he asked hesitantly and then saw

the priest emerge from the shadows. Fr. Hippolytus was a very pale, thin, effeminate man with a bullet-shaped head. Zorig swore obscenely under his breath.

"Do you have the book?" the priest asked in his high-pitched voice.

"Inside this bag!"

The priest grabbed it with his delicate and well-manicured hands. Satisfied, he told Zorig, "You may come after vespers to collect it. Go now!" He turned, disappearing through a door on the altar's left side which led to a small office. Zorig watched him leave and then went out through the main door.

Hippolytus inspected the volume. The cover was in black leather with gold-tooled letters on the back, the words written with black ink on thick, high quality paper, certainly handmade - initially he thought perhaps in Japan but on one page he spotted the watermark of Fabriano, the most ancient paper mill in Europe. The handwriting was entirely readable, especially for him, since he was used to old documents. The first three pages were white and there was a warning to the readers, presented as an introduction. Hippolytus called a boy and ordered him to produce two copies.

That same afternoon he would hand them over to his superior, Monsignor Paulo de Andrade, who had shown an extraordinary interest in the book while warning him not to read anything. Not even a line! Hippolytus had never seen the Monsignor so impatient and excited before, and thus his own interest was aroused. Hippolytus was a fastidious and curious little man who thought it his right to read the book to understand what all that fuss was about.

He took the first fold of pages out of the copier, and while the boy was carrying on with his task, went back to the church and sat on one of the wooden benches under a pulpit close to the chapel where the Holy Mary, Mary Magdalene, and Mary of Clopas were wailing under an agonizing Jesus on the Cross.

He thought for a few seconds about old legends connecting Mary to Cleopatra and looked up at the suffering women, feeling contentment, no pity nor displeasure. They were just a baroque representation of nothingness.

Shifting on the bench, he thought that Jesus should have been more diplomatic and smart by holding back his fiery tongue. Preaching the Kingdom of Heaven was fine, but he was far too blunt - *I would have managed better than him*, he thought, pleased with himself and getting close to condemning Jesus to the Cross for a second time. He put on his glasses and carried on reading without regard for the words of his superior. Prohibitions just make things more exciting. *He told me not to read the book*, he thought, glad to possess such a witty mind. *Well, I am just reading a photocopy. Fuck all superiors!*

He went quickly through the first two chapters penned by Gino Montecorvo, Mogul's father, then turned to the other pages, where the real story began to unfold. He went on for about half hour, then was suddenly stopped.

"How is your reading, Hippolytus? Engrossing, exciting? Or is it perhaps disobeying my orders that excites you most?"

Hippolytus warily stood up and turned around. Monsignor Paulo de Andrade, quite unexpectedly, had entered the church, moving silently behind the benches, and he was now staring down at him from his imposing height with a face full of dreadful sternness, reminding him of a certain baroque picture of God on the day of the Last Judgment.

V
Macau: Friday, September 9, 2011. 2:00 p.m.

"I am sorry, Monsignor, have pity on this poor sinner," he stammered.

"You are a fool, a dirty fool. You will pay for this. You ruffian, you traitor! Was I not sufficiently clear?"

The Monsignor hissed these words and stepping forward, violently smacked Hippolytus's face with his heavy hand. The priest, recoiling and utterly humiliated, cried as though a child caught red-handed stealing candies.

The prelate snatched the pages from his hand and demanded, "Where is the rest?"

"There, Monsignor, follow me," Hippolytus squeaked.

They went back to the utility room where the copier had been installed and found the floor covered with ripped pages. The boy and the book had disappeared and the door leading to the road was ajar.

Paulo de Andrade took his mobile phone out of his black vest and dialed a preset number. "A bloody disaster, Fatty, they've stolen it!" he said crossly. Looking down at the trembling priest, he said, "You are an idiot! At least make yourself useful for something. See if you can put all these pages together."

He left him to collect the scraps and went out onto the road where he saw a boy sitting outside, visibly shocked, with blood dripping from his right ear. The Monsignor asked if that was the boy working at the copier and Hippolytus confirmed it.

"What happened, son? Have they beaten you? Please, speak. . ." demanded Paulo, putting on a seraphic smile.

"Yes, Monsignor. They hit me on the head and stole the book. I am so sorry, Monsignor!"

"Don't be sorry, it was not your fault. What is important

is that you are not badly hurt. We'll call a doctor and then you will receive a reward for your trouble. A thousand patacas. Are you happy now?"

"Yes, Monsignor. Thank you!"

"Now tell me who stole. . .who hit you on the head?"

"Two beautiful girls, Monsignor. Not Chinese, not Portuguese. They had strange faces and were talking in a foreign language. I tried to resist but one hit me."

"Good boy, good boy. Come to me and collect your money when you feel better. Now, can you walk?"

The boy nodded, "Yes, I can walk."

"Good, go down that road, it is the Calçada do Tronco Velho, there you will see Doctor Mercado's ambulatory, go and ask him to check your ear and give you some medicine. He can send the bill to my secretary. Good boy." He patted the boy on the head with his large hand and went back inside the church.

The Monsignor redialed the same number and said, "The two Mongol girls you mentioned to me. . .yes, they have it. Ask your people to find where they are before they leave Macau, check the ferry and the Portas do Cerco - they mustn't leave Macau! Yes. . .We also should take care of Hippolytus; he read the beginning. . .Yes. . . It's not that urgent, we can wait for a few days. . .I know. . .yes, I know. . . It was my mistake…because of his dirty life, I thought I had him under my control, but I blundered."

The Monsignor spoke again to the trembling priest, "They are looking for the two thieves. Now go back to St. Joseph's seminary and lock yourself inside your cell until I order you to come out. What did you find in here?"

"Monsignor, I read only the first two chapters and there is absolutely nothing in it, just a stupid Italian story. . . Things that happened more than a century ago. We have nearly half of it but some other pages have been ripped off and I am afraid that it will not be easy to patch them together."

"Shame on you! You have no idea how big is the hole in which you have sunk. Let me tell you, it's the hole that leads straight to hell, yes, to fire and brimstone! Give me the pages left and burn all the unreadable fragments!" the Monsignor thundered, feeling a new surge of rage because not only had Hippolytus read it, but he allowed it to be stolen.

"Oh, I am so sorry!" the weeping Hippolytus said, joining his hands and kneeling in front of his superior.

"Finish your work here and then lock yourself up in your cell and pray, pray, pray! I forbid you to put your nose out and to speak to anybody about this matter!"

Paulo de Andrade turned on his heel and walked out of the portal of the church, moving with slow, imposing steps. He felt his thighs rubbing against each other inside the cassock. At fifty, being six feet and two inches tall, and far above his ideal weight at 265 pounds, he needed trimming his expanding waistline. At the same time, to his faithful, especially simple women, he represented the classic image of the saintly and dedicated high priest. His heavy, black-rimmed glasses resting on his Greek nose added gravity to his hieratic looks.

In the sunny churchyard, he felt the need for a refreshing bath to wash away the sweat causing his vest to stick to his chest. Joao, his Chinese driver, was waiting in his black Mercedes parked in front of the theater. Paulo got into the car and asked to be taken to his villa at the Chun Tok village, on Taipa Island.

While in the car he went through some of the salvaged pages, but had to stop reading because the twists and turns of the road were making him ill.

VI
Macau, Taipa Island:
Friday, September 9, 2011, 4:00 p.m.

"Here we are, Monsignor," the driver said, after driving into the well-kept garden of the prelate's villa.

"Thank you, Joao. You may pick me up at eight tonight."

Paulo walked slowly inside where his cousin, Maria, an old spinster, was waiting for his return. He did not speak to her nor acknowledge her presence, but went instead straight to his bathroom.

While the tub was filling, he took the clammy garments, off, hanging them on a peg; they were stinking and wet. He had been sweating too much. He threw some perfumed salts into the water, switched on the Jacuzzi flow, laid down in the bath, and carried on reading. He left his telephone on the floor with the ringer at maximum level, waiting to hear when the two Mongol girls would be nabbed.

After some time, the telephone rang, and the Monsignor woke up with a start. The sun was setting, and the room was darkened by shadows. Paulo had fallen asleep but was unable to understand for how long; he had been having powerful erotic dreams and was remembering the sweetness of strange androgynous, celestial creatures in vivid detail. This was not the first time he had been buggering angels in sleazy dreams!

While grabbing the ringing phone, he thought of Goethe's Faust where Mephistopheles was distracted by the angels' derrieres, thus being deprived of seeing Doctor Faust's soul leave his body.

"They will not distract me," he thought, surprised that he could still be haunted by sweeping erotic dreams despite the tension in the past few days. He thought about visiting a massage parlor where he could relax a bit with some of those cheap, young prostitutes flocking in from China.

"Chastity is not for me!" he concluded, while pressing the green button on his phone.

"About time you answered the fucking phone! Damn! We have found the girls," said Fatty Ng, speaking Cantonese in a sharp voice.

"Good. And where might they be now?"

"One is dead, the other slipped through. They put up a strong resistance, three of our boys are in the care of a doctor."

"Poor girl! And is the book with the dead or with the living?"

"We do have the book. Two new copies have been made and the original will be returned to Zorig."

"Do it yourself this time. What about the body?"

"I have arranged for an honorable burial at sea."

"Is it the one with the dragons engraved on her ass you were talking about?" While he was asking, he felt his small brother getting harder, emerging from the foamy water.

"Oh, I see my little story made quite an impression on you. They checked her out, and she had several tattoos, but not the dragons down there."

"Good, then, perfect job. I would like to have a copy not later than tomorrow, for this evening I have an important Mass at the cathedral. Then the boys must take care of Hippolytus, but in a discreet and natural manner. You know what I mean."

"It is dangerous; do we really need to do this? You told me he had read a few pages, let it go. . ."

"It is not about the pages he read, it is because he knows that I am involved. He'll speak and blackmail us, and besides, I cannot suffer that little prick anymore!"

"Very well, sir, then tomorrow we'll fix this problem."

"You will give me the Xerox copies of the book tonight. Also, the one which has been treated, clear? I'll pass it to Richard tomorrow."

"Copies are on the way; you will get them tonight or early tomorrow morning."

Paulo de Andrade looked at his prick pointing skyward and thought it was high time for him to get a couple of young girls. He would book a relaxing massage in his favorite place, a discreet sauna parlor.

He stood up and began drying himself with a towel. He felt content and excited because he was living the life he had always dreamt. Power and intrigue - nothing could be more exciting!

VII
Macau: Saturday, September 10, 2011, 6:00 a.m.

Paulo had a particularly long session of filthy sex with three, not two, young Chinese girls - possibly underage - while watching Japanese pornography on a big screen for inspiration. He collected the diary's two copies while handing the original back to Zorig, who placed it inside the safe box at Mogul's villa. Paulo slept inside the sauna parlor for a few hours, woke up at six, and called his driver.

First, he left his own copy of the diary well hidden in his personal library at the Matteo Ricci House then he was driven to the ferry pier to board the first helicopter bound for Hong Kong. He wore a gray, clergyman's jacket, but he removed the white collar. With his black leather handbag, he looked like a respectable American businessman.

Once he landed in Hong Kong, he boarded a taxi and went straight to the grand villa of Richard Chan in Kowloon Tong. There was a small garden in front of it - a great luxury in Hong Kong - with a fountain of red marble from Verona.

Paulo de Andrade removed his sunglasses while facing the two Nepalese Gurkhas who were standing guard there and watched as they checked the contents of his briefcase. They let him pass the threshold, giving him a military salute.

The Monsignor moved into the waiting room. There was a very large and colorful Persian carpet on the floor, with a bulky, round, mahogany table resting over it, and a crystal chandelier lighting the windowless room. After a few seconds' wait, a door opened and a beautiful young lady entered. Paulo, on sizing her from the feet up, thought she was far too attractive and well-dressed to be a simple servant. She was in fact Blanchefleur Chan, Richard's granddaughter.

"Please, come in, my grandfather is waiting," she said and escorted the Monsignor into a dimly illuminated corridor with jade-green lights on the walls.

A long series of old gouache paintings of Chinese men and women lined the passage. They were clearly ancestors of the owner of the house and, judging by their varying attire and hairstyles, Richard's family stretched back a thousand years, at least to the Sung Dynasty.

Upon reaching a reinforced steel door she touched it slightly with her knuckles. A camera above them came alive, slowly rotating.

Evidently, thought Paulo, *the old man needs precautions.*

As an electric lock clicked, the girl pushed on the door, and it slid open smoothly. Paulo entered Richard Chan's studio while she silently withdrew.

Paulo's legs were trembling, and he was again copiously sweating, seized by an uncommon bout of anxiety. It was not fear but a strange malaise never felt before as if his body was no longer following his mind's commands.

Richard Chan was sitting behind a slender Ming-dynasty desk of Zitan wood. On the walls were paintings of the China Trade, known to collectors as *Chine de Commande*, the fruits of the artistic interactions between Europeans living in Macau and Chinese craftsmen.

If I suspected the old fool loved this trash, Paulo thought, amused by the quaint array of objects, *I would have fished something out of our church warehouses as a gift for him.*

On the far left was hanging a vaguely erotic reverse painting on glass representing a Chinese woman dressed in embroidered clothing, breastfeeding her baby on a canopy bed.

Richard's desk was clear of documents, with just a few calligraphy objects standing on it; an ancient ink stone, greenish in color; a porcelain water dropper; and a *bitong-*holder for brushes with a shining underglaze of sapphire-blue decoration.

Richard invited his guest to sit down. With a faint smile and a sweeping sign of the hand he said, almost apologetically, "a man must have a hobby."

Paulo's eyes lingered on the brush holder; a representation of quiet mountain scenery with a river and two anglers.

"An attractive piece, isn't it?" asked Richard, following Paulo's eyes and adding, "Transitional porcelain produced at Jingdezhen during the dynastic change from the Ming to the Qing. The Qing were Mongols. We Chinese had been beaten once more; trampled by the hooves of the barbarians' horses!"

"I am no expert on old porcelain but, yes, it looks nice." Paulo, still wet from cold sweat, took out a handkerchief to dry his face.

"Is it too warm for you in here? We keep the temperature at twenty-five degrees Celsius."

"No, it is not. This is my problem. I have had this damned sweating problem for a week. Perhaps I should see a doctor," said Paulo.

Richard nodded and asked, "Do you have the papers?"

"Yes, we managed to get the book and make a copy."

Paulo opened his briefcase and put a sealed plastic file on Richard's desk. Inside was a thick bunch of pages kept together with a steel spiral. Strangely, the paper gave out a yellow metallic gleam under the spotlight of Richard's studio.

Paulo swore silently and his sweating doubled. For the first time, he felt a strange sense of impending doom and dizziness. He collected his thoughts and said to Richard, "Sorry but they used old stock paper to produce this copy. Our dioceses are poor and we save on stationery."

"Never mind the paper. I hear there were unexpected complications, even though you and Fatty handled everything properly."

"Yes, Fatty tied all the loose threads."

"What happened?"

"Two Mongol girls. . ."

"I see. If there is another party involved here, then we are in danger," said Richard.

"I wouldn't bother. We have nothing to lose, have we?" Again, Paulo wiped his face with the handkerchief.

Richard thought his answer perplexing. "This isn't a joke. We all have something to lose unless you value your life like that of a mouse or a mosquito. I just hope you haven't made another copy of these papers. Has Fatty seen them?" He looked intently into Paulo's eyes. "The more people get involved, the more dangerous it is for us."

"This is the only copy, believe me, I am not a fool."

Richard kept on staring into his eyes, sizing him up, then he pushed a button under the table and opened the door. The same girl was standing there, waiting to show Paulo out.

"You may go, Monsignor. Your money will be deposited into your bank account. We'll let you know when we need something. Go on a holiday out of Macau, it will be good for you."

The meeting had been shorter than he expected and Paulo humbly answered, "Thank you, Dr. Chan. I will think about your advice." Following the girl, he stepped into the corridor.

Yes, I might take Richard's suggestion after all, Paulo thought. *A stay in Phuket for a month will do me good, but only after this job is finished. The money this fool is willing to pay is big, but not when all the complications and the risks are included. My copy of the book will keep me alive and could be a source of further money. I'll always be on top of this game!*

As soon as the Monsignor was out of the studio, Richard placed a call to Fatty Ng.

"I have a copy, Fatty, and now I have finally met this big *guailo*[1]. Your plan has worked fine but your Monsignor

---

1 Cantonese for *foreign devil*.

must have one copy too, how do I know? He was scared and nervous. He knows the importance of the matter we are dealing with. . .Yes, my years of experience tell me this. Otherwise I would be history already. I must tell you that this man, whom you seem to trust so much, looks just a bloody fool to me. Yes, we need to keep our eyes open. As you know, the Mongols are also involved. I think that this game is getting too big for us."

"Don't worry now, Richard. As Chinese patriots, we must play our part until the bitter end, right? This was our agreement since day one."

"Yes, but I still feel bad betraying Mogul. Have you spoken with your friends in Beijing?"

"Yes, of course, I spoke to them. Never mind if Paulo has a second copy. Soon this matter will be settled and closed forever, like a grave. We are not money-minded perverts like him."

"Then why did the Mongols get involved? I can only think of a leak in Beijing, or do you have a better explanation?"

"Yes, possibly a leak but we should take some risks. I just hope to get Aldo on our side, after all, his mother is Chinese, like ours. I have people coming up from Shanghai to speak to him," commented Fatty.

"About what?"

"A great industrial conglomerate owned by the PLA is willing to invest in his Mongolian mining project."

"We should not harm Mogul and his son. I have an uneasy feeling that this business is slipping out of our hands."

"I also love Mogul, don't worry, and my contacts in Beijing want a clean job, no loose threads, no noise, but also, no afterthoughts."

"So, you still think that we are dealing with an important relic related to Mongolia?"

"I've got to look at Mogul's book when you've finished it, haven't I? But I do suspect that here we are dealing with *the* relic, not just *a* relic. Mongolia's Holy Grail, as Mogul put it. The involvement of those two Mongol girls is a sign of this but we might get further confirmation by reading the diary. After going through it, please give me a call, then we'll talk again with our friends in Beijing."

"Fine, no harm in reading it. I'll call you as soon as I finish."

"Yes, please, and have a good and peaceful read."

As Richard put down the telephone, he had a feeling there was something wrong in the tone used by Fatty; he was normally more submissive. With a frown, he opened the file and went through the pages, full of excitement, thinking, *A secret, a great mystery here, under my nose. . .*

The pages were thicker than usual as well as dry and stuck together, so he frequently needed to put his thumb to his mouth to wet it. He went quickly through the first chapters about the war in Africa and Gino Montecorvo's departure to China, then sipped tea from a cup, feeling a strange and unusual bitter aftertaste. He called for an orange juice and saw that the next chapter was the one that Mogul had read to them the month before in Fatty Ng's flat, describing his father's meeting with a Mongol princess near Beijing.

VIII
On a flight to Hong Kong:
Monday, September 12, 2011, 6:00 a.m.

The lights of the business class cabin were switched on.

"Omelet or fruits?" asked the hostess.

"Omelet, thank you, and some coffee, please," answered Marco Sforza, pressing the button that lifted the back of his seat and stretching his legs. Being tall was always a problem on a plane.

They had left Milan's Malpensa airport the day before on Cathay Pacific flight CX234 bound for Hong Kong. Marco's mother, Elisa, had called him a few days before from Mantua, where she lived, asking him to go immediately to Hong Kong because there was a matter of the greatest urgency to attend to. His uncle Aldo would pick him up at the airport and explain everything.

That morning, Marco kissed his girlfriend, Clara, and hurriedly left. He called his father while in a taxi, headed to board a direct train to the airport in Milan's Cadorna Square. His father, a retired professional photographer, met his mother in Hong Kong in 1973 while working for the Italian magazine, *Panorama*. After a few months, they were married and settled in Italy, but they separated three years after his birth.

Marco had felt happy and excited to get back to Hong Kong and had asked for some days of vacation, a request granted by the general manager of his bank.

On the flight, he watched the movie *Contagion* with Matt Damon and fell asleep. After breakfast, he opened the overhead locker and took out a book on the history of Hong Kong to read.

"First time to Hong Kong?" asked the passenger sitting next to him, with a broad smile.

"Well, no, not the first time, and you?"

"I have lived there for more than thirty years."

He was a middle-aged man with a humble air.

"Are you here for employment or tourism?" The same man restarted the conversation after the coffee.

"A visit to relatives. And you, what are you doing?"

"Oh, I am in the rag business, shirts and down jackets."

"I know it's a crazy business. I have a friend doing it in Milan."

"Quite so. Fashion changes so quickly. Sometimes I think it was better when everyone was forced to wear only the garments of his own profession or social status."

"Ah, an interesting point, and when did things change?"

The man stretched his arms and with a sigh exclaimed, "With the French Revolution!"

The man seemed serious but closed his eyes and lay back on the seat.

Right at that time the hostess collected the trays and a red light signaled the passengers to buckle their safety belts. Soon afterwards the pilot announced the descent into Hong Kong. Landing was expected twenty minutes earlier than scheduled, at six-forty in the morning. The pilot added that the sky was cloudy and rain was expected.

The Boeing 773 descended over the waves, nearly grazing them before land appeared under the wheels and they touched the tarmac with an almost imperceptible whistle. A recorded message started immediately with the usual recommendations for the passengers, and after passport control, Marco collected his luggage and went out to the waiting hall.

The beautiful airport, designed by Norman Foster, was immersed in a bright light, like a cathedral built of crystal and steel. Marco glimpsed Aldo on a screen. He was beyond the doors, talking with two men who looked like peasants from Red China. He was wearing a pair of designer jeans, faded and broken, with a yellow shirt and a blue jacket. Aldo was his uncle, the son of his grandfather and his second wife, a former Miss Hong Kong finalist. They looked like brothers, in spite of Aldo's strong Oriental features and Marco's dark blond hair that he had inherited from his father.

They met at the end of a corridor.

"How was your journey?" Aldo asked, hugging him.

"Perfect. Look, I am sorry that you had to wake up so early because of me. Next time I will take care of myself."

"No problem. I had to accompany some customers flying back to Shanghai. But you look in good shape."

"You too, you haven't changed a bit since last time, eight years ago."

"Eight years, true! Already eight years, I remember I was on a vacation from New York."

"Aldo, do you have a car?"

"No, I took the train."

Aldo grabbed one of Marco's suitcases and they walked to the fast train connecting the airport to the center of Hong Kong. As soon as they sat down, the doors closed and the train departed.

"How is your mum?" Marco asked.

"She is well. She is waiting to join us for a breakfast on the balcony of our flat. And your mother?"

"She is also fine, thank you. Do you know why there was all this hurry to have me here?"

"I would also like to know," answered Aldo, throwing an absent-minded look outside the window.

"Really?"

"Yes, but we'll know shortly. We should be more patient."

"Something very mysterious, apparently. . ."

"We just need to wait."

IX
Hong Kong Island:
Monday, September 12, 2011 7:30 a.m.

Marco switched on his Blackberry and found a long, well-structured farewell message from Clara. She was dumping him with an email! He looked for a message along the lines of "I miss you", or "stay well and take care of yourself", that sort of thing; but no; she said she wanted to move on with her life, she was going to stay with one of her old acquaintances. "A friend and just a friend", to whom she had explained her predicament. She was sorry to have terminated their relationship in such an abrupt way but she hadn't the heart to talk to him directly before his departure and hoped the news would not affect him too terribly.

"Important news?" Aldo demanded, seeing him frown and concentrate on the words written on the small screen of the electronic device.

"Nothing, just something from a friend. . ."

Marco felt a weight had been lifted from his shoulders and was happy, not displeased. Later, he decided to send a message complying with the split and praising her brave decision.

"Good!" he thought, relieved, putting down the phone.

The train was moving at the speed of a bullet. They crossed the long bridge which links the island of Lantau to Ma Wan and reached Tsing Yi in fifteen minutes, then turned towards Kowloon where they made a second stop. Afterwards, they entered the tunnel which connects the Kowloon peninsula to the island of Hong Kong, then reached their final destination, Central Station under the IFC Tower. There was a short line of taxis waiting. Aldo told to the driver to drop them at number 41, Conduit Road. The old taxi driver had the air conditioning at full power and his radio was tuned to a channel broadcasting Cantonese music of the fifties. With his left hand, he engaged the first gear, and up the slope they went, finding the road jammed with cars.

"It's not always like this," noted Aldo.

"Is today special?"

"Ah, don't you know? It's the Mid-Autumn Festival."

"What is that?"

"Well, I spent most of my time at Harvard and in New York but my mother taught me traditional folklore. In accordance with Chinese folklore, tonight's moon will be the most outstanding of the whole year, reaching the zenith of its orbit. It's a time when the locals eat lots of moon cakes. You must have tasted them before: they are made from duck eggs, lotus seeds, and walnuts. Legend has it they were used in the fourteenth century to hide messages of rebellion against the Mongol invaders - small pieces of paper were inserted into the cakes, urging people to rise at midnight on the fifteenth day of the eighth moon and, furthermore, this is the year of the hare which is strongly associated with the moon."

"A hare on the moon?"

"An old belief is that the hare can only deliver its leverets when the moon is full, but there is also a connection with Lord Buddha. In the Lalita Vistara, one of his ancient biographies, there is a parable which tells of a hare which speaks to an old hermit."

"And what did the talking hare say?"

"If I remember correctly, the hermit was hungry, and he wanted to leave the mountain where he was meditating. The hare urged him to persevere, offering her own flesh as a meal. She was a good hare, wasn't she? Perhaps a bit suicidal. . . this will be the eighth moon, the harvest moon. A benign moon compared to the previous one which was the moon of the hungry ghosts."

"Hungry ghosts?"

"Yes, today ends the month of hungry ghosts," remarked Aldo with a wry smile. "At midnight, the doors of hell will close, and all the hungry ghosts wandering on Earth will depart. For a month, they have been able to enjoy free food, drinks, operatic music, and prayers. We hope that, satisfied and tamed, they will quietly return to hell where they belong, without lingering among the living. For this reason, on the streets, you see offers of food and cards burnt in their honor. Inside the temples, Buddhist sutras will be chanted, bells rung and offerings made. Then tonight all children will light lanterns in their honor. Yes, it will be a great farewell party for all the ghosts, forcing them to go in peace," concluded Aldo.

They traveled to Garden Road and turned left, engaging a steep ascent and reaching Conduit Road, a quiet street with several tall buildings. After about 500 meters, they reached number 41 and turned again to the left.

There were five towers in a residential complex called Realty Gardens, built in 1970. They proceeded slowly until they reached the last tower, named after the city of Vienna. Those buildings had been built after the demolition of an imposing villa, formerly owned by a rich, Chinese merchant family which has since become the Foreign Correspondents Club. Aldo picked up Marco's suitcases from the trunk of the cab and they took the elevator to the twenty-first floor at the top of the building. Aldo pressed the bell, and the maid opened the door, welcoming them inside.

The floor was covered with teak wood polished like a mirror, and after passing through a small corridor displaying the ancient Thai paintings illustrating episodes of Buddha's life, they walked into a lounge flooded by the sun which had by now appeared in the sky. On the walls hung two nineteenth-century oil paintings of Sicilian landscapes. Marco recognized Taormina as one of the subjects.

There were antique bookshelves full of ancient books and a Venetian chandelier made of blown glass hanging from the low ceiling. Sliding glass doors led to the balcony, looking towards Hong Kong Harbor, with ships and small barges crossing the bay. It was like the Canal Grande of Venice.

"Please, do sit down, Marco. I will ask for a coffee while the maid puts the suitcases into your room. She will unpack them and put your things into the wardrobe. My mother will be here shortly."

A CD was playing the soundtracks of James Bond movies. Shirley Bassey was singing *Diamonds Are Forever*. The air was crystal clear, and the sun illuminated the city, still wet from the morning rain. Far away in the background, tinged with the violet light of the morning, rose the majestic Lion Rock. The tip of the Kowloon peninsula was also visible beyond the bay, with the *Star Ferry* and the China-Hong Kong Pier, where hydrofoils were docked and ready to sail.

The balcony was full of flowers planted in large porcelain pots, and a round table had been readied for four people. The base was made of colorful majolica of Deruta, painted with lemons and grapes.

"Here is our dear Marco!" Aldo's mother Cathy exclaimed, stepping onto the balcony. She was an attractive lady wearing a salmon-colored satin robe.

"Cathy, you look wonderful!" Marco said kissing her on the cheeks.

"Thank you, my dear. We will serve breakfast shortly; we are waiting for Aldo and for another person."

"Ah, you have a guest, perhaps I know him already?"

"By name only."

"I will drink some tea and l will taste a slice of that apple pie."

"And Elisa, your mum, how is she?"

"She is well. Always busy with her charitable work."

"That is the key for staying young and healthy. We should

keep ourselves busy with good deeds. Here is Aldo with our guest; please, do sit down, Marco."

Marco saw Aldo coming out of a room. He was helping an elderly man with a bald head, following him with great care and holding his arm like a young priest assisting an old bishop. He helped him to take a seat, never taking his watchful eyes away from him.

The old man straightened up, looked at the landscape and after a deep sigh, exclaimed, "Fine place this, isn't it, Marco?"

Marco, surprised by the unexpected confidence, probed his memory trying to remember where he had seen him before. Some of the old man's traits were indeed familiar but he could not connect them to a single person. When the old man turned to the left, their eyes locked. They were grey, like those of his mother.

He reminds me of someone, a distant relative, thought Marco, but he was unable to focus on the swirling images crowding his mind. Then some of those images became sharper and clearer. At first he discarded them because they were absurd; the man he had in mind had been dead for a long time and although the drowsiness caused by the jet lag was still strong, Marco felt he knew him, but it wasn't possible. He felt his heartbeats increasing.

"Yes, you are right, Marco," the old man calmly said. "I am your grandfather, Ferdinand."

"My grandfather Ferdinand is buried in the cemetery," answered Marco. "I saw his grave with my own eyes!"

"That is a cenotaph, technically not a grave. Your grandfather Ferdinand is here, sitting before you, and he is not a hungry ghost who will vanish at the stroke of midnight. The story of my passing away was made up to protect me, your mother, and you."

X
Hong Kong Island:
Monday, September 12, 2011, 9:00 a.m.

Marco was disturbed and frightened by the revelation, yet he had to admit the man facing him was the same man in the photograph that his mother kept in the library.

"You should know, my dear Marco, today is the birthday of Ti Tsang, the king of the dark city, as we call the Hereafter. Ti Tsang is the winner of hell and a benign god. He has eighteen arms and in one of his hands holds the bolt which closes the doors of hell; in another he holds a pure jewel which reflects the light of the Buddha's teachings on the poor souls dwelling in darkness, full of fear. He can defeat the infernal powers using that bright jewel as a mirror to reflect the purity of Lord Buddha's doctrine."

"Father is always telling us tales of Taoist folklore," Aldo said, with a wry smile, perhaps wanting to reassure the pale-faced Marco. Marco felt the hairs lifting on the top of his head, as drops of sweat were running down his shirt.

"It is not good to talk about these matters today!" objected Cathy.

"You are right, my dear Cathy. And yet these stories, as you know, have always fascinated me. Anyway, let's have a quick breakfast, as we are finally happy to be together in peace and harmony. I believe Marco is tired - better for him to take a shower and then go to sleep for a while. This evening we will have a dinner at the old Mandarin Hotel and after that we'll go to watch a performance of Pekinese Opera. Then, at midnight, you may return here while I will go . . .oh no, not back to hell," Mogul laughed and added, "Well, not yet. I will return to Macau and we will meet there a few days later. My dear Marco, now that I look at you at such close range for the second time - the first time you were just one-year old when I visited Italy incognito - I can say that you look better in the flesh than in the pictures your mother sent. After a few days, you will know all you must know."

Once he had completed that surreal breakfast, Marco went back to his room, and before taking a shower he phoned his mother. It was three o'clock in the morning in Italy but she was still awake, waiting for his call.

"Marco, is all well?"

"Rather well, yes . . ."

"I know but please don't be upset; it has been never easy, even for me. You will understand. It is better that we don't discuss such matters on the phone."

"Mum, are you afraid of phone tapping?"

"I cannot discount that. Have you called Clara?"

"Yes, done already," Marco lied.

After his shower Marco tried falling asleep but it proved impossible. His heart was still pounding faster than usual. He switched on the television and watched one of two stations broadcasting in English until six-thirty then they prepared to leave. Mogul was walking with the help of a stick, wearing a well-cut, elegant suit of pale gray flannel combined with a regimental tie, dark blue with red bands, and a white handkerchief inserted into his breast pocket. Their driver awaited them near the elevator and lent a hand to get Mogul into the back seat of a Jaguar with the registration plate 9999, a very much-desired number in Hong Kong where *kau,* nine in Cantonese, sounds like longevity.

The car turned behind the buildings, heading to the old Mandarin Hotel on Connaught Road, where they had reserved a room in their famous Chinese restaurant on the twenty-fifth floor.

After they had settled down, champagne was served. A dozen people were sitting there, all close friends and relations. At the end of the table, Mogul beat a chopstick over his glass, catching everyone's attention, and stood up to deliver a short speech.

He officially welcomed his grandson and spoke about the future, saying that unforeseen accidents excepted, this would be their last festival together. Cathy had tears running down her cheeks. Marco's impression was that he was really planning to vanish with the ghosts at the stroke of midnight. Marco was puzzled and could not grasp the meaning of that speech but thought Mogul was joking because he pronounced those words without betraying the slightest emotion, as if talking about another person, not about himself.

Then he announced dispositions for running the business of the family, like a manager about to retire and leave the tab to a new generation of directors. Marco guessed that, with all the years weighing over his shoulders, Mogul thought it best to be ready for the worst and, probably, this would even have a propitiatory effect.

Mogul concluded with the words, "Marco had a little shock this morning and I do apologize for that but I do know that he is a strong man. During the following days, he will have to be resolute and steadfast in all his endeavors, for danger and responsibility will weigh heavily on his shoulders, not only on those of Aldo. I have watched his progress and I can tell you this much: My grandson is a brave and honorable man!" He smiled at Marco and added, "I welcome you into our business as a bright and honest man." Everybody applauded. Only Aldo looked askance and raised his glass in a toast to Marco.

It was a great supper, worthy of the occasion. They tasted the rarest specialties - Abalone, Siumai, and Wagyu beef - and by eight-thirty moved to the lobby where the old Italian hotel manager, on spotting Mogul, went to greet him, calling him James.

They went back to their car and took the road to

Kowloon, going through the Western Tunnel in the direction of Tolo Bay. A benign yellow moon looking like the yolk of an egg smiled down from the clouds, lighting the air. In some of the crowded estates on the roadside, they saw scores of children playing with multicolored lanterns.

"Where are we going now, grandfather?"

"You can call me Mogul, Marco. Perhaps one day you and Aldo will also carry my nickname. What do you say?"

"You are the only Mogul, father. And you will always be," intervened Aldo.

"Thank you, son, but our little dynasty should continue. Tonight, we go to a magnificent place reserved for privileged persons like us - Plover Cove. Marco, do you know Pekinese opera?"

"I don't know anything about it, sorry, but I once saw a Cantonese opera performance, and frankly speaking, found it tedious."

"It is not like Italian opera where the words are also part of the melody. You should understand Chinese. Do you intend to study Chinese?"

"Do you think that it is important?"

"Absolutely, and you should begin tomorrow morning. Better concentrate on Mandarin, forget Cantonese. I should have asked your mother to give you some lessons."

Marco pursued his line of thought, asking, "Mogul, I couldn't understand what you were saying earlier. Why were you talking about leaving soon? What did you mean?"

"You will understand next week after reading a special diary. If my time is over and my mission accomplished, why linger longer on this shore?"

"I have just found you and I am losing you again?"

"No, not so soon, not completely. . ."

"Mogul, please, stay alive until the end of the world!" Aldo exclaimed, rather emotionally.

Mogul looked at them, moved by their tender affection,

and said, "I have to go, my dear boys. My world is coming to an end and I feel that even my friends are deserting me."

They reached their destination in about twenty minutes. It was a poor fishing village. They entered a house with chipped walls, squeezed next to other buildings in great disrepair close to the beach. It had possibly been used as a hangar for the construction of fishermen's ships in the past. It felt as though they were inside a large gymnasium, with a stage covered in shiny red silk satin erected at the far end.

Around fifty people were already assembled there and a young lady was welcoming them. When she saw Mogul, she headed straight for him, "Sorry Mogul, my grandfather could not make it tonight. He is not feeling well and Fatty just phoned to say that he will miss this year's performance."

"Oh, I am sorry," said Mogul. "I hope it is nothing worrying. Blanchefleur, may I introduce to you Marco, my grandson who arrived today from Milan, and of course you already know my son, Aldo. Blanchefleur is the granddaughter of Richard Chan."

"It seems just a slight indisposition, nothing serious," Blanchefleur said and added, while shaking Marco's hand, "my grandfather will be fine soon. So very nice to meet you, Marco!"

Marco was impressed by her charm and beauty. Her English was perfect. She was dressed in the style made famous by the local stylist Shanghai Tang, looking like a slender cover girl. Her face had faint Western traits but strangely, her eyes were of a deep turquoise color with a violet hue, like those of some exotic cat.

"Come here, Marco. Let's sit, do stay close to me," said Mogul, using a warm tone of voice. "I want you to remember her grandfather, Richard Chan. He is a very influential man in Hong Kong, even if he is ninety-years old. Among us, age still carries weight. Here, here, let's sit, I will explain to you what happens on stage. Aldo, please sit on the other chair over there."

With a grimace, Mogul fell on an armchair reserved for him. He felt tired and with his hands massaged a hurting leg.

"What about tonight's opera?" Marco asked.

"It is a well-known piece of the Pekinese repertory. The title is *Yangmen Nujiang* and it is about the women generals of the Yang family, a sort of historical drama divided into several episodes and set at the end of the Song Dynasty, in the twelfth century. Northern China had been invaded by a Mongol race, the Liao. They killed the male members of the Yang family. The remaining women, not wanting to abandon their homeland, defeated the enemy under the command of their centennial matriarch. The actors are all from China, and I guess they are the best available. Richard paid a small fortune to offer us such performance, so it is a pity he couldn't make it here. Look, the actors are getting on stage!"

The generals had four flags planted on their backs and were moving with firm steps to the rhythm of tambourines and wooden castanets. Women and intellectuals moved with short steps and cast their eyes chastely down. Their costumes were magnificent, made with gold and silver embroidered silk. Their faces were heavily made up to conceal that they were men. Following an old tradition, the feminine roles were taken by male performers who sang in falsetto. The orchestra was composed of Chinese violins called *huqin* with two cords and with guitars having three cords, as well as gongs and flutes. They played loudly, provoking a deafening clatter that made the glass in the windows shake. It was a small band of musicians, placed at the right side of the stage, who underlined only the most dramatic moments of the story.

"This type of opera has a recent history," explained Mogul, whispering to Marco. "It was created for the celebrations of the eightieth birthday of the Qianlong

Emperor in 1790. These performances were suspended during the Boxer Rebellion, when all the theatres of the capital were burned down by the mobs. In 1963 this happened again, because of Jiang Qing, Mao's wife, who banned all the ghost dramas, as they were then called. Deng Xiaoping, a great fan, resurrected them in 1978, thus marking the end of the Cultural Revolution."

"Mogul, does this story represent historical facts?"

"Well, yes, at least partially. It is the story of the mettle shown by the twelve mothers, wives, and daughters of the Yang family. They wore cuirasses left by their dead men and led the army at the battle of Jinshatan. This will be a reduced version summing up all the best parts of the four episodes and will last only an hour. Nothing to worry about, although if you are not able to follow the words, it may be boring."

"Is the drama set in Beijing?"

"No, the Chinese capital at that time was in Kaifeng."

The mastery of the musicians and the actors in their splendid attire were working a miracle, breaking all linguistic barriers and bridging the cultural and temporal divide: Marco was not bored at all, even if his eyes were lingering more on Blanchefleur than on the actors on stage. Twice their eyes met. The first time she looked away, but the second time, she smiled warmly back at him.

At the end of the performance there was a rapturous applause. Sweets made of rice and nuts were offered with warm wine from Shaoxin.

Blanchefleur approached Marco to ask if he had enjoyed the show. Then they drifted apart, mixing with other people, but attracted by a magnetic force, came back together. She spoke flawless English with an Oxonian accent. She fascinated Marco. She was different from the other young girls, not just because she was taller with finer features, but because she belonged to a different world. They exchanged a few more words, and before they parted, she dropped a perfumed calling card into Marco's pocket, wishing him good night and whispering into his ear, "If you call me I will show you some mysterious corners of Hong Kong which no one else could show you."

When everyone was getting back to their cars to return home, Aldo's phone rang. It was Fatty, who told him that after his meeting with the investors from Shanghai and the signing of a contract for the mining venture in Mongolia, they had changed their minds and were no longer willing to honor what they had guaranteed.

Aldo, stunned by the news, became agitated and asked Fatty why they had changed their minds. He was extremely upset because he had placed an order for their shares that morning and paid a deposit with money he had borrowed from the bank. A huge amount.

XI
Hong Kong Island:
Tuesday, September 13, 2011, 9:00 a.m.

"Are you awake, Marco?" asked Aldo, looking through the door.

"Good day, Aldo. I have been awake since four o'clock. I am afraid I have not yet recovered from the jetlag. Not even two pills of melatonin helped, or perhaps it was that girl that we met last night, Blanchefleur Chan. I think I dreamed of her."

"Nothing pornographic, I do hope," Aldo said with a smile, "Blanchefleur is Richard Chan's favorite grandchild. A very attractive girl indeed, but if you want my unbiased advice, I believe she is like an edelweiss. . ."

"And what does that mean?"

"I mean that you would have to risk your neck to pick her up and then would realize that the trouble and the risk weren't worth it. They say she is very moody. . ."

"All attractive women are. The sole exception was, perhaps, Cinderella."

"You say that because you never met Cinderella after she married her Prince. Who knows? Perhaps she mistreated the servants when in a bad mood!" Then, turning serious, Aldo added, "If you like, we can have a coffee and I can take you out. It's nine o'clock. I need to see Fatty."

"Oh, then I should get up immediately," Marco answered, lifting the bedsheet and jumping out.

The house was empty, and they sat close to the kitchen. The large blades of a ceiling fan were moving slowly, refreshing the humid air.

"Is grandfather gone?" Marco asked.

"Mogul?"

"Ah, sorry, he is your father. OK, let's call him Mogul."

"He left for Macau early this morning. He owns a junk called *Pantelleria* with a crew of two men. Are you still wondering about what he told you yesterday?" asked Aldo, looking into his eyes.

"Well, I have to admit, yes, it was something unimaginable for me. My mother never mentioned anything."

"I received stern warnings from a young age never to mention Mogul to other people. My dad was a businessman called James. But I guess we will understand more when we know the beginning of the story. One shock at a time!"

"There are still so many things eluding me. . ."

"Me too, and they could be more than what we both think. You heard what Mogul said last night, he wants to see us and tell us the full story."

"When?"

"It's already fixed. We will be going to Macau tomorrow. Don't arrange any other appointments; we shall sleep over there, returning on Thursday morning."

"Well, I am impatient to see him again."

"What is your program for today?"

"I have nothing to do, I am totally free. Perhaps I should give a call to Blanchefleur. What do you say?"

"Ah, I see, you have been bewitched. Please do listen to me, forget her, it is better for both of you. With her family one needs to be careful, you don't know. . ."

"I accept what you're saying but with little enthusiasm," a crestfallen Marco answered.

"Today we can take a stroll in the city."

"If you are already engaged, I can find my own way around. I can manage by myself."

"Today is a festive day and I am at your service. I just have a big headache to tackle but that's why I need to see Fatty. You will like him, strange guy but trusted by Mogul."

At eleven o'clock they went down to Conduit Road,

descending to Sheung Wan. The sun was blazing and the humidity in the air was high, even if a light breeze was somehow mitigating the unpleasant dampness. They turned around an old colonial building, the YMCA, once a military hospital, and entered the Man Mo Temple for a quick visit. It was crowded and on the road two buses were parked, ready to pick up Japanese tourists. They turned left on Upper Ladder Street, known to all Chinese antique collectors around the world as Cat Street.

"Have you ever been here before?" demanded Aldo.

"No, never. I can see a lot of shops selling junk."

"There are even more on Hollywood Road but here we should meet Fatty, his flat is down there. I understand little about antiques but he is a real expert."

After five minutes, Fatty appeared, walking slowly in their direction. He was wearing sandals, short khaki pants, and his usual Hawaiian shirt worn loose over his wide waist. He sported a pair of large, dark sunglasses and looked like the actor Jack Nicholson.

"Good day," he said, shaking hands. "Ready for a tour into the past?"

"Aldo was telling me you are a great expert."

"I was but now I am just a retired man without a retirement pension."

Aldo interjected. "He is just teasing you. He doesn't need a pension. If he wants money, he just needs to sell one of his ancient pieces. He could go on for months."

"The point is that I don't want to part with any of them. A true collector dies poor but content."

"Collector of what?"

"Assorted things, except money!"

They laughed and walked up the road, cluttered with stalls and shops placed at the base of damp buildings. Fatty took Aldo aside while Marco went ahead. "I am sorry for what happened, Aldo. They called me last night. They said they found something wrong in the contract. The money was already approved but for some reason, the division head vetoed the deal. You know how China is."

"Ok, that's what happens in China, but now I am in trouble with my bank."

"Did you order the shares already?"

"Yes, exactly the large amount they demanded. We may have to sue them for breach of contract."

"Don't be stupid, they are a branch of the PLA. Who can sue them? Not even Jesus!"

"Then, you tell me what I should do!"

"Are you ready to settle for a compromise?" demanded Fatty, holding his arm tight and looking into his eyes.

"Yes, I am. If I cannot solve this mess, I'll be ruined anyway, I did stake my ass on this deal."

"Let me call them, I know a retired general who can change water into wine."

"That's easy. . . not sticks into snakes?"

"I do hope so, but I can't guarantee."

"Oh, thank you, Fatty!"

"Don't say thank-you now, perhaps later you will curse me."

Fatty went ahead and spoke to Marco, an effortless about-face into a cheerful mode. "See, this was a zone of brothels and opium dens after the last war. Now we have this stuff. It can be described as a gate that leads into the afterlife. Sometimes I imagine a tent at the back of one of these shops through which we could pass and travel back in time."

"Sorry, what do you mean?" Marco looked puzzled.

"I mean that here we can find artifacts created 3000 years before the birth of Christ. Artwork owned by people who do not exist anymore, but thanks to these shops, are still lingering around. This, after all, is a spirits' road and precisely because of this reason we have this strong feeling, or better say, illusion, that immortality is close at hand."

"But is all this stuff really ancient?"

"No, absolutely not. They are nearly all fakes. We can say that ninety-nine percent are fakes, and a large part of the remaining one percent is worth less than a farthing. We need to be educated, and we need to know what to look for. For instance, that green container over there is two thousand years old, but it's worth nothing - not attractive, not even rare. . ." He pointed his finger toward a window, "That pot on the left is a fake. The bowl on the right is a copy costing only a few coins."

Fatty entered a shop, small in spite of its name, Giant Antiques. On the ground floor, they saw shelves with visibly fake articles. A minute old man sat at the bottom of the room reading the program for the next horse races but as soon as he saw Fatty, put it down and stood up, smiling courteously and signaling ceremoniously to go to the upper floor. They ascended by a small wooden staircase and there they saw pieces laid over green shelves, protected by glass.

"This gentleman has excellent pieces. They are guaranteed, with reasonable price tags," stated Fatty. "These are fat ladies from the Tang Dynasty. You see, Marco, that was the ideal of feminine beauty during those times: a plump and ruddy wife was in the dreams of every man. Today we send them to the gym to lose weight! Here are the same women playing polo, riding ponies."

"To which epoch do they belong?"

"Tang, as I said, about eight centuries after the birth of Christ. That was a period of great magnificence for China, while the remainder of the world was sinking into obscurity, China was the richest, most highly cultured country on the planet with the highest per capita income. The government had a steady income from a value-added tax applied to salt, everybody needed salt but the supply was tightly controlled and regulated. We exported silk, tea, and manufactured articles along the Silk Road from Ladak into Afghanistan and by sea to Indonesia, the Philippines, Arabia, and Egypt. All the silver of the world flowed into China while the West was greatly impoverished. A bit like today. Europe and the United States spend too much and China saves too much. India attracted gold and China, silver, which provoked various financial crises in the West, but you could not immediately realize that the root cause of the problem lay in the drainage of precious metals flowing east. It was as if China had taken up the silver thread and begun to roll a ball. The same crisis presented itself again during the eighteenth century, and to balance the books, they found the perfect solution - opium and military aggression!"

Marco was attracted to a large blue and white dish, about seventy centimeters in diameter. He thought it would cut a splendid figure when hung above the fireplace in his home. Fatty, with a surge of collector's passion, took it into his hands and described it to Marco.

"This dish is made of white, milky porcelain, with dark figures of deep sapphire blue. On the edge, we see twelve storks in flight with their wings opened within clouds and at the center are the three friends of the winter: the plum tree, the bamboo, and the pine. This is the traditional representation of resilience by intellectuals in times of hardship because those trees are the last to wither in a harsh winter."

Fatty took it into his hands and observed it at close range, using a magnifier from his pocket. He turned it upside and observed the foot, concentrating on the point of union between the glaze and the biscuit.

"The bottom never lies, as with women!" Fatty exclaimed and went on, "The intensity of the degrading color and above all, the twisted shape of the pine tree which takes the form of the character longevity, gives away the dating, even if it has no reign mark. This piece belonged to the Ming Dynasty, more precisely to the period of the Jiajing Emperor.

The cavetto is a bit recessed inside and the blue under the glaze has penetrated the paste. All marks, including the free flowing of the painter's brush, indicate this is not a copy. That sovereign reigned from 1522 until 1566. He was an eccentric Taoist and therefore the imperial kilns had no choice but to adapt to his peculiar tastes. This seems more than a dish; it is a charger, a tray. It was produced and sold to serve meats and vegetables. The symbols communicate longevity, communality, and resilience.

These are all unique pieces, even though they were chain-produced. This may have passed through as many as forty different hands. Every craftsman specialized in only one operation which could be painting trees, or birds, or edges, and were basically left free to improvise within certain limits, especially when no reign mark was applied. Pieces of such dimensions were exported in large quantities on the maritime Silk Road. I believe there are a couple of similar items at the Topkapi Serai Museum in Istanbul, even if these symbols are typically Chinese; therefore, the leading customer base of these pieces had to be the Chinese people, or Sinicized barbarians, perhaps in Thailand or the Philippines. Do you like it?"

"It's magnificent!"

"Indeed a miracle that it has reached us in such good shape," then added, "No restorations, will you be interested?"

"Yes, greatly but I can't afford it. I guess it costs a lot of money."

"Not easy to give a fair valuation of such kind of pieces. It all depends on how much one desires them. The price for such artwork can vary from 5,000 to 20,000 US dollars; it depends."

"That's well beyond my meager means."

Fatty summoned the owner of the shop and using a friendly voice asked some questions in Cantonese. While talking to him, Marco looked around, studying other pieces of beauty and antiquity on display. He turned behind a small wooden desk used by one of the shop's partners, absent at the time. The drawer was partially open and Marco's eye caught some old photos with officers in uniform and the Forbidden City in the background.

Since Marco had excellent eyesight, he could read the heading of a newspaper cutting written in Italian. It was the first page of an old edition of the *Corriere della Sera*, an Italian daily newspaper, speaking about a murder, with the words *VITO MODUGNO* in capital letters. The name sounded new to Marco, even if the surname Modugno did belong to a famous Italian singer, Domenico Modugno, who died in 1994.

Fatty looked at Marco suspiciously and because of this he moved away, not wanting to appear indiscreet. Then the small man took the porcelain piece and began to wrap it in white sheets of rice paper.

"Why is he wrapping it?" Marco asked, alarmed.

"He says he wants to give it to you as a gift. He knew your great-grandfather, Gino. He will have it delivered to your house. You don't need to pick it up now."

"But how much does it cost?"

"For you, nothing. . ."

Aldo's telephone rang. He answered, stepping away from them, and after exchanging a few words in Cantonese, he said, "Sorry, but we should go by my office. Two of the girls are there today. We have an emergency and they want to see me now. Let's thank the kind owner of this shop and Fatty for his historical presentation. We must get a taxi."

Aldo shook hands with Fatty. "Sorry, Fatty. It's about what we discussed. . ."

"Don't worry, Aldo, business first," Fatty answered with nonchalance. After they boarded a cab, he walked back to his flat, but on the way, he made a call on his mobile.

"Yes, Monsignor, he's gone back to his office. He's going to get fucked by his partners. We have him by his balls!" Fatty gave a cold laugh, "We'll talk later about this matter."

XII

Hong Kong Island:
Tuesday, September 13, 2011, 1:00 p.m.

Aldo asked the taxi driver to drive them quickly to the Central Plaza in Wan Chai. The cab traveled up Arbuthnot Road, then down Garden Road, passing alongside the new scat of the government at Tamar.

They went into the Central Plaza building, a triangular granite skyscraper surrounded by imposing buildings and hotels. The escalator took them up to the marble podium, where they entered an elevator. It was swift, despite the thick marble slabs lining the interior. It ascended to the mezzanine and to another elevator, which took them to the sixty-second floor. An aluminum plate bore the name of Aldo's company engraved in red letters: *Little, Montecorvo, & Down Limited*.

The windows were facing the bay and a dazzling light was flooding in. It was a splendid sight. The peninsula of Kowloon was in full view, and afar, being a windy day, even parts of the New Territories were visible. The floor was made of large slabs of Carrara's white *calacatta* marble streaked with gray. Only two girls were in the office due to the public holiday, but as soon as they entered, Aldo's assistant, a Chinese lady, ran up to him and handed over a file containing sheets of paper. They were mostly copies of emails and minutes of telephone conversations.

"Do you want a coffee?" she asked, thoughtfully.

"Thanks, one for me," Marco answered.

"I will get it immediately," and talking to Aldo, she added, "I spoke with Shanghai just a few minutes ago. They say there are big problems. It is all written here but I am afraid that this is a difficult situation. . ."

"I know already. Fatty called last night. I am going to handle it, Cecile. Thank you. Let me first read these papers. Marco, there are some books and magazines but most of them are about finance and economy."

"Carry on as if I am not here," answered Marco, stopping in front of a white bookshelf and gazing with interest at the spines of the books.

They seemed to be valuable, starting from the ancient world and passing through the nineteenth century up to the current times. The names of the authors were well known: Adam Smith, Irving Fisher, Von Hayek, Keynes, Piero Sraffa, and Milton Friedman. There were also some titles on topics of the most sophisticated speculative mechanisms as well as manuals dedicated to short selling, futures and credit swaps.

On the left-side he noticed a long row of books dedicated to Mongolia, some of its history and others about its mining resources.

When Aldo finished reading the emails, he asked Marco to step into his office and sit down. Looking very upset, he said, "We have booked shares of the Mongol Mining Corporation, a giant registered in the Cayman Islands. Their IPO was supported by J.P. Morgan and Citigroup, collecting close to a billion dollars. They were the first Mongolian company quoted here on the Hong Kong stock exchange. Mongolia is a country very rich in natural resources."

"Rich in what exactly?"

"In almost anything you can think of, but what were most attractive to the Chinese investors were the iron deposits of Bor Tolgoj. Those should give us a rapid return on the investment. I would say in four years if the steel market holds. Soon Mongolia will become the Switzerland of Asia, even if what they really lack is a long-term plan."

"Are the Chinese also interested?"

"Yes! That's why we handled the shares on their behalf, but now they have reneged on their obligations and have torn up our contract. I can only assume this was because of political interference. The Chinese consider Mongolia one of their lost provinces because it managed to snatch back independence in 1921.

In 1956, the Chinese built a mausoleum to honor Genghis Khan in inner Mongolia. It was made in a quasi-Chinese style, but the Mongols rightly saw it as a sign that they were planning to claim Mongolia. Luckily, the Red Guards destroyed the temple and disposed of all the historical relics stored there. The Chinese had wanted to claim Genghis Khan to be able to claim Mongolia."

"OK, that's history, but what does this matter right now?"

"We booked a lot of shares for the Chinese, guessing that as soon as the news of China's involvement broke, this would bring about a fall in value, which has happened. Now I could buy them using China's money, making a hefty profit to be shared with the Chinese counterpart, and letting them walk away with forty percent ownership of those mines. . ."

"And. . ."

". . .And the Chinese now say they were kidding. I don't have the money to honor my booking, thus I am ruined. I'll have to declare bankruptcy. . ."

"Ask Mogul to help you."

"No, I don't want to trouble the old man and I don't think he can help me. The amount of money is staggering. You have no idea."

They looked at each other in silence when Cecile entered Aldo's office, telling him Fatty was on the line. Aldo took the call. His face turned white as he listened. He raised his voice, getting angry. They were arguing. "How can they ask me to do that? Yes, I know you told me that I have to compromise. . . ah. . . OK, then take it or leave it as they say. That's where we stand at the moment, take it or leave it. . ."

He lowered his voice, sent formal greetings, and slammed down the receiver. He looked suicidal.

XIII
Hong Kong Island:
Wednesday, September 14, 2011, 10:00 a.m.

"I can't do that! I can't betray Mogul. He is my father!" Aldo screamed down the phone.

"But what do you care for that old piece of trash?" Fatty answered. "If the Chinese want it, then let them have it. This could mean your fortune or your ruin. You will go bankrupt and end up jailed, and they will get what they want anyway, perhaps harming Mogul, your mother, and Marco. What can Mogul do against China?"

"I know, damn. . ."

"Then order Zorig to pick up the Sulde from the safe and have it delivered to our men in Macau. Then all will be settled. I threatened him but he still refused."

"How can you guarantee that?"

"Trust me, the money will be released. It could be transferred tomorrow. I have no personal interest in this deal. I just care for you because you are like a son to me. This is a matter of national security, not money. Do you remember when you were small, and you called me daddy? Remember? So, now trust me. Ask Zorig to pick up the Sulde because he won't listen to me. I was able to convince him to lend us the diary of your grandfather but that superstitious brute is refusing to hand over the Sulde. If I ask him to hand it to you while you are in Macau, he will do it."

"I have to trust you, Fatty, I have no other choice. Let's do it. But what is in my grandfather's diary, after all? What is this fuss all about?"

"A love story between your grandmother and your grandfather, but the most important point is the way they got the Sulde. That's all. So, can I trust you, Aldo?"

"Yes, you can trust me." Aldo felt he had been caged

and he could see no way out. "But how can we arrange this thing?"

"Simple. Zorig will pick you and Marco up in Macau. He will have the Sulde in the car for you. You will instruct him to pass it to one of our men waiting for him in Largo Camoes after dropping you off."

"That's all?"

"Yes, and tomorrow the money will be delivered from Shanghai to your company's account in New York."

"We have a deal, then!"

"Yes, *you* have a deal."

Aldo closed the telephone conversation, put his hands over his head in desperation, and cried, thinking he was a great fool to trust Fatty and to have accepted such a highly speculative deal offered by his friends.

Marco woke up hearing Aldo's agitated voice speaking on the phone inside his room. He rose from bed and went to the bathroom, switching on his blackberry, where he found this email:

From: <u>Mogul@mogul.com.mu</u>
To: MarcoSforza@vodafone.BlackBerry.net
cc: Aldo.Montecorvo@netvigator.com

Sept 14, 2011 9:35 AM

Dear Marco and Aldo, I am waiting for you at home. Aldo, be so kind to accompany Marco. Zorig will pick you up at Macau's pier. Hugs!
Mogul

Sent from a mobile device.

Late that morning, together with Aldo, they boarded one of the helicopters connecting Hong Kong to Macau. They took off from the Shun Tak Center in Sheung Wan on the island of Hong Kong, and after a fifteen-minute flight, disembarked in the former Portuguese colony of Macau, right in the middle of all the vulgar casinos which had sprouted up like mushrooms over the last fifteen years.

The journey had been smooth, with a fine sun shining over the large ships trailing against the waves, their decks loaded full of containers. Macau, known as the Las Vegas of the East, lies forty miles from Hong Kong. The city thrives on gambling and prostitution, mainly because the nouveaux rich in China play there and buy cheap sex at the saunas.

Mogul sent Zorig to pick up the boys and carry out the formalities for customs inspection.

"Do you have that thing?" asked Aldo with Marco only a few steps away.

"Yes, it is in the trunk. How should we handle it? I don't feel good about it but Fatty said that the only way to protect Mogul was to hand it over to you."

"He told you the truth, but it is better to pass it over to another person for safekeeping. They will call you soon. Marco must not see it."

Zorig did not say another word, only answering with grunts and snorts. He was unconvinced. He drove his car in the direction of Mogul's villa, receiving a call a few minutes later.

After exchanging few words and reaching the destination, Zorig said to Aldo, "I am not sure that I am doing the right thing here, even if you are involved. I need to go to see a friend on Ferreira de Almeida Road for an urgent matter. Please tell Mogul that I'll be back shortly."

Aldo nodded.

Mogul's sumptuous villa was painted in the traditional Macanese colors of white and apricot. It was hidden behind a wall of trees and set in a garden in full bloom and built according to the architectural style common in the colonies of the Far East. The veranda had white marble columns and was rather wide, because the architects had wanted to capture the tiniest gusts of wind and shift them into the house to cool the interior. Fluttering on the flag poles planted on the lawn were two flags - the red one representing the People's Republic of China and the other, Macau - green with a lotus flower and five stars.

Two old maids appeared to escort them into the villa. On the floor of the sitting room lay a large Tibetan carpet, representing a lama's head seen in profile. Magnificent oil paintings hung on the walls. Finally, they entered a bright attic where Mogul was sitting on an imposing armchair.

"Here they are, my two boys!" Mogul said, warmly welcoming them and adding, "Please, do sit down and let me ask for some fresh orange juice for you."

The servants went to the kitchen.

"They are Burmese-Macanese," Mogul commented, speaking to Marco.

"Ah, I was unable to guess where they were from."

"Here in our house all the domestic helpers are from Burma, or Myanmar, as the Burmese generals now call it."

"Burmese?" Marco asked, looking around that wonderful place.

"They had a hard life in their country and I wanted to offer my small contribution, so I moved three Burmese families here. There is an old link with Macau since we sent a small contingent of soldiers there in the seventeenth century. The commander was Filipe de Brito and they went down there to fight as mercenaries on the side of the King of Ava and Pegu, but then our man began his own business, so to speak, founding a private kingdom there and building a stronghold on the Irrawaddy River, near Yangon."

"Sounds like a Joseph Conrad novel. How did it end?"

"Badly, very badly. He was impaled in 1613 because he had plundered some Buddhist monasteries."

"That, I daresay, is not the best form of death."

"I do agree with you but anyway, the descendants of those soldiers are Christians, and they call themselves *Bayingys*."

"Does the driver who picked us up also come from there?"

"No. Zorig is Mongol," Aldo said, anticipating Mogul's answer.

"Right. Zorig is from Ulaanbaatar as it is called today."

"By the way, Mogul received a call. He will return in an hour," Aldo said.

"Fine. Meanwhile we may talk a bit about our history."

"I am impatient to know more," Marco said.

"Curious?" demanded Mogul, winking at him.

"Yes, I am."

"Right. . . you know already that was my father who first came to China."

"Yes, but I don't know the story in detail. I only know he arrived in China with the Italian army, and not wanting to return to Italy, he set up a trading firm here. Am I right?"

"The story is far, far more complex than that, but instead of me telling it to you, I will let him speak. . ."

"Is he also alive?" demanded Marco, surprised.

"Oh, unfortunately not! But he has left his diary for you."

Mogul extended a hand towards the desk by his side and picked up a black book.

"Here, *tolle et lege*. It is for you and Aldo. Then we'll talk again. My father wrote a short record of his youth in Sicily and in Africa, then about his departure from Italy to Beijing, Hong Kong, and Macau, up to the sixties."

Marco opened the book, quickly thumbing through to the end. There were about 200 pages.

"He wrote it in English on free pages. He corrected them, and when he thought they were ready, he copied it using an old Waterman fountain pen and bound the pages together in a single volume."

"I think that I will need a couple of days," concluded

Marco, after having opened it. "The same for Aldo, I guess."

"You will be staying here, and you will have all the time you need to read it in peace and quiet. Do not feel upset or disturbed by what you will find there. My father was a great gentleman, even if sometimes he was immersed in things too great to be faced with equanimity. Now, what do you know about Genghis Khan? Who, by the way, is our direct ancestor," Mogul continued.

"Our ancestor? What do you mean?" Aldo and Marco were surprised.

"My mother was a Mongol princess and a direct descendant of Genghis Khan. So . . ."

"He was a mass-murderer, right?" Marco demanded.

"Yes, he was, by modern standards. He lived in a different era and followed the laws of his days. Alexander the Great, Julius Caesar, Augustus, and Napoleon; all mass-murderers. You see, Marco, once you accept the principle that a defensive war can be justly fought, then it is just a matter of setting the standards."

"But the other men you mentioned, they created something good, something we may call civilization. They left something behind while Genghis Khan was a sort of god of wrath, a master of useless destruction. Or at least, this is what they teach us at school. . ." added Marco, rather unconvinced.

"I disagree with that. I believe that Genghis Khan was one of the most remarkable and intelligent men who ever existed." Mogul smiled. "He was a military and political genius, tolerant and patient by the standard of his times in spite of all contrary appearances. We know something about his character because of the Secret History of the Mongols, a text known to us for centuries but which has been difficult to interpret, being a Chinese transposition of a story spoken in ancient Mongol. Furthermore, a complete understanding of this text has been hindered by the fact that in Mongolia, under Soviet occupation, it was forbidden to speak of Genghis Khan.

In 1962, Daramyn Tomor-Ochir, vice president of the Mongol Council of Ministers, approved the issuance of a series of stamps and the construction of a small monument to commemorate the 800-year anniversary of Genghis Khan's birth. His decision provoked a bloody purge that led to the imprisonment and assassination of historians and politicians who supported his ideas. He himself was abruptly dismissed and sent to work in a factory, very much like Dubcek in Czechoslovakia. One day, in 1985, they found him dead, his head split open, apparently with a hatchet. His assassins were never caught."

Continuing his dissertation, he said, "Most of the negative legends surrounding the Mongols and Genghis Khan have come from Muslim historians, while others were spread by Europeans in the nineteenth century. For example, some believed that the facial features of unlucky children affected by Down's syndrome, called mongoloids, were derived from the fact that their ancestors in the thirteenth century had been raped by Mongols!"

"Stupid thinking!" Marco remarked.

"The idea stemmed from misrepresentations of the race. The characteristic Mongolian eyelids are better suited to resist the sands of the desert, and bow legs are typical of people who, since childhood, had to live on horseback. Oval faces and squat noses are better adaptations to the cold and dry climate of the steppes. We were called Tartars, a corruption of the name Tatars, one of the tribal groups derived from *Tartarus*, a Biblical term synonymous with hell. In 1924, a British doctor, Francis Graham Crookshank, published a book entitled *The Mongol in Our Midst*, in which he tried to prove scientifically the argument that we are an inferior race. The Jews, in his opinion, fell into the same category, having lived in the eastern territories and thus exposed to Mongol influence. His book was translated into German and a copy found its way into Adolf Hitler's library."

XIV
Macau: Wednesday, September 14, 2011, 2:00 p.m.

They drank, and then Mogul went ahead with his history lesson.

"The truth is, Genghis Khan, with only 100,000 warriors, conquered the then-known world, defeating hostile nations hundreds of times more populous than our own. Only 100,000 men!"

"Fascinating," said Marco. "Can you tell us more about him?"

"He was born in the year 1162 on the shores of the River Onon and when he died in 1227, he had united part of China and India with Russia. His Indian descendants reigned until 1857 and Alim Khan, Emir of Bukhara, was still in power in 1920.

Genghis and his successors employed scores of craftsmen, mystics, and doctors. He used catapults, primitive cannons, and flamethrowers provided by the Chinese engineers. He was quick to grasp the value of scientific innovations as his mind was free from racial prejudice; not bad for an illiterate hunter of the steppes.

He promoted the founding of schools and industries in all the conquered territories. Edward Gibbon remarked that, under the *Pax Mongolica,* the world went through a period of exceptional prosperity and progress. They issued passports, like those used by Marco Polo. They moved German miners and French hydraulic engineers to China and the Chinese herbalists moved to Persia and Afghanistan.

They planted lemons and carrots in Korea, sold carpets in Turkey, taught the Germans how to cook sauerkraut. They promoted the use of paper money outside China because it was difficult for them to transport all the gold and silver they were collecting. Their war cry was hurrah; the word horde comes from *urdu*, a camp. I could go on and on."

"But I still cannot imagine how Genghis Khan could manage to transform a band of hunters of the steppes into an invincible military force," mused Aldo.

"He invented the theory of the delegation of command, *Auftragstaktik*, and lightning strikes - *Blitzkrieg*, long before the Germans. All of Genghis Khan's officers knew pretty well what he wanted from them, often without receiving direct orders and instructions. War was preceded by meetings which lasted for weeks where motives and objectives were discussed on an individual level. He took suggestions from his troops. His army made systematic use of espionage, what we call intelligence today. He created a special department for false information, like the propaganda and *dezinformatsiya* of the Soviets. Most battles were won using stratagems, feints, and withdrawals followed by sudden attacks.

We needed stratagems because we were so few and we had no racial or political agendas. If an enemy agreed to feed our horses, he was accepted as one of us. We were tolerant about religion. Our god was Tengri, the eternal blue sky, even if some converted to Nestorianism. The name Jesus reminded us of a lucky number, nine, yesu in Mongol."

Marco thought about the numbers of the license plate on Mogul's car, 9999, as he continued to listen.

"We reached Vienna, Budapest, and Venice and we could have easily conquered the rest of Europe led by the best among the Mongol generals, Subutai, but we became distracted by the death of Ogodei Khan's in December of 1241. Without the scheming of our court, we could have reached Rome, Paris, and perhaps London, though they were worth little back then. European armies at that time were composed mainly of infantry and were no match for our archers on horseback."

"Fascinating, and how did we enter Europe?" demanded Marco.

"In March 1241, General Subutai sent a column of

40,000 Mongol knights under the command of Ogodei Khan's grandchildren, Baidar and Baidu, towards Poland and Germany. We raided several Polish cities. Henry II of Silesia fielded an army of 30,000 German and Polish soldiers and met the invaders at Leignitz. The day was the 9th of April, 1241. Germans call it the Wahlstatt - chosen place. German troops, composed of Teutonic knights, were repelled by arrows.

Upon their second assault, we turned and fled, scattering in all directions. We were using an Oriental strategy of false retreat, unknown in medieval Europe. Marco Polo gave a good description in his book *Il Milione*, noting that we pretended to lose in order to win. We reassembled, mounted fresh horses, and turned to attack.

That day the Germans and Poles lost 25,000 men, the flower of their nobility, then we withdrew to prepare the next blow, leaving behind the impression that the sacrifice of Duke Henry II had saved the continent. In reality, he had done nothing of the sort. We were aiming at the green plains of Hungary, which could provide abundant fodder to our horses.

Twenty-thousand knights commanded by Batu and Subutai advanced in two columns, entering Hungary and burning everything in sight. As intended, this spread panic and pushed refugees ahead. King Bela IV left Pest with his army of 70,000 on the same day as the fall of Leignitz.

We halted and slowly withdrew, looking for a suitable place to engage battle and finding it at Mohi, on the banks of the river Sajò. The Hungarians tried to storm a bridge but were repulsed. They barricaded inside a great enclosure behind palisades and chains. During that night, we forded the river to the south. Subutai moved 30,000 of his knights, then turned and galloped north toward the Hungarian camp, catching them by surprise at seven in the morning of April 11, 1241. We catapulted barrels of incendiary oil, real bombs, and large firecrackers, provided by Chinese engineers, which exploded with loud bangs. That was the first artillery attack in Europe.

"Terrorized by the explosions, the Hungarians ran outside the enclosure and discovered there was a side left unguarded, so they ran headlong in that direction and it soon became a stampede. It was a trap, and our knights galloped on their flanks, hitting them with arrows and finishing them with spear thrusts. They were massacred like corralled cows.

The Hungarian king took refuge in a fortress on the Adriatic Sea. Historians Thomas of Split and Rogerius estimated on that day 40-60,000 men, mostly Hungarians, but also Austrians, Italians, French and Serbs were killed. According to some European historians those defeats marked the end of the heroic period for European chivalry and of the mystique that surrounded the aristocracy. They fell prey to panic because they had no idea where those mysterious knights, coming out of the steppes, were from. They must have resembled Martian invaders. Some believed that the Mongols were the advancing armies of the Antichrist. Crazy preachers told people to attack Jews, leading the masses to believe the Mongols were punishing mankind because they had accepted the unfaithful within the city walls.

We could fire an arrow every fifteen seconds. Multiply that by 10,000 bows, and you have 40,000 arrows per minute. Mongols' bows could shoot an arrow at 500 yards. Having been trained all their lives, they were capable of great precision, even on horseback. We had developed the special technique of releasing arrows while galloping: we found that the moment when a horse rears on all fours, there is a point of stability which results in the greatest precision."

"Mogul, do we know where the grave of Genghis Khan is?" asked Aldo.

"Ah, his grave! I think it doesn't exist, not as we may imagine it. I believe he was buried in an unmarked pit inside the Ikh Khorig, the Great Taboo. This would have been around the end of August or the beginning of September of 1227. A huge area there remained closed, even when Mongolia was occupied by the Soviets. There are no roads, only a military base for MIG planes and tanks. According to the Mongols' beliefs, mortal remains have no importance. They thought his spirit would survive inside the Sulde, the war banner."

"A trident with the horse's mane?"

"Precisely that. The spirit, the soul of Genghis, should survive inside there."

"Where is this Sulde?" asked Aldo, hesitantly.

"It vanished. . . Some say in 1937, but I know for sure that it was much earlier. That is why you should read my father's memoirs. Prince Lob-Tsen Yet-Tsen, my grandfather, was the last head of the Darkhad sect guarding the sacred relic. Yes, we are descendants of the Sulde's guardians."

"So, is it like the Holy Grail for Christians?" asked Marco.

"I see it more like the Ring of Professor Tolkien," concluded Mogul, smiling. "A relic possessing a quasi-magical attraction which when badly handled, could push men to murder. . ."

"Ah, Tolkien, I love his books!" exclaimed Marco.

"I read a couple of them myself, they are very entertaining. Sorry for my long digression but now you have the book and you should read it to know some of the details. Then we'll decide our next move. . ."

"What will happen if the Sulde reappears?" asked Aldo.

"Difficult to say what will happen, but leaving aside all the supernatural implications it will certainly strengthen the national identity of Mongolia, something which Russia and especially China won't like. To the Russians now it matters little but it will greatly bother China, because they fear a resurgence of the Mongol spirit, even in Inner Mongolia and Tibet. And other people might think that a reappearance of the Sulde will herald a period of strife and war. People tend to believe in negative myths. Look at Hitler's fascination with Longinus' spear, or the story of the reopening of the grave of Tamerlane, another of our relatives, and the curse which was found engraved inside. This happened two days before the Nazi invasion of the Soviet Union."

"Is that a true story?"

"Yes, that is a true story but I can't guarantee that it was a clear-cut case of cause and effect!" Mogul said, with a laugh. "I tend to believe the Nazis prepared the invasion of Russia some time in advance, certainly longer than two days, but millions still believe in the truthfulness of that story, oblivious to the fact that Tamerlane's sarcophagus had been already violated in 1740 by Nadir Shah. He wanted to steal the great slab of jade that covered it but it broke into three parts, so it was left there."

While they were about to stand up and move into their rooms to read, they saw a policeman running into the garden. He was breathless and spoke nervously with one of the maids who had run out to meet him. She covered her face with both hands and began to cry, then raced across the lawn towards the entrance. The second maid joined the policeman, looking at the windows where Mogul and his two visitors were watching.

"A great tragedy has befallen us," said Mogul, lowering his head and awaiting the arrival of the maid, foreseeing what she would say.

"Who?" Mogul asked her as she raced in.

"Zorig," she said. "They tried to rob him but he resisted and was stabbed in the chest."

"Who did it?"

"This policeman says some Chinese gangsters."

Mogul turned slowly to Aldo and Marco, who were staring at him, and told them, "You must return to Hong Kong on the first available helicopter. Or rather, Aldo should go with a helicopter and Marco with a hydrofoil. I do not want you two to get involved in such ghastly matters. The local police may withdraw Marco's passport and ask too many questions."

"But that policeman has seen us here," noted Marco.

"No, he is our friend. You'd better move now and don't waste time. We will meet again in a few days. Leave the book behind, I'll put it back in the safe, it is too dangerous to carry to Hong Kong."

"Do you have a suspect?" asked a white-faced Aldo.

"I think I have. Zorig had serious problems. . ." answered Mogul, with a grimace. With a sign of his hand, he ordered the maid to accompany his guests up to the gate.

"A taxi, put them in a taxi, they should return immediately to the pier."

They flagged a taxi, a black Toyota, which in ten minutes delivered them to their destination. The next helicopter was a half-hour wait, so they decided to depart immediately by hydrofoil, despite Mogul's order to travel separately. They bought two first-class tickets and went through customs where the staff inspected Marco's passport and scanned Aldo's ID-card. The large boat moved slowly through a zone of low depth marked by floats, picking up speed towards the island of Lantau. Within ten minutes, they were out of Macau's territorial waters.

Once they reached Hong Kong they went home where they had tea with a slice of apple pie and some cheese sandwiches. The Ming charger had been delivered for Marco and the domestic helper had put it in his room still wrapped in paper.

"Marco, I should leave soon." Aldo was looking badly shaken by what had happened to Zorig. He seemed absent-minded and Marco watched as he talked to himself in a rage.

"I must see Fatty about our investment in Mongolia. Time is ticking by for my company, even if the loss of Zorig is a terrible blow," Aldo said.

"I understand. . ."

"My mother will not return home tonight. She will stay in our villa in Discovery Bay. If you feel hungry or thirsty, just ask for the domestic helper. I hope to be back by midnight. Then, we should talk again. I am sorry I can't spend more time with you, Marco, but I need to attend to these matters. I do apologize."

"See you later and good luck with Fatty."

Marco was still feeling hungry and asked the servant to prepare some more sandwiches. His mobile rang, and he answered, recognizing at once the sweet voice of Blanchefleur, the charming granddaughter of Richard Chan.

XV
Hong Kong Island:
Wednesday, September 14, 2011, 8:00 p.m.

"Hi, Marco, how are you? Am I disturbing you, are you in the middle of something? It seems the intrigue of the mysterious Hong Kong do not interest you at all."

"Blanchefleur! How are you? How did you find me?"

"I Googled you."

"Ah, yes, right. I thought about calling but there were so many complications."

"I would have wanted to be part of your complications. I am a very capable riddle-solver. Always the first out of the maze."

"You are so nice, thank you."

"Only nice? I am not normally called nice. By the way when will you take me for a drink? I am thirsty, but not for blood," she said, laughing at her little joke.

"I should check my appointments, but for sure we can have a drink, I do promise that."

"Ah, I believe I know what happened. Aldo told you to leave me alone because of my grandfather. Are you afraid of him, or is it just me?"

"Why? What's wrong with your grandfather? Why should I be afraid?"

"Very well, a good actor here. . ." she laughed again, then slyly continued. "I am not an ordinary Hong Kong girl. I won't think that you want to marry me if you invite me for a coffee."

"Oh, hear this! A straight talker! Will you be available Friday evening?"

"Now, that's better. Friday evening, I will cancel all my appointments and have a dinner with you. Where?"

"Felix, on top of the Peninsula? I went there the first time

I visited eight years ago, and it was good."

"Good choice. Dinner, then. I agree. Then, we'll see each other at eight Friday evening in the lobby of the Peninsula. I'll make the booking. If you don't show up, I'll have you shot," said Blanchefleur, laughing again.

"Well, Blanchefleur, being shot is a risk I cannot take."

"Oh, my grandfather is calling me. See you then," she said putting down the phone.

Marco went on reading about the history of Hong Kong and fell asleep with the book in his hands. When he awoke, he could see that it was the middle of the night, and he went to the toilet. Near the telephone he found a note that the domestic helper had scribbled on a piece of paper. Aldo had phoned to say he would not return home but would spend the night at his mother's villa in Discovery Bay.

Richard Chan couldn't stay in bed as he still did not feel well. Dizziness and a strong headache troubled him. When he finally got out of bed where he had been laying, eyes open, he went back to his studio. There, again, he picked up the pages left to read. He continued for half an hour, stopped, raised his head, and stared at an oil painting of old Macau hanging in his studio.

He drank a glass of warm medicinal tea that was supposed to be good for stomach ailments but thought he should see a doctor soon. The story of Mogul's father was getting close to the conclusion with the revelation of its final secret. He wanted to reach the end quickly, even if the pages were getting stickier under his fingers and had to wet them more and more frequently as his headache and nausea were increasing. He thought that perhaps this was due to the shellfish he had eaten a couple of days earlier, but looked at his hands and noticed a strange yellow color. They looked paler than usual and the pad on his index finger had turned dark. With horror, it dawned on him what might be the source of his health problems: arsenic!

Shrieking, he pushed the copy of Gino's diary away, throwing it down from the table. Faltering, he stood up and opened a drawer containing a large array of medicines. He looked frantically among tablets and potions, then gulped down four pills of Dimercaprol in a concentration of 500 milligrams. It was his first shot to neutralize the spreading of the poison into his cells if arsenic was the cause of his ailments. He was well equipped for all manner of ailment. *Damned, this could not be the work of that Monsignor. This must have been Fatty's idea. I am sure he took it straight from the Jin Ping Mei.*

The *Jin Ping Mei,* also known as The Plum in the Golden Vase, is a lascivious novel written at the end of the Ming Dynasty by an anonymous literato, and in accordance with an old tradition, the author put a great deal of alluring immorality in it to make it more readable and then applied poison to the pages to dispense of a hated censor whom he suspected of being a hypocrite.

"He will pay dearly for having done this to me!" Richard hissed. Then he told Blanchefleur to call a specialist in poisoning.

"Murder! Fatty and the Monsignor have poisoned me!" he screamed at the top of his voice to his white-faced granddaughter.

XVI

Taipa Island, Macau:
Thursday, September 15, 2011, 9:00 p.m.

Monsignor Paulo de Andrade went out onto the lawn of his villa where he found his driver sleeping in the car. He knocked on the window to wake him. The man raised his seat, switching on the engine. Paulo thought it was getting dark faster in Macau than in the rest of the world. . . or so it seemed to him. He remembered well that it was quite different in his native Portugal where the same sun hung in the sky for a long time before plunging into the ocean.

"Take me to the Ricci Institute and pick me up early in the morning. I'll give you a call."

The Matteo Ricci Institute, a yellow and ox blood-colored colonial building, was in the busy Avenida Ferreira de Almeida. Once he had reached the place, Paulo got out of his car and crossed the road nearly being hit by one of the many passing motorcycles. Stepping inside the gate, he stumbled into the director, Father Manolo Fok, who was just leaving. Paulo was so deep in thought he did not notice him and went straight to his private studio, adjacent to the main library dedicated to the eighteenth-century Jesuit Tomas Pereira.

Paulo had the key for a locked shelf containing several precious incunables. All valuable, ancient books left to him personally by a deceased collector, a merchant of textiles going by the name of Pedro Lee. The two had never met and Paulo didn't know of his existence until a few years before when his testament was read aloud to his relatives. They were stunned when they learned that all his precious books were going to the Monsignor in exchange for the remission of his sins, he wrote of covetousness and lust above all the others. This was for the salvation of his soul, having spent most of his money on the pursuit of rare books, thus denying a decent life to his children and long-suffering wife.

Those books, around 100 of them, built an impressive collection of works. Most had been printed before the year 1500. The pride of his collection were the perfect and exceedingly rare copies of *Hypnerotomachia Poliphili*, by Francisco Calonna and Poliphilo's *Strife of Love in a Dream*, an extraordinary erotic novel with fine woodcuts of ruins, inscriptions, hieroglyphs and gardens. They were printed in Venice by Aldo Manuzio in the year 1499, and considered by many discerning bibliophiles to be the most beautiful book ever produced.

The welcome news had greatly surprised Paulo, who could not explain why that deceased man mistook him for a holy man. Was it perhaps because he was a Monsignor and thus possessed status and authority within the Church? Or because of his deportment and apparent gravity? He could not find a convincing answer; what the bibliophile had certainly ignored was the not-so-saintly way Paulo had achieved such an exalted position.

Twenty-five years earlier, Paulo de Andrade had been posted to Macau fresh from the seminary in Portugal. At first he had a dull and humdrum life without sex - a burden too heavy for him to carry - and subsequently began contemplating the idea of getting rid of his priest's cassock. He thus thought about abandoning the Roman Catholic Church and accepted a job in Macau as an accountant.

It was then that he met a Spanish priest in need of protection. He was a young lad with delicate and perfumed flesh like a young virgin and was even better than a woman in bed. They became lovers, and he introduced Paulo to a circle of homosexuals, some of them powerful clergymen.

They were well connected politically and well off economically, so much so, that he joined their circle and began assembling files on each of them. He gathered photos, recordings, even films, which he used for blackmail while enlisting some local thugs in his hideous enterprise. Fatty, himself part of that circle as a Chinese spy, became his partner in business, for he had useful contacts with China's secret service and the local 14K Chinese triads.

All the people blackmailed by Paulo were initially terrified, but after their shock subsided, seeing he acted in a stern but professional manner, they became his obedient servants - granting him whatever was in their power to grant.

His Spanish lover, the first victim, was a special envoy of the Vatican. Upon discovering what Paulo was up to, he rashly told him he was going to denounce him to the police. The saying goes that the first death is the most difficult for a murderer, but those that follow become much easier - in Paulo de Andrade's case, this rule did not apply. He had no problem dispatching even his first victim, calmly staging an accident after inviting him on a short trip over the Chinese border. He pushed the young man down from the bell tower of an abandoned church they were visiting - then just slept there for the night. The case was quickly closed by the Chinese police after an intervention of some of Fatty's friends.

Paulo took down a Fifteenth-Century folio edition of Saint Augustine's *City of God*, printed in Venice in 1475, placed it on the table, and released the metallic clasps. Inside were sheets from the second copy of Gino's diary he had been reading already the day before. Then he took out a smaller volume, *The Life of Father Carlo Spinola of the Jesuits, Murdered for the Holy Faith in Japan*, printed in Rome in 1671.

Spinola was a Jesuit father who, while in Macau, laid down the plans for construction of the Cathedral of St. Paul and then died a martyr in Nagasaki in 1622. Paulo selected that book as a reminder to be prudent in his dealings, to neither end up in jail nor share Spinola's fate.

He lifted a folded plate representing the plan of the cell where the blessed man had been detained in Nagasaki. Under it, he carved a five-by-five-centimeter hole with a paper cutter, passing through 100 pages and making a secret compartment for some white powder to be hidden. He picked a small pinch of it with his fingers, laid it on a page, and using a straw, deeply inhaled the crystals into his nostrils.

A bit of this shit will help me to calm down and stay alert, he thought. *I must find what we need quickly. It must be here. I just need to read these pages as carefully as I can.*

He closed the book on Spinola, turned on the fan over the table, and immediately felt the kick of the drug working its wonderful effect. It was like switching on many small lights in his brain. His sweating ceased and his mind cleared, then he eagerly went through the pages.

After about one hour of deep reading, a young and clearly distressed priest came running down the corridor, disturbing his concentration. It was Father Vicente.

"Monsignor, Monsignor!" he screamed from behind the grating.

"What do you want?"

"Awful news, Monsignor. Father Hippolytus is dead!"

"Dead? Oh, poor son, what happened?"

"We don't know yet, the father superior opened the door of his cell and there he was, hanging by the neck!"

"Any note?"

"We don't know yet. Policemen are inspecting the place."

"Thank you, Vicente, go back now. Be strong. We mustn't overdo it now, what's dead's forgotten. Go and pray for his soul. Go now, I need to be alone, I'll also pray for his soul."

"Yes, Monsignor. . ." Vicente, still sobbing, went away with quick steps. *Never mind that fool, he should have listened to me,* Paul thought, and continued reading at high speed for a few hours until he felt the urge to go to the toilet to relieve himself. When he returned to the study, he decided to walk down to his customary massage parlor, where he reserved a special room. He would return later and carry on with the few remaining pages. Before going out, he took off his white collar, put on a large Panama hat and a sporty jacket, and replaced his glasses.

XVII

Macau: Friday, September 16, 2011, 5:00 a.m.

The sun was rising over Macau, the city of sin and perdition, as it was known all over the world in bygone days. Monsignor Paulo de Andrade left the massage parlor and returned to his cell, but before entering he called Fatty, waking him, and yelled into the phone that he had been waiting for his news all night at the Ricci Institute.

"Can't we speak tomorrow? What time is it?" Fatty moaned.

"Five o'clock in the morning. I thought that the relic would have been delivered to me this night. Have we got it? Why haven't you called?"

"Some complications. We had to kill Zorig, and I was kept busy calming down Aldo, who freaked out. But we have the box."

"Damn it, why did they kill him?"

"He smelled a rat and resisted, then assaulted one of the boys."

"Does Mogul know this? I mean about the Sulde?"

"I think he must know by now."

"Well, now we may play this game in line with our rules."

"What, which rules? What are you talking about?"

"I believe that some people are willing to pay top dollars for this thing. Higher than the pittance your Chinese friends are offering."

"Who? Some of your friends? Let me tell you what the game is here! China, with Genghis Khan's Sulde, could lay claims on Mongolia. This is the game, the only game. Can't you see it?"

"Exactly, but given its importance we can ask more than the twenty million they have offered us."

"You can't be serious. Do you intend to renegotiate this

deal? Are you mad? They will not like it!"

"Yes, we must renegotiate before passing it over the border. The Mongols are also trying to get it, I know, along with Hong Kong's 14K, but with Richard Chan out of the picture, we should be safer on that side even if the cat is out of the bag by now."

"Which cat?"

"It's just a saying, beast! Haven't you woken up? Get a cold shower. I need to get the Sulde this very morning!"

"I'll arrange a couple of our men to carry, the cat."

"Fine then, get up and go walking somewhere. While you slept, I was working for you! Now I must go."

"Yes, I can imagine where you were working. . . But thank you for your advice," said Fatty, putting down the phone and thinking, *whom the gods would destroy, they first make mad. Richard was right after all, this Monsignor is a fool!*

Fatty had no intention of handing over anything. He'd send a couple of men to finish the Monsignor off, for he received orders from Beijing to erase all traces of their involvement. Then Fatty would have to move to Chengdu, China, where they had already prepared a villa for his retirement. He would never return to Hong Kong. Then he went back to sleep.

After speaking to Fatty, Paulo resumed reading nonstop until everything was clear in his mind. He could understand the reason for all the interest in that politically charged memorabilia: it was something like the Iron Crown of Monza or the Holy Shroud of Turin, both of which he had admired a long time before. They filled him with awe when with other young seminarians he was taken to see them on a bus tour of Italy.

The stakes were high, involving a mix of politics, national pride, religion, and it was worth a fortune, or in another sense, it was priceless. With Richard Chan out of the way he had nothing to be afraid of. *I don't care for those Chinese and*

Mongolian heathen idol-worshippers. I just care for money, and I want a lot of it. Tomorrow, I'll pay a good assassin to get Fatty murdered. Twenty thousand dollars will do; I know a guy who works clean and safe. It will be money well invested. . . Fatty is no use to me now, Paulo thought with a smirk.

Only then did it down on him that he had taken too much cocaine and should have used it more sparingly. Paulo's driver took him home. He had not eaten anything since the day before, with only the drug keeping him going. Paulo felt far too alert and excited, even if he had possessed two young Chinese girls when at the massage parlor, performing the filthiest acts on their thin, bamboo-like bodies. Moral considerations aside, it had been quite a feat for an overweight man of fifty like him. With the second of them he felt his heart getting out of gear, like the gears of a car scaling from fifth to first speed while on a highway. For the first time in his life he had to stop and lie down for ten minutes, taking a breath before finishing his job, out of duty.

Paulo was hungry and went to the kitchen to look for food. He opened the fridge where he found a lasagna casserole with an iced bowl of fruit salad sprinkled with Grand Marnier. He put the lasagna in the microwave oven and after ten minutes sat down to eat. It was far too generous a portion, but he wolfed it down in five minutes, followed it with a large iced beer then devoured the large serving of fruit salad.

He stood up, released a couple of thundering burps, and went to take a shower, his mind racing like a rocket, darting back to the past then springing into the future. *How much should I ask for? Perhaps fifty million US dollars will do, half cash and half gold ingots. Or perhaps a wire transfer to my personal account in Singapore? Then I'll retire to a quiet villa on Phuket Island, very green and discreet, a few servants, plenty of young girls and boys for my entertainment. Every year I could visit my village in Portugal just to show off my wealth to my miserable folks. Ah, what a pity that dad and mom are no longer around to see me! They would feel proud of my wealth after having spent their lives in wretched misery. I will pick up painting again, I was good at that when I was at the seminary, but then I stopped. Why did I stop? I can't remember. . .*

Paulo entered his bedroom, and, satisfied with his day's work, lay down under an embroidered linen sheet to sleep for at least a couple of hours. The light was filtering through the half-closed windows, announcing the beginning of a new and busy day. He felt reassured. Another morning was dawning, and he remembered the happiness he felt as a child in Portugal when his mother prepared breakfast for the family.

Paulo's pale and obstinate eyes were closed but his brain was still working at full speed, a lingering effect of the drug he had taken. His heart was beating fast, pumping and pumping more than the usual flow of blood into his veins. That inexplicable sweating with the skin rash returned to bother him. Then he felt a sudden stab in his back, just behind the right scapula. He tried to get out of the bed but felt suddenly very weak. He tried to call his cousin but was unable to scream. He knew it was a serious symptom, for he tried to make the sign of the Cross as a sort of protective charm, but his right arm refused to move. like Samson with his hair shorn. He felt as though falling into a dark vertigo while the sweating increased tremendously.

Seized by panic, he knew what was happening: a massive heart attack. After a couple of long minutes, he felt a new stab, deeper and sharper into his chest, and finally crossed life's last threshold, giving up the ghost.

XVIII

Hong Kong Island:
Friday, September 15, 2011, 11:00 a.m.

"Fatty, is it you?"

"Ah, Blanchefleur. Yes, it's me, how can I help you?"

"My grandfather is dead. The doctor confirmed that it was arsenic poisoning."

"I am sorry to hear that. It should be a good day for dying, a friend of mine in Macau just passed away. I just received the call."

"Are you sorry that you arranged to have him poisoned? You did it, right?"

"Not really."

"He told me before dying that you have the Sulde of Genghis Khan, is it true?"

After a few seconds, Fatty slowly answered, "That is not completely true. I have it but I don't own it."

"Were the stealing of the Sulde and the murder of Zorig arranged by you? I am sure you also poisoned my grandfather."

"Soldiers steal and kill for their country. . ."

"Which is your country, Fatty?"

"Do you have any doubts?"

"I can pay to get it back."

"Then you don't get it, do you? It is not about money, and besides, I can't give back what I don't own."

"You will pay for what you have done to my grandfather. He mistook you for a friend!"

"Oh, spare me this music. I understand your rage but I had to do it. I had to betray Aldo, Richard, Mogul, and everybody else to serve my country. I had orders to follow. I am sorry but the stakes are far too high. Now I have to go down to visit a friend." With these words he abruptly closed the conversation and left his flat.

He went down to Hollywood Road and turned onto Square Street, passing in front of shops selling coffins, on one side Chinese and on the other Western styles, then entered a dirty-looking flat, descending some steps to its basement. He knocked on a rusted iron door, and upon entering the dark, he could see Aldo, manacled to a steel pipe.

"Fatty, why are you doing this?" Aldo asked, as soon as he saw him entering his prison. "Why are you keeping me down here?"

There was a strong stench, almost unbearable, coming from a sewer. Fatty sat in front of him while two young thugs kept a close watch over the prisoner.

"We are close to my flat, and after you were drugged last night we brought you down here. You trusted unscrupulous people, are you aware of this? My people want nothing from you but the Sulde because you are a worthless piece of flesh to them. I am sorry for this, but I am powerless, though up to now, I've managed to save your life. They wanted you to disappear Hong Kong-style, with stones tied to your waist, sinking down to the bottom of the sea. I had to fight, temporarily, to make them change their minds."

"Do you want money?"

"Not really, and I know you don't have much. They just want to cut off all the loose ends, and you are one of those ends."

"Please, ask them to release me, I won't talk, I promise!"

"Not that easy, son. . ."

"I don't understand."

"It doesn't matter. Now I have to leave. But I'll return tonight to see you, if I can."

XIX

Hong Kong Island:
Friday, September 16, 2011, 7:00 p.m.

Marco took a shower and put on a white shirt of superfine cotton poplin, a pair of carrot-colored pants, and a blue jacket to create a strong contrast with the white handkerchief which he put into his breast pocket. Then he took his credit card, a brown, 500 Hong Kong banknote, and two red 100-dollar bills for the taxi and other petty expenses. He looked at himself in the mirror, passing his own test, though at the same time being slightly ashamed of his vanity. He thought about the Mongol warriors who only washed themselves properly when they were born and when they were dead. Certainly, they would have mocked him.

The telephone rang. It was Blanchefleur Chan.

"My grandfather is dead. . ."

"I am sorry Blanchefleur! Do you want to cancel the dinner?"

"No, I need to see and talk to you, let's go on with it," she said.

"I am just about to leave, see you soon."

Marco checked his watch and saw that it was seven o'clock. He went to the parking lot and called a taxi, asking to be taken to the Peninsula Hotel in Kowloon.

The journey took only twenty minutes because the roads were clear of traffic. Two bell boys opened the great crystal doors of the Peninsula and he went to the reception, waiting there for the arrival of Blanchefleur.

She was punctual. Crossing the marbled lobby in a long, mauve silk dress decorated with shiny crystals, everybody looked at her, from the hotel manager to the most junior bell boy. She wore long cream-colored gloves matching her bag and shoes, and her necklace was of twenty-four carat gold and bright green jade.

Marco was awestruck, as he remembered her being beautiful, but not that stunning.

"It has been difficult to see you but finally, here you are," said Blanchefleur, with a shy smile. Removing her gloves, she stretched out her hand. Marco embraced her, kissing her twice on the cheeks. Blanchefleur was not expecting that, and blushed slightly, then smiled remarking, "Not the standard form of greeting here, but thank you anyway…"

"Where is the Felix? I can't remember. . . Condolences for your grandfather. What happened?" Marco asked.

"We'll talk later. The Felix is here behind the check-in counter. Please, follow me."

"Felix reminds me of an old cartoon with a black cat."

"I've never seen it but I do know they called it Felix as a mark of gratitude for an old Swiss manager of this hotel, Felix Bieger. I met him a few years ago, a nice gentleman."

They entered a wood-paneled elevator, shaped like sand on a beach and designed by Philippe Stark, and went up to the twenty-eighth floor, where they had a magnificent view of Hong Kong Island's glistening towers looking like marching giants.

"Quite a sight, a futuristic image," Marco said.

"The future is ours, if we want it," answered Blanchefleur, rather enigmatically. The chairs were unmistakably Fornasetti, with the usual woman's faces, and a waiter escorted them to their reserved table.

"Sorry again about your grandfather," Marco said.

"Thank you, but his bad karma finally caught up with him. It was only during the last years of his life he realized he had done so many wrong things and had been abandoned by everybody except me. Even his friend Fatty, at the end, poisoned him."

"Are you sure that it was poisoning?"

"Yes, I'm sure, he was murdered by Fatty and that priest in Macau, who is also dead."

"Have you spoken to the police?"

"The police will stay out of this. They have classified his death as natural due to his age. But it's Fatty's work, I am quite sure."

"I am sorry but I know that Aldo was going to see Fatty."

"Ah, and what did Aldo say?"

"I have not seen Aldo for two days, should I worry? Perhaps he is still in Discovery Bay or he is searching for money to keep his business afloat."

"Did you call him?"

"Yes, several times, but I got no answer."

"Then we should worry. Did you inform Mogul or his mother? I called Mogul this morning telling him about my grandfather's passing, but there was no mention of Aldo," Blanchefleur said.

"I have not called Mogul but perhaps I'll call Cathy first."

Marco dialed Cathy's number. She answered saying that she had not seen her son, and it was not true that he had been in Discovery Bay. Alarmed, Marco called Mogul to tell him that Aldo disappeared. Mogul said he was going to find Fatty and would call them back later.

Settling down, Marco ordered a gin and tonic, then ordered Blanchefleur a milkshake.

"I don't drink. I am driving and alcohol makes so many people lose their minds," she said.

"Then I swear that after this I will stop."

"There, a good boy. Tell me now, are you nervous about being here with me? What idea do you have for - later? Tell me, I would like to know. Did Aldo tell you that I am a praying mantis?" She was teasing him.

"Well, what I can see is you're a straight talker! Aren't you afraid of being too bossy and frightful to a plain man like me?"

"Oh, I just do it to mask my shyness."

"Are you shy? I don't believe this."

"You will see if this evening is not our last together. What do you want to eat? The chef here is great."

"A steak."

"I'm vegetarian. I'll ask what they can offer."

"Totally vegetarian?"

"Mildly vegetarian. Dairy products and eggs are fine, no meat, except oysters."

"Poor oysters! What have they done to be singled out and eaten by you?"

"Buddhists in Hong Kong think that oysters have no soul."

"Ah, I understand. No soul. . ."

Blanchefleur ordered some cheese with a salad. She was indeed very attractive, with a pretty face and delicate traits, but her hands seemed to possess a superhuman beauty. They were pure white as if made of Blanc de Chine porcelain.

"It would be better if you would stop looking at me like that, Marco. I find it embarrassing. . ."

"Well, I am not consuming you, just scanning. . ."

"Oh, in this case, then, please, carry on!" she commented, with light irony.

Modern music played low in the background, and the lights were dimmed, to avoid interfering with the panorama.

"A seer was here centuries ago, a wandering poet who had a vision," said Blanchefleur.

"Which vision?"

"He saw a great city where only grass and rocky cliffs were visible, and an explosion of lights with a myriad of boats crossing the bay."

"Really, he foresaw this? How extraordinary - Blanchefleur, do you like Hong Kong?" asked Marco, after a few seconds of deep silence.

"I was born here, and I have seen little outside of Hong

Kong. A few relatives in China, a short journey to the United States and to Australia."

"School at Oxford?"

"Ah, I tricked you. No, from birth I had a governess from Oxford, Miss Hobbs. She always spoke to me in English. My dead mother was Russian on her father's side. She died five years ago - a boozer."

"I am sorry about that. I am guessing she was also very beautiful."

"Yes, she was. You may see in me only a pale shadow of her beauty. My father and mother never cared much about me and I grew up with Miss Hobbs and my famous grandfather." She had a nervous giggle and put her right hand in front of her mouth as well-educated Asian women normally do.

"May I ask how old you are?" Marco asked.

"I am like the woman from Shangri-La; 121 years old. As in the novel Lost Horizon. . . have you read it? If you take me out of Hong Kong, my true age will gradually show."

"Yes, I read that book. Hilton, right? Richard Hilton. I've also watched the movie."

"Spot on. So, about my age, I was born in the year of the dragon. Do the math."

"Hmm. You can't be ten years old, so you should be twenty-two."

"You are good, I am impressed. And what about you?"

"Ox. Born in 1985. I am twenty-six."

"And are you happy living in Milan?"

"Reasonably happy, even if it is a complicated country."

"You should move here then. Go East, young man. Live your Eastern dreams to the fullest. Visit the unfathomable Orientals."

"Now you are being a bit sarcastic."

"Here, look at me. Am I not an unfathomable Oriental girl? Can you guess what I am thinking now?"

Jokingly she assumed a hieratic pose, looking like Guanyin, the Chinese goddess of mercy.

She is delightful, Marco thought, while his heart was jumping.

"Let me see, wait a minute. . .You are thinking that nothing has come out of the kitchen and you are hungry."

"You see, after all, we are not that inscrutable. Waiter, waiter! What happened to our dishes?" she asked.

"I will check immediately, Miss Chan, excuse us for the delay," he answered, racing to the kitchen with a worried expression on his face. Blanchefleur looked into Marco's eyes and asked, "Do you know the story of the young man who fell asleep on the bank of the Ganges River?"

"Not that I can remember. What happened to him? Was he eaten by a tiger?"

"Oh, no. The story would end too soon. He awoke, crossed the river, and entered a village on the other shore. A family gave him shelter and work. He met the beautiful daughter of the head of the village. She was an attractive girl and she fell in love with the stranger, and he with her. Her father, seeing that he was a good man, offered her as his bride. The young man entered the business of the family and because he was very diligent, made it thrive. They had a son, and then a daughter. Everything went well for twenty long years.

But one season the rain grew worse than during all the previous seasons, and at night the river broke the embankment and the village was swallowed up by water and mud. The young man wanted to save his children, his wife, his in-laws, and the people of the village but he saw them perish one by one, swallowed by the river.

The following morning, the sun was again shining in the sky and birds were chirping on the trees. He wandered around and seeing a ruined wall he realized that, until the day before, it had been his house where he had spent so many happy moments. He went up to that wall and bitterly cried. . ."

"Here are your dishes, Miss Chan. I am deeply sorry for the delay but I wanted to prepare them myself." The young chef of Felix was standing in front of them with a contrite expression on his face.

"Oh, thank you, Yoshi. We were just kidding with the waiter, we were not complaining," Blanchefleur assured him.

"Still, I wish to apologize and I hope that the food will satisfy you," and after a deep bow, he went back to the kitchen.

"And then?" asked Marco, wanting to know the end of her story.

"Oh, he woke up on the bank of the river where he had fallen asleep. He had never crossed it. It had been just a dream."

"Ah, I guess there is a cryptic message."

"Several messages. . ."

"Am I that man?" insisted Marco, while cutting his steak.

"A bit of you, a bit of me."

"Blanchefleur, what would you do if you were me? Would you keep on sleeping or would you cross the river?"

"I would cross it," and then she added, laughing, "and I think that even that young man, after waking up, had crossed the river. That's what we call to follow a dream. He would have tried to marry the daughter of the chief but would have been wiser to enjoy life as it came, without worrying too much about the future."

"I see, but perhaps he would have built higher embankments on the river's banks!"

They both laughed and finished dining with a slice of excellent apple pie and an espresso.

"Blanchefleur, what about later? Will you show me some mysterious places?"

"Certainly, that's why we are here," she smiled, adding,

"Now we should go down to take my car."

They crossed the lobby. Blanchefleur gave the car keys to a boy and in a short time he returned with a yellow Lamborghini Aventador LP 700-4, the latest model. Marco had not seen one before. Blanchefleur lifted her vest just slightly before sitting in the driver's seat.

"An ideal car for people not wanting to be noticed," said Marco.

"Oh, this belongs to my father. He runs a large trading company in Singapore. I normally use an old Toyota but this evening I wanted to make an impact on you. . ."

"You don't need the chassis of this car. Your chassis is good enough."

"Hear this. Ah, these sleazy Italians!" she exclaimed, pretending to have been slighted.

"Where are we heading with this - meteor?"

"Do you like it?"

"I am not a great fan of cars. What speed can it reach?"

"It's too fast for Hong Kong. It has a 6.5 liter, twelve-cylinder engine. If I am not mistaken, it looks more suitable for taking off on the runway of the airport rather than going around in a city."

They passed the Hung Hom Railway Station, Argyle Street, and San Po Kong, and then pointed towards Clearwater Bay before stopping at a small hamlet called *Choinansu*.

"This car really can fly. Where do we go now?" asked Marco.

"I want to show you some aspects of my double life."

"Oh, do you really have a double life?"

"Yes, but it is not what you might think."

They parked the car on the road and took a path going into the forest. On one side, there were some old Chinese graves in the shape of a horseshoe, probably built illegally forty or fifty years earlier.

"Where are we heading, Blanchefleur?" It was dark, and she was walking with difficulty in her high heels but she made a sign with her hand to follow.

They reached a shed with a faint light illuminating a window. She knocked at the door and it opened. There were three children, all younger than six, who threw themselves into her arms.

"They call me cousin. Come in, you are going to discover a well-kept secret in Hong Kong - poor people."

In that flimsily built shack, more like a hunter's barn, a dozen people lived, five adults and seven children of various ages. They switched off the small television set they were watching.

"Who are they?" Marco asked.

"A family of immigrants from China. The father is the only person who has a job, and he supports the rest. They are all good people."

"Do you help poor families other than this one?"

"A few families, yes. It costs me very little, but mind you they are all proud people. They will return the money to me."

"And do you believe them?"

"I do believe them. You are now seeing a side of Hong Kong you could have never imagined, nor seen. There are a lot of shack dwellers who live far from the tall skyscrapers, far from the crystal windows of luxury. They are derelicts without a voice and no one wants to see them; they are transparent like crystals as if they do not exist.

Thousands of families in Hong Kong cannot raise enough money to feed their children although the government has a big surplus every year. To eat here in Hong Kong, you need six American dollars per day for an adult and four for every child, and when this is added to the cost of renting a small flat, it's impossible to make ends meet. Our politicians should do more, and yet they pretend that all is fine, turning their heads aside."

They remained there for half an hour while Blanchefleur played with the children. The elder one, a boy of ten years, took out a Chinese violin and gave a test of his musical skills, playing an air reasonably well.

"Verdi? Where did he learn to play that?" Marco asked.

Blanchefleur replied, "Music lessons. I pay for his schooling."

After having tasted some of their tea they went back to the car.

"Should we go drink something in Sai Kung? We can stop at the Ebe Club. We have a yacht there and it is a very informal place. I reckon now we'll find few people there, besides perhaps a couple of drunken sailors."

"Fine with me, but may I ask you something about the Sulde stolen in Macau?" Marco demanded.

He saw her stiffening, and after a few seconds hesitation, she said, "I hope you are not here only because of that. My grandfather told me something about it and now he is dead because of it. I want to tell you something about that. . .thing. Did you know it entered the walls of Beijing in 1215 together with its bearer and for two weeks, death and mad destruction followed? A traveler, who went there a year later, wrote that the roads were still caked in human blood and fat from the victims. Sixty thousand virgins committed suicide, throwing themselves down from towers and ramparts, rather than fall into the hands of those barbarians.

Do you really believe that the Sulde is a positive symbol? I don't think it is. If it were to fall into my hands, I would gladly throw it to the bottom of the sea or into a volcano." She added, "Not only for that reason, for the rape of Beijing. My ancestors were Russian, and as I told you they fled to Manchuria after the October Revolution and settled in Thailand. We are descendants of Prince Mstislav Romanovitch of Kiev. Does this name mean anything to you?"

"Nothing. Why?"

"He was the chief of the Christian cities of Russia which confronted the Mongols in 1223, a confederation that included Smolensk, Galich, Kursk, Volhynia, and other cities. The Mongols used their usual tactics - a clash with the vanguard and then a sudden retreat."

"Mogul told me that this tactic is in Marco Polo's book."

"The pursuit lasted two weeks. The trap set by Jebe and Subutai was sprung on the river Kalka, near the Sea of Azov, fifty thousand Russians, almost all peasants, against twenty thousand Mongol archers."

"You know these historical facts well."

"Considering that I am a woman?"

"Not in that sense, sorry."

"Well, they are facts that touch me and my family. My grandfather spoke to me about them when I was small. The tactic used by the Mongols was known as the quiet attack and was directed using flags. They advanced, trotting, and then stopped. The Russian archers began to hurl their arrows, but their bows could not fire that far. The Mongols mocked them by advancing, collecting their arrows from the ground, and firing them back on our soldiers, who turned and fled. The Mongols pursued, killing most of them. Only one in twenty survived. My ancestor was captured alive with other nobles and generals, and they were carried in cages on the Black Sea, in Crimea. They wrapped them in carpets, put them under the plank of a platform, and danced all night above them, drunk. They died, crushed by their weight."

"I have bad news for you. I heard the other day from Mogul that I am a descendant of Genghis Khan. . ."

She turned on the seat and looked at Marco with fiery eyes but then remembered that history has nothing to do with present life. She softened and smiled at him.

"I am sorry to hear your story, Blanchefleur, and I

understand your feelings, but I should find the Sulde and return it to the owner together with Aldo."

Blanchefleur, instead of answering, turned the key and put the car into first gear, then the second and third, and departed at top speed towards Sai Kung. Her mood was suddenly changing. She did not open her mouth until they reached that laid-back nautical club and sat down.

After a few minutes, she told him, "This is a dangerous game, Marco. I must consider what to do. I have good feelings for you and my heart melted the first time we met. I confess I have had other boyfriends before, but they were different."

"I feel the same for you, Blanchefleur. I have dreamed of you every night since I first met you."

She looked at him with large, sweet eyes, caressed him on the cheek, and said, "We seem to be on different fronts but love has pushed us together. For the first time in my life I am not sure what to do."

"What do you mean?"

"I mean that the cursed Sulde and its dark spell has produced love, but it has already pitted three old friends like my grandfather, your grandfather, and Fatty in a mortal struggle. Now Aldo might also be in danger." She was close to breaking into tears. Marco took her into his arms and offered consolation, "My grandfather told me that Fatty's henchmen were looking for him. He may be detained in one of their prisons, and I pray that nothing worse than that has happened."

"Let me try Mogul again then and let's see if he has found him."

Mogul was still in Macau and said he had spoken with Richard before his death. He had learned of his son's financial worries, which were previously unknown to him. "He should have talked to me about his problems, I could have helped. I have connections with the Mongol government. But I am confident that we are close to finding him, and he is still alive," Mogul told him.

Marco drank an orange juice with Blanchefleur, paid the bill, and they went back to the car. They took the same road, but on reaching the University of Science and Technology, they turned to the left towards Hang Hau, in the direction of the Easter tunnel of Causeway Bay.

"Tell me just one thing," Blanchefleur said, restarting the conversation. "Do you trust me or do you think that I am using you?"

"I trust you with all my heart."

"I love that," and she sweetly put her hand on his knee.

They reached Conduit Road after midnight. "Thank you for the great evening, Blanchefleur, and condolences again for Richard."

Marco was closing the door but with a last look into Blanchefleur's eyes, he got back into the car again and kissed her.

"What happens next?" asked Marco.

"What happens next is that you wake up and cross the river!"

XX

Hong Kong Island:

Saturday, September 17, 2011, 4:00 a.m.

Aldo was still missing and his room was empty. Marco was turning in his bed, unable to sleep. He thought about calling Blanchefleur on her mobile phone, even if he was afraid to wake her up. He decided to try. At the second ring, he would put it down - but perhaps like him, she was also unable to sleep.

She picked the phone on the first ring and said, "I was just getting ready to call you. I have spoken to some friends of my grandfather. They are in contact with Mogul and they say the prison has been located. He is being kept in Sheung Wan on the Island, just behind Fatty's home. It seems that officers of the Hong Kong Special Police Force are willing to mount an unofficial operation to free him."

"Can we also go there?"

"Yes, that's what I was going to ask you, we must go there. Let's meet at the Hong Kong Museum of Medicine on Caine Road, and we'll walk down together. I am going to ask Mogul to move back to Hong Kong."

Marco dressed quickly, wearing a pair of jeans, a T-shirt, and a leather jacket, then he walked down to Caine Road. Fifteen minutes later Blanchefleur arrived in a taxi coming from Kowloon, only a few hours after having separated. She was also wearing casual clothes. They fell into each other's arms and kissed in the middle of the still, empty road. They moved slowly in the darkness down steps built a century before over the open-air cemetery, where thousands of victims of the plague had been hastily buried and covered with lime.

The Museum of Medicine was on their left, but down they went, until they reached the Man Mo Temple, on the left of Square Street, and there they waited. The place looked deserted.

"What can we do now, are the police coming?" Marco whispered.

"Yes, some friends in the Special Force, let's wait for them to arrive. I thought that they would be here already, together with that Mongol girl, Matilda," Blanchefleur said.

They spotted two black cars with their lights off, parked near the Blake Gardens. A man came out of one of the cars, walked towards them, and said, "My name is Eric Wong. I am the police team leader. We have placed two agents outside the apartment where the suspects are hiding, and we have another with special listening devices in place. They are snoring all right."

"How many of them are inside?" Marco asked.

"Two inside a small apartment. They prepared an escape route through the back, but we will wait up there to catch them if they try to flee."

"Are you all policemen?" Marco asked.

"Yes, but this is an unofficial operation of the ICAC."

"The ICAC?" asked Marco.

"The Independent Commission against Corruption. We are independent from all the other branches, and we answer only to the Chief Executive through our commissioner. Really, you have never heard about us? Then you must not be Hongkonghese."

"But what do you expect to find there, besides Aldo?"

"Perhaps cocaine, plus somebody wanted for murder in Macau."

"And if you do not find any drugs?"

"We will find them, don't worry." Eric said with a crafty smile, lifting a small plastic envelope filled with white powder.

At that moment Matilda arrived and ascended on foot to Blake Gardens.

"You two are quite eye-catching," Eric noted, looking at Matilda and Blanchefleur, and without a hint of flattery, added, "Someone may think we are shooting the third Charlie's Angels movie. Don't stick together. I'm already contravening our official regulations by letting civilians near a police operation. If something ugly happens, I'll be in great trouble. I am taking this risk only because of Richard and the old 14K."

The sun had risen over the city and a plainclothesman approached Eric, muttering a few words.

"Well, we'll go in at the signal. Matilda is accredited so she can join us, but she cannot use firearms."

"I don't need firearms. These will be enough," Matilda answered, showing the metallic tips of her shoes. She was eager to avenge the killing of her partner, Betty.

They were facing a rundown building built during the sixties, like most of the others in the area. There were several hanging structures, mostly constructed illegally, a common occurrence in Hong Kong, and all a source of sudden falls and deadly fires.

"This is a zone for cheap prostitution, where they take advantage of poor female immigrants from China," Eric explained. "Before the economic crisis, the fee was forty US dollars, but they have since reduced the fee to twenty for basic intercourse. Handicapped girls are in great demand because they have a reputation for accepting anything."

"I could have never imagined that...Who might be their clients?" Marco asked.

"Any type, you can take your pick. Common workers, salary men, lawyers, doctors, priests, policemen. A few months ago we caught one of the leaders of the Democratic Party. He had to resign in shame. But that was work commissioned by our colleagues beyond the bamboo curtain. He even asked the wretched girl for seven courses!"

Eric turned to his colleague and had a good laugh.

"Seven courses, like at a restaurant?"

"Sorry, I don't want to get into details, but you should know that here in Hong Kong, men are generally restrained with their wives, who, apparently, are not very interested in sex."

Eric nervously lit a cigarette, but squashed it under his foot after only two puffs. He looked around and whispered, "Ready now!"

He looked nervously at his watch: "Time to enter. We'll use the staircase to go down one floor. They may have installed a video camera. Let's enter one by one. If there is anyone on guard, he will think we are just looking for prostitutes. We should descend at the same time as two policemen and Matilda will break in through the door. Knowing our suckers, they may try to flee through the back. I'll go first, then one by one, every five minutes, you will follow me," ordered Eric. He crossed the road and entered the crumbling building, imitating the waving of a drunk and leaning against the wall. Blanchefleur got closer to Marco, whispering to him, "I am afraid, stay close to me."

"Don't be, they seem professional, and Matilda is a strong girl, a true Mongol warrior," Marco said reassuringly.

"Go ahead, don't stay here. Go up, the road is free," said a policeman, speaking into a walkie-talkie, "Green light! They've signaled they are still sleeping."

Matilda and the policemen who were there already made a sign not to talk and went ahead. After entering the gate, they descended the irregular and filthy stairs, then she pointed at the door.

Eric pointed toward the rusted gate, signaling that from there the gangsters may try to get outside, while two policemen moved gingerly around so as not to cause noise and spoke slowly into walkie-talkies. Eric returned to the main door and gave the sign they were one minute away from the break-in while the grating at the door was silently moved away and the police placed a plastic explosive on the lock with a radio detonator. The explosion would certainly open a wide hole there.

The moment arrived. The policemen, wearing protective armored plates, took out their revolvers and gave a last look at the floor plan of the rooms where the two gangsters and the hostage were sleeping. A plain-clothed man sent the signal that activated the detonator. The floor vibrated with a deafening sound and the whole building was violently shaken with the sound of broken glass and objects falling. The door was unhinged and did indeed fall inwards. The policemen entered, guns aimed forward and shielded by the blinding lights of special halogen lamps.

One-armed boy, almost naked and covered in tattoos, came out from one of the rooms with an automatic pistol in his hand.

One of the policemen yelled at him to drop it, but instead, he aimed. The policeman fired two shots, hitting him in the legs. The other gangster entered the room with access to the rear gate but was hit between the ribs by a vicious kick by Matilda, breaking two of them. He fell on the floor wriggling, his face twisted in pain. They found Aldo tied to the steel pipe, but Fatty was not there. Marco went to Aldo while a policeman armed with a saw helped to cut him free from the chain. Aldo looked distressed, frightened, and confused, but at least he was in one piece with no wounds.

"Congratulations, a perfect operation," Aldo said to Eric with a breath of relief.

"Are you hurt? No? Now let's search for drugs."

The apartment was a true haunt. Everything was in disorder; there were several pornographic DVDs, and some food bought at a nearby supermarket scattered around, among empty cans of beer. An ambulance arrived while policemen put crime tape on the staircase to keep away other tenants who had rushed out to see what had happened.

"Here, here!" exclaimed Eric and from a white envelope hidden in a drawer appeared some white powder, which he tasted with a finger. "Crack-heroine. Twenty years in jail are guaranteed. The magistrate will give a discount to the one who speaks first about the killing in Macau. Case solved. Bingo! Can you look around and see if you can find the relic? This place is small, so you should find it pretty fast. . .Better rush because journalists will be here in about half an hour."

They searched between the closets and it was there that Blanchefleur found the yellow box. It was hidden inside a drawer under some shirts. Taking it out and opening it, Marco discovered that it was empty.

"What is inside that beautiful box?" asked Eric, watching it from a few steps away.

"It is empty!" Marco said, disgruntled.

"What did you expected to find there?"

"It was stolen in Macau - a very important piece but now it's gone!"

"Fatty took it. I saw it a few hours ago," said Aldo. "He came and went away, putting it into his rucksack."

"Aldo, how are you feeling?" asked Marco, passing the box to Blanchefleur.

"I am well, but perhaps it would have been better if they had killed me. What am I going to do now?"

"Don't say that! Let me call Mogul to tell him you are in good shape. He'll be very happy and relieved."

"No, wait. I am still feeling ashamed. I cannot face him after what I have done. . ."

"Don't be silly, Aldo. He said he knows how to solve your financial worries and we think that you were cheated by Fatty, falling into the diabolical trap he set up. Have they beaten you?"

"No, no beating, only death threats."

After they went out into the street, Aldo and Mogul

talked for quite some time over the phone. Aldo was crying and apologizing to him. After that conversation he looked greatly relieved. The last stars were going out and the narrow roads around the building were already filling with people. Steam from the kitchens of small restaurants could be seen rising over the tenement blocks. People were cooking dumplings and rice for breakfast and the shops were reopening, putting out their merchandise. People were briskly in motion, though some were curious, lingering around, trying to guess what was going on with the police.

Marco's phone rang. It was Mogul calling again. "Marco, I am coming up there by car to speak with you. How does Aldo look?"

"Shaken, but better now. Has he told you the Sulde has disappeared? We only have an empty box. . ."

"I am greatly relieved for Aldo and for the golden box of the Sulde. I'll be there in five minutes, don't worry about that."

"We'll wait for you in front of the Man Mo Temple."

Mogul's car arrived and his driver parked it in front of the Confucius Society house on Hollywood Road, just before the Man Mo Temple. Mogul went out to embrace his son and remained close to him until he left, boarding an ambulance called to take him to the hospital for a medical assessment and then on to the police station to make a report. Blanchefleur and Marco entered Mogul's car to return to their home on Conduit Road.

"Blanchefleur, I am sorry for your loss. With your grandfather, I have lost a great friend. . . I'm sorry all this was provoked by Fatty's scheming. But in his defense, I have to say it was Fatty who gave away the location of Aldo's prison, so he wanted to save my son, even though he knew that orders had been issued to kill him. Because of this, and despite everything, I am greatly indebted to Fatty."

"Fatty took the Sulde away, and perhaps it is already in

Beijing. He must have crossed the border with it. Now the Police, the 14K, and the Mongols are looking for him, but he may be out of reach already. We'll never see him again in Hong Kong," Marco said.

"Yes, what should we do now? Having the Sulde fall into the hands of people in power in China is the worst possible scenario," Blanchefleur added.

"Well for that particular Sulde it doesn't matter; it's only a copy made by a Japanese swordsmith before the last war. Poor Zorig, he did not know. We had a closed-circuit system installed, so after I saw him taking the book, I replaced the original Sulde with a copy. The real Sulde is still in Macau with me. . ."

"That's great news, but we should move it out of Macau into Hong Kong," Marco said. "China may step in officially as soon as they discover their people have been duped."

Mogul gravely nodded.

"Yes, we should have it delivered by plane back to Ulaanbaatar as soon as possible."

XXI

Airport on Lantau Island, Hong Kong: Monday, September 19, 2011, 10:00 a.m.

Aldo, still suffering and bruised, was at the airport waiting for his flight bound for Ulaanbaatar. Letting him keep his passport, the police asked him to report back in a week. At the hospital, he was discharged almost immediately and after a conversation with a psychologist, tablets of tranquilizers were provided, to keep his nerves in check.

Marco gave him a call before his departure.

"Aldo, how do you feel?" he asked. "I am sorry that you cannot get any rest but I'm sure this trip Mogul arranged for you will bear good fruit."

"I am all right now, except for some sudden flashbacks, but they told me that after a few weeks and a course of tablets the symptoms should disappear and I'll forget it. It has been a very hard ride, but I cannot complain too much, since I put myself into this predicament. I see it as a lesson which has changed my priorities in life."

"I understand, Aldo. Well, in the meantime we are still looking for Fatty, and if anything new comes up, we'll inform you."

"I feel sorry for him. When they find out it's a fake, they will be furious. I heard him speaking to the jailers. He said he was going to deliver it to people over the Chinese border and disappear forever in China. Just before he went out of the door, he whispered to them that now they could freely dispose of me. That was the worst part of all because I knew what their plans were...And I had mistaken him for a good man, a second father."

"Mogul still thinks he is a good man, and he probably tricked your jailers by alerting him to your whereabouts. You are safe now. And now he knows that he too is a loose thread to be cut. He's aware how ruthless his masters can be. . ."

Before boarding the plane, Aldo received a second call from the minister of commerce of Mongolia, bringing great news for him: he reassured him that his economic worries about the placement of the mining shares he had subscribed to were over. They had found new investors willing to put down the money and they could offer him a profitable way out.

The Mongol Airlines flight took four hours to reach the Chinggis Khan Airport of Ulaanbaatar, where the airplane parked alongside one of the Russian line Aeroflot.

The airport was eleven miles from the capital of Mongolia at an altitude of four-thousand feet. After passport control Aldo went to a teller machine and with his Cirrus card withdrew some Tugrug, the Mongol equivalent of five-hundred American dollars, for his incidental expenditures. Outside, there was a car waiting for him sent by the Ministry. He had no suitcase, only a large leather bag. The driver confirmed that the minister himself was waiting. The temperature was low, only three degrees above zero, but Aldo's padded jacket protected him from the cold, dry wind sweeping the plateau.

"Which hotel has been reserved for the night?" Aldo asked the driver.

"The Kempiski was full and the new Hilton is not finished. We reserved a room for you at the Bayangol Hotel. I hope that it will satisfy you. I will take you there after the meeting with our minister."

"Perfect. I know the place. I spent a night there last year."

It was getting dark. The electric lights were not strong enough to illuminate the mostly unpaved streets. The big buildings in that city were constructed in the ugliest possible Stalinist style of architecture. Windows and doors were protected by iron gates to discourage thieves. There was a strong smell of burnt coal in the air. When they stopped at a crossing to let a truck go by, a group of five urchins, no more than ten years old, gathered around the car, beating on the windows and extending their coal-blackened hands for charity. The driver lifted a disk with the word police written on it, screamed at them to get away, and accelerated forward, nearly running one of them over.

They crossed the Tuul River then entered the main road of Ulaanbaatar, Peace Avenue. They drove over Sukhbaatar Square, where well-lit windows of deluxe shops like Louis Vuitton, Zegna, and Armani were clearly visible. Within fifteen minutes they reached United Nations Street, where five gray, cement blocks were standing. The Ministry of Industry and Commerce was the second block after the Ministry of Finance.

The driver found a parking lot and escorted Aldo to the entrance of that building, then returned to his vehicle. Two soldiers armed with AK-47 assault rifles stood to attention, letting him inside. He ascended a staircase to the second floor and walked along a corridor. The offices were on the right side, with all the doors ajar. Inside, men and women were busy at work in front of their computers.

The Minister of Commerce, Bat Badamsuren, was talking to a secretary. He wore a short-sleeved shirt, despite the cold, and a black tie. He was overweight, wore a pair of steel-rimmed glasses, and had a jolly face, round like a full moon.

"Ah, welcome, Doctor Montecorvo. Was your travel peaceful?"

"Calm and peaceful. Please, call me only Aldo, it is easier to pronounce and I am no longer sure of being a doctor in anything. . ."

"Ah, thank you," the minister laughed and shook his hand. "We are very busy during these days, facing great problems with the Tavan Tolgoi project. To put together Russians and Americans is much more difficult than was initially supposed. But, please, do follow me. Let's move to the meeting room. We have two people from the Ministry of Defense waiting for us. Please, do follow me."

"Is it about the Sulde? Have they been briefed already?"

"Yes, a certain Fatty Ng went to speak to Beijing and in turn they spoke with experts on Mongolian history, but some of them have special connections with us, so to speak, and we were informed almost immediately. That is why we activated two agents in Hong Kong. You met them, Matilda and Betty, the latter unfortunately killed in action recently. We even received a call from a priest in Macau a few days ago who wanted to negotiate a deal for a lot of money. This is a great thing for us and I think that you understand it well, because after all, your family is partially Mongol."

He then took Aldo by the arm in a friendly manner and they walked down the corridor. He opened a door, and they entered a large meeting room with an oval table which could accommodate fifty people but only two were sitting there, an old general and one very attractive girl, no more than thirty years old. They had in front of them two large mugs of tea, and as the Chinese normally do, they were holding them in their hands to warm them up as they waited.

"We have some problems with the heating here. Naughty people say we do it deliberately to reduce discussion times," joked the Minister, and the two guests laughed. He then made the presentations, talking in Mongol and English.

"Aldo, allow me to present to you the Deputy Minister of Defense, General Batukhan." The general stood up and saluted with his hand over the visor of his hat, then took it down and shook hands. He had a skin reminiscent of brown parchment, with narrow eyelids and half-closed eyes observing Aldo through tiny cracks. He was like the robot in Orson Welles' *War of the Worlds*.

"This charming lady is Colonel Altankhuyag. She was a Miss Mongolia finalist in 2004, and is now in charge of the security of our country. As we say, beauty can be a weapon as well; she speaks eight languages and is director of the foreign section of the GIA, our secret service which answers directly to the Prime Minister."

"Enchanté, mademoiselle," Aldo said, kissing her hand.

"Je vous emprie, Monsieur. Asseyez-vous," she answered, indicating the chair and smiling, a bit amused. Aldo was very impressed by the young woman who was wearing a black suit, not a uniform, with a gold brooch pinned on her chest. It was a small Sulde.

They sat down and the lady at once asked what she was looking for. "Is our Sulde, the original one, still in Macau?"

"Yes, it is."

"Not too bad," she breathed a sigh of relief, "if Fatty had had his way it would have already been in Beijing by now."

Aldo added, "The problem came to a head with the arrival in Hong Kong of Marco, Mogul's grandson, and the stealing of Gino's diary."

"I see. . . can I simply call you Aldo? You seem not too shaken by what has happened, a great sign of fortitude. You are a strong man and you know how to mix charm with intelligence. We are sorry for the death of Zorig in Macau and Richard Chan in Hong Kong but we have to act following our national interests. The Chinese might have broken into Mogul's house, harming him. That's why our agents stole his diary and copied it. One of them was later killed by their brutish thugs. Mogul is very precious to us, like you and Marco, being the only two male living descendants of Prince Lob-Tsen Yet-Tsen. We don't want anything happening to you. You are living treasures for our Mongol nation."

"Well, I have never been spoken to like that before but I am not at all displeased. Thank you."

"What should we do now?" the general asked.

"We must get the Sulde back to Mongolia before China

realizes that the one they have it is a fake. Do you think that we should get help from the Hong Kong government?" the lady, a bit naively, demanded.

"Hong Kong is part of China. They know who their new masters are," said the general, shaking his head.

"We should get it back ourselves, perhaps using a diplomatic courier," noted Aldo.

A short silence followed.

"Aldo, may I follow you back to Hong Kong? I can help you with our contacts. I wish to express our feelings clearly. This matter was debated by the top religious and political authorities in our country, the Sulde mustn't get into China's hands. We would even prefer to destroy it, smashing it to pieces if necessary. I am sorry to say such a thing which may sound like blasphemy, but if China gets it, it would spell great trouble for our young nation."

"I understand this point very well." The general added, "If China gets the Sulde, tensions between our nations will increase. Some years ago, a conflict between South Korea and China was averted at the last minute because some Chinese textbooks claimed that the Kingdom of Silla was Chinese, not Korean. We watched that story unfold very closely, studying Beijing's reactions."

"I'll be glad to have you in Hong Kong, Colonel. Should we leave tomorrow morning with the first flight available?"

"I have already reserved seats."

"How efficient. . . I love to travel in good company."

"Me too, but only when I am on a working mission."

Minister Badamsureng nodded then added, "Very well, having settled that, I have to go. Aldo, please excuse me but I cannot entertain you for supper. I should prepare for a meeting with the Undersecretary of Commerce of Kazakhstan."

"I volunteer to take care of our guest," the colonel said.

"You cannot complain, it went well, Aldo," the Minister

jokingly said, patting his back. "And as for that investment of yours, as I told you over the phone, I have spoken to our American partners and they agreed to step in as new investors. They will provide the necessary funds you need and subscribe the shares you had booked. This is the gift we have prepared for you. See, you are having a very rewarding trip this time!"

He tapped Aldo again on the shoulder, winked and then went out. Aldo felt greatly relieved as his bankruptcy was averted. He turned to the army officer and said, "General, we would like to have you join us tonight."

"Thank you, that's very kind of you but no, I have my wife waiting for me at home with my grandchildren. Perhaps next time."

The young colonel looked at Aldo and asked, "Where do you want to go tonight for supper?"

"I do believe there is an Italian restaurant inside my hotel called the Bellagio."

"Ah, that is an excellent Vietnamese restaurant. Names, like appearances, can deceive."

"May I ask you what your full name is?"

"My first name is Sarangerel, meaning moonlight. Colonel Altankhuyag Sarangerel."

The same name of my grandmother, perhaps a good omen! Aldo thought.

XXII

Macau: Tuesday, September 19, 2011, 8 a.m.

Mogul returned to Macau and invited Marco and Blanchefleur to join him. Once they got there, they had a light lunch together and then picked up the fateful yellow box, which was heavier than before.

"You should take this home with you. You may imagine what it contains. I trust you."

"How can we get back to Hong Kong, any suggestions?" Marco asked.

"It will be risky if you return by the regular route, so what I will ask you to do is go to China through the Porta do Cerco, together with tourists and traders. No one would consider you so foolish as to do it with the Sulde. I think they have not yet found out they were duped, but this peaceful lull will not last for long. I believe that, within the next hours, they will discover it is just a clever copy. Once in China, you may get back to Hong Kong by taxi."

"Are you sure it will be all right, Mogul?" Marco asked, very worried.

"Not totally sure but almost sure - yes. You may go now."

They left by taxi and walked through Chinese customs. When they reached the other side, Marco applied for a one-day tourist visa. They flagged a taxi, asking to be taken to Lok Ma Chau, a new secondary border crossing. It took them almost four tense hours in the taxi to get there. Upon leaving China and re-entering Hong Kong, they were greatly relieved. The gamble had worked perfectly well, and they immediately gave a call to Mogul to inform him they were back in the former British colony.

"Good, young Mogul, I am proud of you. From now on you have to be extra careful. I received a call from Fatty a few minutes ago, and he said that Chinese experts in Beijing have realized the Sulde in their hands is a fake."

"How could they have found that out so quickly?"

"Well, after all, it is not rocket science. They simply tested the steel of the blades and the mane hairs. They correctly estimated it to be Japanese-work made in the swinging twenties and not a thirteenth-century Mongolian one."

"How is Fatty?"

"He is in deep trouble - he is possibly going to meet his end. I told him to come here to Macau where I would provide shelter for him, but he refused. He is in Hong Kong - he did not go back to China."

"I feel sorry for him after all that has happened, but what should we do now?"

"Listen to me now. You must go with Blanchefleur to the InterContinental Hotel in Tsimtsatshui and wait there for Aldo. He is on his way back from Mongolia. Afterwards, I'll send my boat, the *Pantelleria*, to pick you up and take you back to Macau. We'll have to celebrate!"

"We should reach the InterContinental in twenty minutes."

"Then you'll have time for an afternoon tea before seeing the *Pantelleria*."

The InterContinental is a five-star hotel in front of the Peninsula Hotel, overlooking the bay on the tip of Kowloon. Marco and Blanchefleur sat down in the splendid lobby, facing its tall and luminous windows over the bay. In the distance, they could see the Peak towering over the City of Victoria as Central was once known. They had sweet fruits and excellent brioches filled with chocolate, then two large cups of coffee.

Aldo reached them an hour later, together with Sarangerel. They rushed into the lobby, and after the presentations, sat down with Marco and Blanchefleur, settling in with a couple of sandwiches and beer.

"Marco, Blanchefleur, we are going back to Ulaanbaatar,"

said Aldo. "They are waiting for us to pick up the Sulde. Our flight will leave as soon as we reach the airport. The Mongol government has chartered a small plane for us."

Standing up he hugged them, and they promised that as soon as they reached Mongolia, they would call confirming that all was well. They picked up the large black polyester handbag containing the yellow box with the Sulde and left quickly, boarding the limousine they had booked at the airport.

After an hour, Marco and Blanchefleur saw the *Pantelleria* appear on the left side of the harbor, sailing towards Wanchai. They went out to the walkway dedicated to the actor Bruce Lee, waiting for it to get close to the embankment. There was no need for docking as they quickly stepped on board with the crew's help. The boat departed westward, in the direction of Macau, at full speed.

As soon as they were out of Hong Kong's territorial waters, they were challenged by a speed boat of the Hong Kong maritime police, manned by five soldiers in uniform. They thoroughly searched the vessel using a portable metal detector. The captain of the *Pantelleria* phoned Macau, where the ship was registered, but the police stated they were powerless in international waters.

Soon after, another boat belonging to the Chinese military police approached. The mainland Chinese were a sight to behold, with no shoes, worn-out uniforms, and rusted AK-47 assault rifles on slings. They were so menacing that Marco and Blanchefleur were grateful for the presence of the Hong Kong police. The Chinese from the mainland wanted to redirect the *Pantelleria* back to Guangzhou, arrest them, and search the boat thoroughly, but the Hong Kong police refused to comply, defending the crew and the passengers. A shouting match between the Hongkonghese and the mainland Chinese captains ensued, with the Hong Kong captain screaming more than the mainland Chinese.

After establishing contact with Guangzhou, they recognized that, without a permit, they could not seize a Macanese-registered boat in international waters; grudgingly they left.

Marco and Blanchefleur found Mogul in his villa, sitting peacefully on the sofa where they had left him that same morning.

Mogul exclaimed, with a wide smile on his face, "Now I can see that Zorig and Richard did not die in vain, despite their bad Karma. Their sacrifice has created a new couple and a new Mogul. In a way, their sins are redeemed! Blanchefleur, you know very well that to Richard you were the light of his eyes, but as the poet said, we are merely the bows and you two are the arrows. Both of you are flying into the sky, and considering you come from a Mongol bow, you should fly far.

I intend to retire to a lamasery and spend my remaining years in meditation and prayer. I'll have to leave this world but I'll feel content with you and Aldo taking up my place. Alas, during my long life I have wasted time in useless endeavors just because of my sense of filial duty. Now that the Sulde is returned to Mongolia, all my obligations are over and I may abandon this world."

He looked out of the window, perhaps searching for the right words, and added, "As the Buddha said, the bait is desire and the hook is death. Lacking desire, death ceases to exist. I did not achieve Nirvana during my life and I fear that a new reincarnation is in store for me. I need to make good use of my remaining time."

"Where are you planning to move, Mogul?"

"Oh, not really far. There is a monastery in Hong Kong, on Lamma Island. I'll take a small cell there. I know the Abbott. He is a kind man."

"We'll visit you during the weekends, Mogul," said Blanchefleur.

"No, that will be not possible because I shall be totally

immersed in my preparations and will not be distracted. You will not see me again. Not alive," he smiled, "but don't be sad. We should all be happy and rejoice. Is Aldo doing all right with his Mongol girl?"

"Yes, Mogul, they should be back in Ulaanbaatar with the Sulde. They look like a fine couple to me," Blanchefleur said.

"They are not a couple, not yet," Marco pointed out.

"I have seen the way they look at each other; I am sure that they are a couple!" Blanchefleur insisted, with a smile. Mogul smiled back.

"Good, the magic circle will be soon closed. I feel so happy for my mother and my father because their mission will soon be accomplished. One last thing remains. It is to give you the diary of my father and a sealed letter from his colleague, Vito Modugno."

"Vito Modugno, again that name. . .I remember, I saw a newspaper cutting with his name in Cat Street."

"Giant Antiques? They are very close to Fatty. Possibly the name was on stuff which had been stolen from our home after my faked death in Macau, when they broke in and took away some of my things. Here is the book and here is the sealed letter from Modugno, which my father never wanted to open. It was sealed the day of Modugno's death and he left it behind in Singapore. After reading my father's story, according to your judgement, you may open it or just burn it unopened. You must decide.

But for now, let me give you some preliminary information about what you will find in this book and what happened after my father's death.

First, you should consider that the government of Macau in those years was a lame duck against China; they were powerless. . . Because of this, the last defensive action taken by my father to protect me and the Sulde was to entrust us to the only force then available, the 14K. They were financially secure and maintained a certain code of honor.

I am talking, of course, about honor among thieves. They refused to deal with the Communist Party of China, with which they engaged in a deadly struggle. Organizations like the 14K can exist only because they can solve the problems of ordinary people, and Maoism was a problem for many. The trouble is, these kinds of secret societies, created to foster unity and nationalism, can easily get out of hand, creating different problems. Some even worse than those they are intended to solve.

My father, Gino, approaching the end of his life, went to see Richard Chan, the young and brilliant new head of the 14K, asking for protection for his only son. He told him that we were under suspicion in China for financial and political reasons. After my father's cremation ceremony, celebrated in Macau in 1964, his ashes were put together with those of my mother and taken to Italy, where they were scattered on the beach of Gadir, on the island of Pantelleria. My father had always wanted their spirits to linger there forever because he felt close to that tiny volcanic island where his mother took him as a child. They had been back there after the end of the Second World War and my mother had fallen in love with the place too after their visit."

"You were alone at that point."

"True, I was alone, but by then I had officially joined the 14K. I was accepted into the Tin Tei Wui Lodge, the Association of the Earth and Heaven. I remember the large red room where I was initiated. It was called the *City of the Poplar Trees*. The initiation was a very complicated business, even more than those used in Masonic Lodges. The elderly members were there wearing red garments with small yellow flags in their left hand and the Sword of Sincerity and Justice in their right.

I could recognize some directors of banks, well-known industrialists, and a couple of artists. The master of ceremonies held a white fan with black characters on it that were written by Sun Yatsen, the father of the Chinese Republic.

In a bronze brazier, they burnt some yellow cards, and I had to swear sincerity and secrecy in Cantonese, on pain of death, thirty-six times. It was a complex, tedious and solemn business which went on for three hours. They gave me the title of *Tai He*, Great Brother, and the office of *Pak Tsz Sin*, that is, Great Advisor. They told me even Sun Yatsen had been through that ceremony, and therefore I should not be ashamed. The father of China, while living in exile in Honolulu, was one of their officials, holding precisely the same degree. After the ceremony, we sat down to eat salted fish, congee, and a glass of warm water - the lunch of poor coolies! After that, I was officially enlisted, and I could enjoy all the privileges reserved for members of their organization. I had become one of them, I could call myself a man of Hung, like all the other brothers. That name derives from their legendary founder and first emperor of the glorious Ming Dynasty, Hung Wu."

Mogul paused to drink some tea and went on with his story.

"Richard never knew anything about the Sulde. He did not know we were its keeper. We led him to believe that the attacks were motivated by our wealth and by the fact that I was the only male descendant of Prince Lob, with solid claims to the Mongolian throne."

"And grandmother, what happened to her?"

"Your grandmother, Amalia, my first wife, died in an accident a few years after the death of my father. I thought your mother had told you."

"Yes, she told me it was a boat accident."

"She was on a boat from Macau to Hong Kong which sank. I am still convinced the boat was intentionally rammed."

"Who did it?" Marco demanded.

"I don't know and I can't say, but we were all tightly monitored. Luckily your mother was away to study. Yes, the circle was shrinking and shrinking around us. Back in Hong Kong, the brilliant idea of Richard Chan was that he would have me killed. Yes, a fake killing in a road accident, on the island of Coloane in August 1974, before my second marriage. The roads on that island were infamously known for the number of traffic accidents, even if there were few cars on the roads."

"Ah, that explains the empty grave!" exclaimed Marco.

"One evening, I went for supper with an Italian orchestra director who had been in Shanghai for forty years where he met my father. With us was a Tuscan sculptor who built the nearby Church of *Our Lady of Sorrow* in a leprosarium and who was a long-time resident of Macau. They took a taxi while I drove my car home.

A tropical storm was approaching, and I pretended to have drunk two bottles of wine, faking drunkenness just to let the other customers notice my state. I left alone in my car, and at a certain point stopped where a man sent by Richard got into the car.

Upon reaching a bend, we pushed the car down a steep slope, then I was picked up by a waiting car and moved to a secret location. Two policemen, also affiliated with the 14K, prepared a false report and a doctor produced the false death certificate for Ferdinand Montecorvo.

I then assumed a new identity, James Osborne, an Anglo-Chinese industrialist who moved to Hong Kong in 1949 from Shanghai. The coffin was quickly sealed putting inside a mannequin filled with stones. The next day, obituaries appeared in the Chinese and Portuguese papers of Macau. A funeral with plenty of flowers, trumpets, and people lamenting my sad demise was rapidly arranged. August is a very warm month, and it is normal to bury the dead as quickly as possible, so no one questioned the reasons for such hurry. The coffin was transported to Hong Kong to avoid a last-minute search and placed in the Roman Catholic cemetery of Happy Valley.

The Hong Kong police trusted the death certificate, why would they not? As for me, I had new documents and moved to a new residence, taking up new Burmese servants. I shaved my hair and surgically altered the profile of my eyebrows and my ears. On the night of my funeral, thieves entered our former residence, but they were unable to find the diary and the Sulde; however, they did take away files and old memories of my father and my mother."

"Ah, perfect timing!"

"Yes, indeed. . . but now my mission is coming to an end, and you will understand why I am going to enter a lamasery. Now, get the book and the letter, and return to Hong Kong by helicopter. They will not send warplanes to intercept you in the sky. Remember, if you want the good things of the past back, you need to change the present. Have a safe return!"

XXIII

Hong Kong:
Tuesday, September 20, 2011, 6:00 p.m.

Back in Hong Kong, Fatty Ng walked up Hollywood Road, passing the Man Mo Temple. He stepped inside, lighting a couple of incense sticks to the infernal gods. He loved that temple because it reminded him of one he had visited as a small, poor war orphan, living with his uncle in Canton. Fatty's parents had been murdered by the Japanese invaders in 1944, and as a child he had never failed to visit it every evening, asking the gods to return his mother. Seeing that the gods did not deliver, he lost faith in them and threw in his lot with the Communist gods - Marx, Lenin, and later Mao.

On that day, he requested them to arrange a space close to his parents, because he would be visiting soon. *I must take responsibility for my mistakes, and I'll end my life in style, like a Ming Dynasty scholar who has displeased his Emperor. It is about time for me to mount on the heavenly dragon. . .*He thought, certain that they could arrange that.

Fatty was heading to the Foreign Correspondents Club on Lower Albert Road, an old building full of memories. He had been a member for fifty years, and in a way, it was his second home. Among his fondest memories were the nights spent with great journalists like Richard Hughes, Guy Searls, Donald Wise, and Tiziano Terzani, just to name a few, but he particularly cherished the passionate discussions with Father Ladany, the Jesuit who was publishing the *China News Analysis*.

Fatty had been spying on the China watchers during the seventies and eighties, drinking with them and going home to report his findings to Beijing. Clever as they were, they never had the slightest suspicion there was someone watching their every move. The most entertaining part for him was feeding them false, but cleverly constructed scoops, broadcast around the world.

Plain misinformation for a good cause, he thought. *That, after all, was always my true specialty. Funny and glorious years, with something new coming up every day!*

The weather was wonderful, with a brightly lit sky and a warm wind blowing in from the west.

"*Mundus senescit*. The world is getting old," he sourly whispered, for even the road he had always lived on was changing, with new shops, cozy bars, and restaurants for young people.

Strangely, the police had not yet issued a proper warrant for his arrest - perhaps hoping he would be murdered by assassins from China or by the 14K. That could be the reason they were resisting pressure from the justice department.

Fatty booked a private table at the Chinese restaurant inside the FCC, ordering a whole and extra-fat Beijing duck. At the top of the stairs he was greeted by the restaurant manager, and after sitting down, he selected the most expensive bottle of Mouton Cadet available on the wine list, knowing full well that the bill would be settled by someone else. After finishing the first bottle, he ordered a second, and after drinking half of it, summoned a waitress, asking for a small teapot with hot water.

"I need a strong tea," he told her. When that arrived, he calmly took from his pocket a silver capsule the size of a lighter, containing tea. It was a 300-year-old fermented *pu'er* tea, which he dropped into the hot water. He waited for the color of the brew to turn brown, poured the liquid into a teacup, drank it, and, filling it for a second time, gulped down more.

Then he called for the manager. "My dear friend, would

you mind calling an ambulance for me?"

"Are you not feeling well, Fatty?" the good man asked, slightly alarmed.

"Right now I am feeling great but in less than two hours I'll be dead."

"Fatty, are you joking? Is it the wine?"

"Have I ever joked with you about anything?"

The manager understood. His face paled, and he went out to call the ambulance. Fatty waited patiently at his table for the effects of the poison he had mixed with that excellent tea to work its lethal effects. His last will was laid on the table of the kitchen. His properties would go to the People's Republic of China, for he had no close relations nor friends, having become with advancing age an impervious loner, frequenting only the few opera performances staged in Hong Kong.

Still waiting for the poison to take effect he raised his eyes to look at the simple Chinese decoration of the restaurant and thought about his two great lifelong loves: China and Italian opera.

It was not long before he felt the first symptom of the poison, a strong and painful acidity in his stomach. Right at that moment, he felt like Mario Cavaradossi, facing the firing squad on top of Castel Sant'Angelo in Rome while Tosca was looking at him with eyes full of love, and he distinctly heard her whispering from afar, *gli occhi ti chiuderò con mille baci, e mille ti dirò nomi d'amor!*

He turned to the restaurant manager, who looked terrified, and asked, "How long for the ambulance? I don't want to make a mess here."

"Five minutes, they said."

"Remember to smash this teapot." Then his jaws stuck together as he lost control of his muscles. He would not be able to talk again. He thought it was somehow funny that the puzzling words about smashing the teapot would be his last. *Well, no worse than sacrificing a cock to Aesculapius.*

Puccini's melody flowed back into his mind and he heard Mario's clear and powerful voice singing, *parlami ancora come dianzi parlavi, è cosí dolce il suono della tua voce!*

A waitress rushed in with the bill in her hand, wanting to ask Fatty to sign it, but the manager stood in her way and sent her back with a disapproving look.

He sat at the table facing Fatty with tears running down his cheeks, and he took his hand. Fatty felt comfort in that human contact, while his body slumped on the chair, floating into nothingness on the wings of that wonderful melody. Then he heard shots from the firing squad on Castel Sant'Angelo and Tosca's thrilling and fearful voice, *Là! Muori!. . . Ecco un artista!*

XXIV

Ulaanbaatar, Mongolia:
Tuesday, September 20, 2011, 8:00 p.m.

The Chinese Ministry of the Interior ordered officially to the Hong Kong government to act in securing the Sulde, but it was far too late since the plane carrying it had already flown into Mongolia's airspace. There were rumors that the chief of the Hong Kong police would soon be dismissed, and even their confidence in the Hong Kong chief executive, a man they had never completely trusted because he was devout Catholic, was faltering.

The airplane carrying Aldo and Sarangerel, arrived in Ulaanbaatar that afternoon, and the pilot received instructions to move inside a large hangar for military planes on the far side of the runway. The sliding doors were closed and all the lights were switched on.

Members of the Mongol government were there to greet them, shaking their hands as soon as they had descended the steps.

They explained that the secrecy was due to tense wrangling which had been going on during the past hours between the government of the People's Republic of China and those of Mongolia and Hong Kong. In Beijing, after having realized they had been duped, they were extremely upset with Fatty and the way in which he had handled the operation.

All the key members of the Mongolian government were there with the highest religious authorities, and Aldo had the honor of delivering the yellow box with the Sulde into the hands of the President, a Harvard-educated Democrat. Then the President delivered the sacred relic to the head lama standing near him. He reverently took it, and handling it with enormous respect, carried it away.

The President exchanged a few jokes with Aldo, since they had studied in the same faculty, and they shared memories of their old professors.

"We want to thank you and your father for what you have done for our country. We would have liked to have arranged a special welcoming ceremony, but it will be impossible this time. We'll officially deny that we have received the Sulde. Our secret service," he said looking at Sarangerel, "will spread rumors that indeed something was received - but it was just another fake."

"Then what are you going to do with it?" Aldo asked.

"It will be kept in a temple, hidden away, for a few years. A sort of temporary shelter in a secret location, its whereabouts unknown even to me, and when the waters have calmed, a special temple will be built to store it. We have to wait perhaps ten or twenty years, I don't know, but when everything has been settled, I promise you that your name and deeds will be acknowledged."

"We understand, Mr. President, and we'll maintain our secrecy about the affair," Aldo confirmed.

"Very well, and that is what I was going to ask you. Don't speak about it with anybody. Now let's go to the city and have a late dinner to celebrate. The cars are waiting outside."

Marco and Blanchefleur had an uneventful flight from Macau to Hong Kong. They flew in a pitch-black sky, but after fifteen minutes, they saw a red and white spark appearing over the horizon. The spark then opened like a flower made of pure light - a combination of a billion lights - getting larger and larger. The helicopter veered sharply to the right over Hong Kong among the skyscrapers, and then gently touched down on a platform over the Ferry Pier on the Shun Tak Center.

The diary that Mogul had passed to them was in a bag which he clutched tightly. They were hungry, but decided to return straight home, believing it would be safer than any restaurant. The driver was waiting outside to take them to their house on Conduit Road. They were still nervous, wary of all the cars overtaking them, and felt safe only when they entered their home, greeted by the helper who awaited their return.

"Home sweet home!" Marco said with a deep sigh.

"Can you prepare some spaghetti and salad for me and Marco?" asked Blanchefleur and then she threw her arms around Marco. They felt secure there, and after dinner, they lay down on the bed, very tired but not too much so to keep them from making love for the first time. They fell asleep in each other's arms exhausted, but they could not wait to wash away the dust and sweat accumulated during that long, sweltering day.

Very early the next morning, they awoke to birds chirping on the balcony and the sunlight filtering through the windows. They had forgotten to pull the curtains before falling asleep.

After a breakfast of cheese, toast, and coffee they went up into Aldo's study and sat on a comfortable sofa where they could finally start reading the elusive diary written by Marco's great-grandfather. They were curious to know how such a small book could have caused so much tragedy and passion. Marco read it very slowly and loudly to let Blanchefleur hear, and when he was tired of reading or out of voice, Blanchefleur took over, carrying on with what they wanted to be a non-stop reading session.

PART II

Americans are real freebooters. Trilby hats in hay color, black shirts of wool, khaki trousers, and leather boots. They all have an easygoing air but there are some real crooks among them. Of the Germans, I don't speak because we all know them and because they are always the same, here, in Europe, in the colonies. . .

We, Italians, are nice people and at the same level of the best, although we look like beggars.

- Colonel Tommaso Salsa, Tianjin, September 6, 1900

I

My name is Gino Montecorvo and I will turn ninety-four this year. It is about time for me to put down my memories while still possessing all my mental faculties whereas my bodily faculties are declining by the day. I mean to leave a brief recollection of what happened to me and to Sara, my beloved wife, expounding the strange circumstances which brought us together as keepers of a relic which was entrusted to us. My testament was drawn up a long time ago and left to the notary Jorge Preto in Macau; after my passing, you need to go to him, and he will provide it.

I was born in the town of Enna, in Sicily, in the year 1868. Our family was prominent and respected; we owned a small palace there, close to the Janniscuru Gate. My parents told me when I was a child that the Montecorvo were descendants of a knight who in 1088 had escorted Adelaide del Vasto, bride of King Roger I, from the northern region of Monferrato down to Sicily.

My father's name was Domenico; he was a good man though he spent his youth loafing, which in those times was mistaken for a mark of nobility. He married my mother very late in his life when he was forty-five and she was eighteen. Now that I am much older than him at the time of his death I can see his character in a better light. He was a shy and provincial man, afraid of making mistakes, a quality which provoked several mistakes. Poor father, I am passing such a harsh judgment on him, but I don't love him any the less because of any of this. Not a single day passes without my thinking of him, and I still feel sorry that I was unable to speak to him or help him as a good son should have.

My father made only one big decision in his life. He joined Giuseppe Garibaldi's army of the Thousand which united Italy under the northern Savoy monarchy. Father had been smart enough to understand that, after Garibaldi's landing in Sicily, nothing would ever be the same again, and he enrolled as a simple soldier, but by the time they reached Naples he had been promoted already captain of the Red Shirts and was close to another officer, the future prime minister of Italy, Francesco Crispi.

Recently a Sicilian friend sent me a wonderful novel written in Italian, *The Leopard*, by the late Giuseppe Tomasi di Lampedusa - I knew his father fairly well, which I read with great emotion, because it vividly describes the changes which took place in our world before it vanished into nothingness.

My mother's name was Elisabetta Requesens, and by birth she was a true princess, with Spanish and Norman blood flowing in her veins. The Requesens had a large house in Palermo and a house with a small plot of land on the volcanic island of Pantelleria. My mother suffered all her life in silence, as women often did in those years, and died of a stroke in 1890 when she was still young, while I was away studying in Turin, and thus I missed the chance to bid her farewell for the last time.

In truth, the single most important thing which shaped my character was the discovery of a library inside our home.

I was pleased to read that the same thing happened - if one were to compare a great man to a small one like me - to the poet Giacomo Leopardi at Recanati. I had known of the library since I was a toddler, but at first I saw it as merely part of the room's decoration, like a drawer in a table. It was inside my father's studio, but he had inherited it from my grandfather, a notary by profession. On the shelves was a wide but haphazard collection of volumes, some in Latin, a few in Italian, most in French and English. I am sure that they had been put there because they were attractive, not because they had been read by anybody in our house; most of them had unopened leaves which I had to cut with a knife. I think grandfather used that collection of books to impress his clients and sharecroppers with a display of his learning, which of course was just fiction.

The texts written in Italian were surprisingly few. There were some classics like Dante Alighieri, Torquato Tasso, Ludovico Ariosto, Pietro Metastasio, and all the works of Paolo Sarpi, but nothing was published after the end of the eighteenth century. On the other hand, I found the complete works of Voltaire, the entire thirty tomes of the 1777 Geneva edition. Then, the twenty-three volumes of the *1780's Voyages* by La Harpe, and the *Histoire Ecclasiastique* by Fleury, in thirty-seven volumes, in an elegant print dated 1691.

In English, I found Sterne and Shakespeare, but to this day my favorite work is *The History of the Decline and Fall of the Roman Empire* by Edward Gibbon in six tomes, printed in 1776. Only Gibbon is still with me in my studio in Macau, as tangible proof that the world I knew as a young man was not a dream, but really existed.

All those books were bound by a bookbinder using the same bright red leather with gold-stamped titles. On the backs, in pure gold, there was a large impression of a phoenix rising above the flames. It was that weird symbol that first attracted my attention. Only later did I begin opening and looking inside them to understand what they were saying, trying to guess what those bewildering words could mean. I suspected they might have contained wonderful fables, like those my mother was telling me.

That proved to be the case when I stumbled across an eighteenth-century Latin edition of Aesop's fables which had many wonderful woodblock impressions., I was smitten. I felt the attraction and the curiosity for the strangeness of those foreign languages. In the years which followed, I consumed those books, reading and re-reading them. I can still recite, now that I am old, whole pages that I committed to memory.

Through them I learned English, Latin, and French. My amused parents, noticing my inclination for foreign languages, employed a lady who spoke French and English and an old priest who visited twice a week and tutored me in Latin. I must say those readings gave me a great ease with foreign languages and a strong faith in my capacity to learn. That later helped me greatly to add Khalkha, Mandarin, and the most difficult of all, Cantonese, to my linguistic repertoire.

The Italian reunification of 1861, to which my father had given his unconditional support, did not bode well for our family's finances. To make things worse, my father wasted away a large part of our patrimony, including my mother's dowry, in rash financial speculations, and it was that, I believe, which proved to be the last straw that broke her heart.

By 1888 my then-impoverished parents, no longer able to afford financial support for my legal studies at the University of Palermo, moved me to the military academy of Turin, where I ended my studies in 1892 with the rank of lieutenant in the Royal Engineers Corps.

The general opinion shared by all Italy at that time was that we had to build a colonial empire like all the other European nations had, and out of a spirit of adventure I volunteered for Africa. The lands of Abyssinia and Eritrea were then under the regency of General Oreste Baratieri, whom my father had known personally when they fought shoulder to shoulder in Garibaldi's ragtag army.

We embarked from Naples in January 1894, and after travelling through the Suez Canal, we arrived at our garrison posts. There the shame of our defeat at Dogali in 1887, was still burning with constant calls for revenge - at Dogali, 500 soldiers had been massacred together with their commanding officer, Tommaso De Cristoforis. The year following my arrival, a new tragedy struck us. In hindsight,

I can say it was another warning which went unheeded: the Amba Alagi massacre. 2,000 Italian soldiers were killed with Major Toselli at their head.

Then there was Adowa. Adowa happened on the first day of March of the year 1896, a Sunday. Negus Menelik II was at the head of an army of 250,000 Ethiopians with 50 Russian advisors who joined in the fight. The battle began in the morning. By midday, it was clear we had lost, while our enemies kept surging forward in waves like madmen, believing that angels were fighting alongside them, recalled by the opening of the Ark of the Covenant.

I can testify that an Ark was there though I can't say it was the one the Queen of Sheba brought to Axum as they were claiming. I saw it in the distance with my binoculars on a hill right under Mount Ecclà. Menelik's blind guardian lifted the lid at his order before the battle. That day I could see no angels at work, but the mere belief of divine intervention strengthened the valor of those fierce warriors.

I don't intend to discuss strategy and tactics here; suffice to say that for reasons of camaraderie with the Ascari - which is what we called our native troops - and to save cartridges, we were given old 70-87 rifles instead of the new Carcano model 91. With the new rifles, I believe, we would have an edge on the enemy, even though we lacked water, medicine, food and were greatly outnumbered.

Any prudent commander put in the same dire straits would have ordered a general withdrawal, but General Baratieri, on receiving orders from Rome to engage, did just that, oblivious of the fact that all the odds were against us. He forgot the precept of his old commander, Giuseppe Garibaldi, who used to say that the best general is always the one who wins, not the one who follows orders. Let me speak a bit more about that day, because as you can imagine, it is still vividly imprinted on my memory.

We were part of the division of General Vittorio

Emanuele da Bormida, who was killed on the spot and whose body was never found. I was at the right wing, close to the valley of Mariam Sciavitù, with a company of native troops mixed with Italians of the Third Battalion led by Colonel Ragni. Our orders were to advance and fall to the left in a pincer maneuver, a movement we were unable to perform because our center was overwhelmed by the sheer number of the Ethiopians.

I believe I killed four or five enemies with my revolver, and I could only come out alive from that carnage by turning and fleeing. I ran, unashamed, together with common troopers, while some of my heroic friends took a stand, dying there as heroes or, as dogs, it all depends on one's point of view. I salute them for their blind courage, but the position was untenable.

We left our cannons behind and regrouped once we arrived at the small town, Adi Caièh, the evening of the third of March. Then, pushing desperately forward, we were in Massaua on the fourth of March. The surging enemy could have easily thrown us into the sea, but inexplicably, they halted and dispersed. Perhaps they themselves had been surprised by their easy victory over a European army; Alternatively, perhaps they did not want to push their luck too far.

As soon as the full extent of our disaster became known, all hell broke loose in Italy. A few days later, with the enemy out of sight and using the banner of the Red Cross, I led a group of soldiers back to the scene of the battle to look for the wounded, but we found none. They had been killed or left to die under the sun and in the freezing nights.

We found one of my classmates from the Turin Academy, Lieutenant Vito Modugno, still alive: he had been hiding for four days and four nights without water or food on a rocky hill. He told us something about his ordeal. One night he managed to kill a hyena with his bayonet while laying down and pretending to be dead, thus getting some fresh meat.

Several of our dead soldiers had been dreadfully mutilated. We found the body of another of our classmates disfigured, with his genitals cut and stuffed into his mouth.

II

There, I came to know the aide de camps of General Baratieri, a man who left an indelible mark on me: Major Tommaso Salsa, a native of Treviso, a northern city. Today, he is almost forgotten, but in my opinion, he was the most capable officer I ever had the honor to serve. A pity that he died of fever before the onset of the Great War, because he would have made a great commander-in-chief, far better than General Cadorna and Armando Diaz.

At Adowa, Major Salsa firmly insisted on withdrawing and not engaging the enemy, but because of faulty intelligence and pressed by politicians in Rome, General Baratieri decided otherwise.

After the battle, I escorted Major Salsa to the enemy's camp to negotiate the terms of peace. First, we demanded we should give a proper burial to our 7,000 dead, then we could discuss all the other terms, like liberating the 700 soldiers and 47 officers they still held. They agreed to everything because they had no wish to escalate the conflict.

I sailed back home in 1898, and there I met my aged father for the last time, but I was impatient to leave again. I was first posted to Palermo, a city that looked magnificent to me after the wilderness of Africa. There, I lodged in the house of one of my uncles.

The most vivid images remaining in my memory of Palermo were those of the evenings I spent at the Bellini Theater watching Eleonora Duse on stage. I can still visualize her acting in *La Gioconda*, a work written for her by the poet Gabriele D'Annunzio. Watching her for the first time in my life, I felt the sweeping power radiating from that great actress performing on stage. It had not been the first time I entered a theater, but that evening was very special for me; all merit was certainly due to the divine Duse, a diva constantly surrounded by gossip of her many passions and affairs. That night, I left the theater bewitched, and returned the next evening, and again the following one.

I felt a great emotion when she recognized me sitting among the spectators on the third night. She looked down and sent a furtive kiss to me, blowing it from the palm of her hand. Since then she has always been in my heart and in my dreams. I followed the path of her career, even when I was stationed in China and afterwards, until her tragic death in Pittsburgh in 1924.

From Palermo, I moved to Venice. Tommaso Salsa, promoted to the rank of Colonel, was also there, then in June 1900, the army was looking for volunteers to be dispatched to China and I signed up.

I met Lieutenant Vito Modugno again, who by then was nicknamed by his men *the hyena-eater*. I mentioned to the lieutenant what Colonel Salsa wanted from me, and he decided to volunteer for China as well, although he had been married only three months before. Later, in Beijing, he would tell me why he had wanted to abandon his young and pregnant wife, but I'll talk about him at length in the following pages.

We were sent to China to free the diplomatic legations of Beijing, besieged by the Boxers. Colonel Salsa had been appointed as one of the commanders of that expedition. We embarked in a rush on the heavy cruiser *Ettore Fieramosca*, the magnificent flagship of our small flotilla, which had a displacement of 3,700 tons. Vito Modugno was also accepted, but he could not join us on the same unit because we were already over the limit. He followed a few days later, boarding another ship departing from Naples.

Once we were reunited in Beijing, Vito told me that on July 19, 1900, the day of their departure, King Umberto of Savoy was in Naples to bid farewell to his soldiers sailing to China.

Stiff and martial as he always appeared in public, he read his farewell speech, which turned out to be his farewell to life. Some of our soldiers were illiterate but had a lively memory. I remember one soldier who, for a cigarette and unintentional comicality, could repeat it - imitating the king's small gestures and tics as well as his words.

His speech had been simple and short, unlike that of the German Kaiser to his soldiers embarking to China from Bremerhaven, who evoked the methods of their ancestors, the Huns, to push them to murder. He said, "Like the Huns 1000 years ago under Attila made themselves a reputation that rendered them immortal, may the name of Germany become known in China, so that no Chinese will be ever able again to raise his eyes on a German."

It was due to such unpleasant words that Germans from then on were called the Huns, a nickname which was to be used well after the First World War.

We left Italy burning with indignation because of what the newspapers had reported: the killing of our minister Giuseppe Salvago Raggi and his family and the grisly details of the massacre of Taiyuan in Shanxi province.

On July 9, 1900, the Chinese provincial governor ordered the massacre of 70 people to include sisters and priests, our old bishop, Francesco Fogolla, among them. We felt proud to participate in such a military enterprise, still smarting after Adowa and feeling like crusaders. We were truly convinced we were carrying our superior civilization to a country full of bloody savages, savages even worse than the Ethiopians who had mutilated our fallen comrades. Of course, we were wrong.

King Umberto had only ten days left to live when he inspected his soldiers. He was shot at Monza on July 29, 1900 by Gaetano Bresci, an anarchist who returned from the United States to vindicate the 1898 massacre of striking workers in Milan; that had been a cruel and unnecessary army operation directed by General Bava Beccaris, who incredibly, received the king's blessings.

Vito told me the king had wide, gray eyes full of sadness, sunk into the orbits above large white moustaches, and he swore to us that he understood the king's premonition of his impending death when he saw a flash of his eyes as he warily inspected his soldiers.

III

I feel you should get an explanation for why we were departing in such haste to China. I'll be brief, since several books have been published on this subject, even though the best account of Italy's intervention remains the one written by my comrade and friend Mario Valli - entitled *The Events in China in the Year 1900* issued in 1905.

The reigning dynasty in China in 1900 was known as Qing, and they were of Mongol descent. They had seized power in 1640, replacing the Ming Dynasty which was ethnically Han Chinese. The Qing provided three great emperors in rapid succession; Kangxi, Yongzhen, and finally Qianlong.

But Lord George McCartney, on meeting Qianlong in 1793, saw the latter ruling a country that was like a magnificent ship in stormy seas but lacking a rudder. After the short reign of Qianlong, his son, Jiajing, Daoguang ascended the Dragon's Throne; upon his death in 1850, it was the turn of Emperor Xianfeng to have a reign full of troubles. Particularly due to a rebellion unleashed by a madman claiming to be the brother of Jesus Christ.

That revolutionary movement, known as *Taiping*, came close to toppling the imperial government. Then in 1860, an Anglo-French army led by Lord Elgin - the son of the man who took the marble friezes from the Parthenon in Athens - invaded China. The Summer Palace was looted and burned while Britain secured the Kowloon Peninsula, adding it to the island of Hong Kong that was annexed in 1841.

That unhappy sovereign died in 1861 at Jehol in Mongolia where he found shelter. On his death, one of his twenty-eight concubines, an attractive but ruthless woman called Cixi (or Yehonada in Manchurian) seized power, placing her toddler-son on the Dragon Throne, thus starting the Tongzi Dynasty. From then on, she acted as regent over the minor emperor, carrying out a true *coup d'état*.

The Tongzi emperor died in 1875 when only seventeen without having produced an heir to the throne. Cixi solved the problem by pushing aside the first bride of Xianfeng and the young bride of Tongzi thus declaring the son of her sister, three-year-old toddler, Zaixian, the new emperor. She, again, nominated herself as his guardian. She was helped in such unlawful dealings by the despised caste of the eunuchs, in control of the levers of the state from within the Forbidden City.

These men were castrated prior to puberty, crippled and greedy, but clever and well educated as well. By force of circumstances they stayed faithful only to those who protected and favored them and tended to stick together as they were often treated as laughing stocks when traveling outside the walls of the imperial palace.

I approached some eunuchs while in Beijing and their garments released the revolting smell of urine their perfumes could not cover. Because of the painful operation undergone as children, most of them suffered from incontinence. This ureic smell also impregnated the walls of the Forbidden City. Not for nothing is there a saying in China, "to stink like a eunuch," since this is an expression founded in fact. I can testify to it myself.

The new emperor was named Guangxu and grew up believing that he was invested with full imperial powers while in fact he was only a puppet in the hands of his aunt and the eunuchs. At a certain point, realizing a disaster about to befall the country, he considered a series of reforms similar to those implemented by Japan. It was a bold program of modernization drawn up by a revolutionary thinker from the Canton province, a man known as Kang Youwei, a learned intellectual but one endowed with little pragmatism.

In September 1889, Kang and Emperor Guangxu kick-started their radical reforms, but underestimated the old woman who having been informed by General Yuan Shikai, ordered the arrest of those hapless amateurs with the help of her loyal eunuchs. Kang's brother was beheaded with five other martyrs, while he managed to flee by sea, assisted by the British.

Emperor Guangxu found shelter at the Italian legation of Beijing, located near the Hatamen Gate. There he had friends, but was soon arrested and relegated to an artificial island in the garden of the Summer Palace, well supplied with opium and surrounded by obliging courtesans who kept a close watch over him. It was a sort of golden cage, where he stayed incarcerated until his death in 1908, probably caused by strangulation or poisoning.

Meanwhile the old empress-dowager lived in comfort surrounded by her reactionary ministers, sharing xenophobic tendencies, who were quite disinterested in making changes. They convinced her it would be possible to exterminate all the foreigners who were noisily at work within the concessions - clamoring all the time for new grants and new privileges - so that the foreign powers could be kicked out of China once and for all.

I met her once for a short audience at the palace, granted with the help of an eccentric Englishman living in Beijing, Sir Edmund Backhouse. He was an extraordinary linguist who had known Oscar Wilde in school and had a fist-fight with Winston Churchill. I am still grateful to Backhouse for the chance he gave me to meet Cixi.

We entered the Forbidden City at sunset and walked a long way through pavilions and up slopes and gilded staircases to the sinister Afternoon Doors, a gate where the condemned had been beheaded for centuries. The strong walls and ditches defending the Imperial Seat were impressive to see. Sculptures of storks, dragons, flowers, and tortoises were everywhere to be seen. The roofs were tiled in yellow and green with glazes shining under the sun. It was indeed like entering a celestial palace.

The empress dowager sat on the throne in a solemn pose throughout our short interview, looking like a wax statue. She uttered a few words in high-pitched Mandarin then dismissing us, had gifts delivered. I received a wonderful porcelain cup, divided into three parts, with a saucer and a lid. In the design, there were sparrows in flight among wisteria flowers. At the base, placed within a square, was the vermillion seal mark of *Guangxu*, and I still treasure it to this very day and keep it in its original red silk box.

Until 1898, Italy maintained two representatives in China. Marquise Giuseppe Salvago Raggi - a Genoese nobleman, and Guido Amedeo Vitale, an interpreter.

Things changed when, in September of that year, the Minister Renato De Martino arrived from Tokyo. He was unfit for diplomatic service being easily excitable, presumptuous, and superstitious. He looked for a spot on the Chinese coast to be claimed by Italy. At his request, Salvago Raggi and Captain Incoronato of the cruiser, *Marco Polo*, met with him for an entire afternoon. Without having done any preliminary study, he placed a map on the table looking for an area to be claimed. They tried to avoid areas considered within interest of the other powers but, jabbing a finger here and there, De Martino persisted to find a spot, any spot, to carry out the occupation.

Three areas were thus selected - Nimrod, San-Mun, and Sam-sa. Captain Incoronato, with the support of Salvago Raggi, prevailed over the rashness of the Minister to allot the necessary time for an inspection of the three spots. Marquise Salvago Raggi had the task of consulting Great Britain to enquire about their views on the matter. The answer came back that they could not see any problem with those areas.

Captain Incoronato left with his ship and De Martino returned to Japan, just five days after his arrival in Beijing.

The cruiser Marco Polo visited Sam-sa, Nimrod, and San-Mun. Captain Incoronato telegraphed that the best choice seemed to be Sam-sa, followed by Nimrod, because of the closeness to Ningbo and Shanghai. The last landing, San-Mun, was not even worth considering, as too much expenditure would be needed just to establish a port.

Renato De Martino, however, for reasons unknown to all, telegraphed Rome to indicate that the bay of San-Mun was the most suitable for occupation. Rome answered, confirming the choice, and the Italian Minister of Foreign Affairs, Napoleone Canevaro, leaked the news to the press for electoral reasons. Soon after, the newspapers ran stories which painted San-Mun as some kind of earthly paradise.

The Italian government dispatched a four-unit fleet to carry out the occupation: The *Elba*, *Etna*, *Piedmont*, and *Vespucci*. The cruiser *Elba*, a unit displacing 2.460 tons, easily got to China because it was already docked at Hong Kong, while the other vessels were soon diverted away by new orders. Commander Cecconi, of the *Elba,* moved to San-Mun, informing the local authorities that Italy had arrived to civilize them and raising our flag.

Renato De Martino moved back to Beijing in March 1899, clamoring for an audience with the Tsung-li Yamen, the equivalent of our Ministry of Foreign Affairs, to present Italy's territorial claims. The Chinese, though badly weakened by their loss to Japan of 1895, refused to take our demands into consideration.

A furious Renato De Martino went back to our legation, put down his requests, and had them delivered officially to the Chinese government. Waiting for their pronouncement, he went to Tianjin to relax in the company of his lover, a Japanese geisha who followed him to China.

Knowing of the contents of that envelope, the Chinese mandarins returned it unopened, a serious slap in the face for the diplomatic world. Indeed, they were surprised that such a small European power, defeated by an army of Ethiopian savages, could dare to ask for so much. They rightly considered it an affront. When the news of the breach of etiquette reached Rome - through Morrison, reporting for *The Times* of London - the Italian press had a field day, and the matter was debated in the Italian Parliament.

Canevaro ordered Renato De Martino to give China an ultimatum, the text was dictated and sent by telegraph. In the meantime, other powers with strong interests in China began to worry that the squabble might escalate, so the ambassador of Great Britain intervened from Rome, asking Minister Canevaro to pour water on the fire, assuring him their alliance would mediate a satisfactory resolution. Convinced by Great Britain and unsure about what to do next, Canevaro sent a new telegram to Renato De Martino, telling him to buy some time and wait for new instructions about the ultimatum.

Bad luck and disorganization decreed that De Martino receive the second telegram first, since it was shorter, while the first one - containing the full text of the ultimatum - arrived second. The order of reception had been inverted and De Martino, close to a nervous breakdown, did as he was told to do. First, he was told to wait before presenting the ultimatum. Later, he received the text of the ultimatum together with the order to present it.

On March 12th, 1899, he duly presented it, asking the imperial Chinese government to answer within forty-eight hours!

IV

The forty-eight hours passed without a word from the Chinese government. A tangled exchange of telegrams ensued between De Martino and Rome, then between Rome and London. The British were incensed with Italy because they thought matters had gone ahead with their advice unheeded.

The bay of San-Mun was lost and furthermore, the new humiliation inflicted on Italy convinced the Chinese that firm resolution would yield similar results in the case of all the foreign powers. Renato De Martino, shamed and accused of being solely responsible for the mess, was recalled back to Italy. Salvago Raggi took his place in Beijing while in Rome the head of the Italian Minister of Foreign Affairs, Napoleon Canevaro, also rolled.

It was at that time that a new xenophobic sect appeared in China, and some foreign residents were quick to blame Italy's diplomatic fiasco for causing their appearance. Most of them were just hopeless and starving peasants called Boxers because of their kung-fu fighting rituals, which they believed made them invulnerable. Their name in Chinese was *Yihetuan*, the fists of the righteous harmony. They murdered a few priests and many Chinese who had converted to Christianity, whom they disparagingly called "rice-Christians," hinting that they had converted only to get free food. During the last months of the dying century, the Boxers spread everywhere in China, starting from Shandong, appearing in village squares, claiming magical powers by resorting to vulgar tricks.

The first Boxers' formations reached the Chinese capital at the beginning of June 1900. Soon after, assaults and arson spread almost unchecked as they enjoyed the tacit complicity of Empress Dowager Cixi, holding secret meetings with

Boxer leaders. The interpreter of the British legation and his wife were roughed up while walking in an alley of Beijing; the same happened to the wife of our minister, Salvago Raggi, but she managed to find shelter inside the diplomatic legation. Worried foreign residents in Beijing found refuge with their families in their respective legations while Favier, the French bishop, sheltered thousands of Chinese Christians within the precincts of his cathedral. Savago Raggi sent eleven of our soldiers to the good bishop, led by Lieutenant Paolini. They were part of the group of thirty-nine sailors who disembarked at Taku on May 30, 1900 from the royal cruiser Elba. They were carrying a Maxim gun and a 37mm cannon which proved handy during the siege.

British Admiral Sir Edward Seymour was in Tianjin, and from there he dispatched 2,000 soldiers to Beijing. They were a small force, composed mainly of British soldiers with 300 Russians, 400 Germans, 25 Austrians, some Americans, and 40 Italians from the ship Calabria, and they arrived from Yokohama on June 1, 1900. Later, an additional 25 Frenchmen and 25 Japanese joined them.

In Beijing, on June 11, a Japanese citizen called Sugiyama was murdered; the same fate befell two Italian engineers at Pao Tin Fu named Cadei and Pesaro, part of a group of Italians employed by a railroad consortium. They were cut to pieces while trying to escape on a barge sailing down the river.

On June 17, the sailors of the ship Elba, together with those of the Calabria, joined to storm the forts of Taku while the Chinese army tried hard, albeit unsuccessfully, to retake Tianjin.

On June 18, our lieutenant Ermanno Carlotto with five of his men were killed, but the defense of Tianjin was successful and the city remained in our hands; mainly thanks to the efforts of an American mining engineer named Herbert Hoover, a man destined to a bright future. Several years later, he was sworn in as the thirty-first President of the United States. His wife, Lou, also helped greatly, showing great mettle.

On June 21, the Empress Dowager declared war on the eleven nations attacking China, including Italy then abandoned Beijing, taking with her the Emperor and some of his concubines. One of them stubbornly objected to being left behind since she wanted to depart with her husband. Following an order by Cixi, her loyal eunuchs grasped the poor girl and threw her, head first, into a well. Some later historians thought this to be just a smear campaign against her, but I know from a credible witness it happened.

Hsu Ching Cheng, a former ambassador to Moscow, spoke to our Sabbione, asking all foreigners in Beijing to leave within twenty-four hours. After a discussion inside the compound, representatives for the foreign powers chose to accept this advice and put themselves with their families under protection by the Chinese Army, abandoning their native servants to the mercy of the homicidal Boxers.

This project was abandoned when on June 20, the German ambassador, Klemens August von Ketteler, was killed by a bullet to the head by a Chinese soldier while on his way to meet the local Mandarins. The German was not very popular among the Chinese after he had mistreated a young Boxer whom he made prisoner and stubbornly refused to hand over to the local police.

The telegraph wires were cut, and from that moment on, the foreign residents of Beijing fought for their lives by barricading themselves inside the legation buildings. Several books were written about the desperate resistance of those men and women during the fifty-five days of the siege, some of which were indeed good although most were bad, full of bitter jingoism and low gossiping.

It was at that point that our newly appointed Minister of Italian Foreign Affairs, Visconti Venosta, sent in our naval squad.

The ship *Fieramosca*, on which I embarked, sailed first, followed by the *Vesuvius* and the *Vettor Pisani* then finally, the torpedo-ram *Stromboli*. More steamboats sailed on July 19: The *Giava*, the *Minghetti*, and the *Singapore*, carrying 2,000 soldiers on board with infantrymen under Colonel Salsa and the Bersaglieri, a force along the lines of special assault troops, under Major Giuseppe Agliardi. Supreme command was given to the bearish Colonel Vincenzo Garioni, a bad choice, as he did not possess the necessary diplomatic and linguistic skills.

The city which impressed me most among all those we visited during our voyage was Hong Kong, where we steamed into port for coal and other provisions, casting anchor at dusk on the evening of August 4, 1900.

The next morning's image of white buildings reflected in the gigantic mirror of a wonderful bay impressed me deeply. It was like an amphitheater with a delicate web of roads, cliffs, and forests climbing on green hills. A mountainous chain was towering over the city with its naked tops still immersed in the nocturnal haze, gently swept away by the rising sun. Deeply moved, I promised to myself that I would return.

On that same day in North China, General Gazalee was made his exit from the walls of Tianjin and marched on Beijing. He headed a multinational group of soldiers, Italians among them. The few detachments of the Chinese army and Boxers they encountered were easily defeated.

In the meantime, we steamed first into Shanghai then Taku near Tianjin. After several delays, our ship arrived, while in Beijing, the besieged legations were liberated.

We tried to land at the mouth of the river Pei-Ho on August 13, 1900, but to our chagrin we found the draught of our ship was too high and we were forced to cast anchor ten miles from the coastline. No one thought of carrying-barges, indispensable for that type of landing operation. We had to ask for them, first from our English allies then from the Russians and the Japanese. Finally, albeit at an exorbitantly high price, we could rent a small Chinese boat named *Shen King* and complete our disembarkation.

The beach where we landed looked like a large black bog, made even more slippery by the rain. During a stop in Shanghai, Admiral Candiani, our supreme commander, bought some horses and a few oxen which helped us pull our carts on the beach. As soon as we stepped on dry land we encountered indescribable chaos, with soldiers of all nationalities cursing and pushing, unable to communicate among themselves, in a sort of Dantesque circle of hell with stray dogs and wild pigs appearing and disappearing in the distance.

By then I had formed a friendship with Lieutenant Rodolfo Borghese, who enrolled me in his unit, commanded by Captain Manusardi, and we marched toward Tianjin. With the sun rising in the sky, clouds of grasshoppers struck, lifting in swarms from the edges of the roads, darkening the sky. We had never seen anything like that; it looked to us like a biblical curse.

After a day's march, we entered Tianjin, where we were welcomed by Lieutenant Premoli, who had been awaiting our arrival. The siege of the legations in Beijing ended on August 15, 1900. Sixty-six foreigners had been killed and one-hundred-fifty injured.

I can confirm that within the imperial court there were intelligent people who recognized that all that blood, contrary to Cixi's best hopes, would spur a negative result and thus tried to sabotage the attempts by the rebels to overcome the diplomatic representatives.

The Chinese had cannons and modern rifles made in Germany; if they had used them effectively, our defense would have lasted a few hours, not fifty-five days. Jung Lu, the

Mandarin troop commander of Beijing, forbade his soldiers to use cannons. Most of their rifles were loaded with blank shots, which made noise but did not cause any casualties.

He despised the Boxers but was unable to stand up to the Empress Dowager during the meetings of the Great Council. Simply put, to disagree with her meant dismissal and the executioner's scimitar on one's neck. In fact, several Chinese high-officials in Beijing saw the stupidity of actions sanctioned by Cixi, and the few having the courage to speak wound up beheaded.

Viceroy Li Hung Chang petitioned the Imperial Throne from Canton, far from Cixi's executioner's sword, writing: *Only a blockhead would throw a stone at a mouse hiding among precious vases of porcelain.*

V

We rested in Tianjin from August 16 to 18. It was occupied by contingents of various foreign troops: Germans, French, Russian Cossacks, and Americans. Outside the city walls, we saw human heads hanging, bound by their pigtails - a sign that Japanese soldiers already passed. The city was destroyed by fire, plunder, and cannonade. Having planned well ahead, French and Russian troops took possession of the salt factories, which provided a secure source of income.

On the evening of August 18, a British officer came to our camp. I did the interpreting for him as he asked if we were willing to cooperate in patrolling the city. We accepted at once, eager as we were to participate in some real fighting, but a few hours later they asked to join other contingents marching on Beijing.

We mounted our carts, crossed a bridge held by the Russians, then pushed ahead up to the railway station where we dismounted and boarded a brand-new train. It was full of soldiers from several nations, ready to advance toward the Chinese capital. They told us that departure was scheduled for midnight, but we only began to move at around five in the morning the next day.

After two hours of slow progress and traveling at walking speed, we paused near a Cossacks' camp in the countryside, and disembarked into a field for breakfast and to relieve ourselves. They told us the track was damaged and therefore we had no other choice but to proceed with carts pulled by horses.

However, because of the soft ground, we made little progress and only with great difficulty. We soon realized the only possibility open to us was to abandon our carts and carry the weapons and ammunitions on our shoulders. We walked under great strain for the whole afternoon, marching close to burnt and abandoned huts. We could see bodies of Chinese civilians lying on the ground.

Exhausted by the marching, we found a camping place at Yang Tsung near a Japanese unit. Darkness had fallen, but we put up our tents right there, nagged by the barking of stray dogs throughout the night. Lights and flashes of nearby fires were visible through the thin canvas of our tents, and every so often rifle shots cracked, perhaps fired by nervous sentries glimpsing shadows.

A nauseating smell of rotten flesh hit us whenever the wind changed direction, and after sunrise, a ghostly show was right before our eyes. There were carcasses of animals and men strewn around the grounds where we slept. It looked like an open-air morgue. Women were raped and butchered; children cut in half; and many bodies with horrendous sword wounds. The air was so heavy that even after many years, I can still smell that foul scent of death in the air as it hit our nostrils.

German officers visited before sunrise, claiming to have collected intelligence that a division of 9,000 Boxers marched in our direction armed with twenty cannons. The news caused great alarm, but we never saw them.

We left, chased by swarms of black flies, troublesome and apparently invincible. They raised from the putrefying bodies lying at the side of the road. We felt their legs when they landed on our skin and shuddered at the contact, afraid of infection. They vanished at sunset, leaving the ground to mosquitoes. We rested, hiding under our blankets and trying with little success to limit their bites.

On August 21, we collected our gear and marched again, trying to tail a German unit on the move. Upon reaching a camp set up by Americans, we decided to rest a while, envious of their fine tents and uniforms and feeling like beggars when comparing those to what we had. We then discovered that some of those American soldiers were, in fact, natives of Italy and our soldiers were able to communicate using some of their dialects.

I still remember a corpulent corporal originating from Bergamo exhorting us in his nearly unintelligible vernacular, to quit Italy and move to the United States of America, and fuck our King and Queen who were starving us, their sons. He screamed that he had an uncle in Arzano, Italy, a village close to Brescia, who could not even feed his children, and two of them had already died because they could only eat cornmeal hash. Our captain took me as a translator to complain to his superior officer about the corporal's despicable language, but we came back empty-handed; he told us the corporal was a good soldier and an American citizen who was exercising his freedom of speech so he flatly refused to endorse any form of punishment or censorship.

Their equipment was first class and the commanding officer, General Adna Chaffee, had a great reputation with his men. We Italians were badly equipped and poorly clothed. We had not even thought about organizing medical assistance for the injured - bizarre when we recall that the Red Cross was created in our own Italy forty years earlier! We sported pith helmets with cork insides on our heads making us look ridiculous. They were fine in the heat of the summer, but did not offer protection during winter when the temperature could drop below zero by several degrees. Apparently in Rome, no one considered that China was not part of Africa.

Working very hard, we loaded our gear onto a junk, intending to drag it forward with our horses, but a few hours later we realized it was sinking and were forced to unload everything in a rush.

On August 22, we departed under the rain at around four in the morning and dragged on for ten hours, until we reached a Buddhist temple full of bronze statues near Hochiwu. Finally, we could enjoy the luxury of having a roof over our heads as we slept inside a pagoda.

We plodded forward the next day, and by evening we reached Matou. There we stopped for a whole day having found another Buddhist lamasery where the lamas welcomed us as warmly as possible, even though they appeared to be frightened. They had good reason to be. We learned later they were shot by a German company trailing behind us.

The sun came back as we sat by the river near that temple and we saw a junk carrying away the wife of our ambassador, Salvago Raggi, the beautiful Marchioness Camilla Salvago Raggi Pallavicino, with her son, Paris. She was escorted by Count Livio Caetani to Japan for some rest after living with the great fear of being butchered inside the besieged legations. On seeing Italian soldiers, she greeted us, shaking her white handkerchief in the air, and we responded with shouts of, "Viva l'Italia!"

The conduct of this grand lady and her husband during the siege was criticized by certain ladies, possibly because of their noble aloofness. However, our representatives never failed to present themselves properly dressed, behaving with great dignity and maintaining a positive attitude, even during the most critical of circumstances. In fact, Salvago Raggi never wanted to take credit for what he accomplished but he had been one of the strongest defenders of the legations; this I heard from several German and British men who lived through the siege.

We marched up again on the same road, passing close-walled cities and abandoned paddy fields. Most of those towns were garrisoned by Japanese soldiers, greeting us with deep bows. Everywhere we could see dead bodies of Chinese civilians, dreadfully mutilated: proof that an army had already preceded us. That evening we reached Tung Chau, only twenty miles from Beijing and larger than the previous cities we had seen. It also looked like a dead city, with no people in sight. It had been stormed on August 12; the bodies had been left to rot in the streets and inside the huts.

What kind of war was this? Why had so many civilians been butchered? Out of utter dismay we were asking ourselves these kinds of questions because not even in Ethiopia had we seen such ruthless butchering of harmless people. We were told that the Boxers were to blame, for venting their rage on their own people, and at first we believed that, only later to discover the truth. Those responsible for the massacres were Germans, Japanese, and Russian Cossacks.

We were met at Tung Chau by Lieutenant Giuseppe Sirianni, who had just arrived from Beijing to escort us there, and he told us that proper accommodation had been arranged. He gave us a quick briefing about what had happened in the Chinese capital and about the arrival of General Seymour.

We entered Beijing on August 27, 1900, passing through the walls of a gate controlled by Russians soldiers. As soon as they saw us they raised their hats, whistling and shouting, but we were unsure of whether this was done as a welcoming gesture or in jest to mock us. Two days later a Russian captain, Nicolaj Leontjev, mentioned, with an insulting smile on his lips, that like me, he was a veteran of Adowa; the difference being that he was on the winning side.

We reached our quarters in the evening because the roads of the capital were cluttered with carts and soldiers. There we met Salvago Raggi quartered in a sort of old mausoleum built to commemorate two eminent Mandarins who had died long before. It was in an area called the Foo, and had an enclosed yard where our soldiers put up their tents while we, officers, made ourselves comfortable under a portico.

The next day, on August 28, a great military parade was arranged for the foreign troops going through the Forbidden City, as a sign of our strength and knowing how bad the Chinese would feel about it. It was arranged according to the number of soldiers, and we Italians were able to march before the last of the Austrian contingent. The only journalist authorized to participate was Arnold Savage Landor, born in Florence but citizen of the world.

After marching, the wives of the diplomats pretended a touristic visit into the imperial quarters, which the powerless Chinese Mandarins had been forced to concede and where the ladies helped themselves to vases, rare jades, paintings, and carvings. Even the wife of the commander-in-chief, Claude MacDonald, did not refrain from the robbery.

Gradually, that great city came back to life, repopulating as soon as the few Chinese who had been left behind saw that the time of indiscriminate violence was over. Then, September 2, our comrades-in-arms from the ship *Fieramosca* reached us, and we were then a battalion of 500 soldiers. Soon, another 2,000 would arrive, and in the end, we numbered 2,453 Italians, out of a total of 65,610 allied troops.

Beijing had been systematically pillaged by Russians and British, with all the prominent mansions systematically looted and their beautiful furniture smashed to get wood for the communal kitchens. The British amassed what they wanted to take away in front of the houses: porcelain, silver, and embroidered vests, guarding it until their carts came to collect the booty for a centralized collection point. Their organization worked like well-greased clockwork. Following their long-established democratic traditions, they put their loot up for auction and their sale went on for three months.

It was there that my colleague, Vito Modugno, finding a mercantile vein inside himself, spent all his money buying articles. He then packed all that stuff, mostly brick-a-brack, into several trunks to take back to Italy with the intention of reselling it for a profit.

When I had first met Vito in Turin he was an awkward-looking young man with a thick moustache, apparently shy but hiding an iron will to enrich himself; his African misadventure further hardening his character. I saw him in action during a punitive expedition organized after our entry in Beijing where he behaved with noteworthy courage.

In Beijing I met a correspondent of the Italian daily newspaper, *Corriere della Sera*. His name was Luigi Barzini, and because of his brilliant reporting he had become famous. I liked him at once. He was intelligent, refined, punctilious, and full of humanity, who was sending home articles in which he described all the horrors committed by the invading armies on defenseless people. In fact, he was one of few reporters who saw through the jingoism so common in those days and pointed out several instances where Chinese people were right and we were wrong.

No one can doubt the Boxers committed unforgivable cruelties, but at times we behaved even worse, while claiming to be civilized people.

Another famous journalist I met was George Morrison, an Australian who reported for London's *Times*, a man with few scruples. Barzini reached China after the liberation of the diplomatic legations, while Morrison witnessed events unfold firsthand, participating in the defense and getting wounded by a gunshot. Luigi Barzini returned to China in 1907 for a sporty enterprise, the Beijing-Paris automobile rally, along with the brother of our Rodolfo Borghese, Prince Scipione Borghese, who drove the whole way, making Barzini more famous all over the world.

On Wednesday, October 10, 1900, we received orders to get prepared for departure to Pao Tin Fu, a city known today as Baoding, for a new punitive expedition promoted by the Germans. The supreme commander would be the Prussian Marshal, Alfred von Waldersee. We prepared our supplies for approximately twenty days; crackers, tins of corned beef, and 120 cartridges for each soldier.

Our column comprised of 400 soldiers under the

command of Colonel Salsa. After two days' preparations, an hour before sunrise on October 12, we departed. We marched through the Tartar city and went through the shacks of this Chinese city, entering a district controlled by the Germans, and as had been agreed, some of their soldiers joined us.

They had horses and one cannon, and were led by Colonel Noremann, to whom Salsa transferred the command. Fifty minutes marching and ten-minutes rest. We crossed the Marco Polo Bridge, and a little further down the first German soldiers began to faint due to the warm weather and excessive speed, as they were carrying heavier equipment than we were.

A few miles later, more soldiers joined our marching column with General Gaselee at their head, dutifully given the supreme command by Noremann. Then two more detachments came up from Tianjin and joined us, one were Frenchmen and the other, Germans. A detachment of Japanese trailed behind.

We camped early that evening and were awakened at seven the next morning. Our plan was to proceed for a further twenty miles. In the afternoon, we reached Liu Tien Kok, where the French had already hoisted their flag. We rested there for the night and departed the following day in the direction of Cho Chao.

On the walls of the city we found bundles of severed heads, all bound together by their pigtails; the Mandarin leader of the place, wanting to endear himself to us, told General Gazalee those severed heads belonged to dangerous Boxers, but many of us doubted his sincerity. Luigi Barzini, who was with us, also wrote of these episodes and of the other events which followed for his newspaper.

On October 15, we stopped in open country because the long-awaited column from Tianjin had been delayed, but again, no enemies were forthcoming. We heard of unspeakable cruelties committed there by the Boxers, but once we reached that place we realized those accounts were exaggerations.

The greatest problems we had to face in those days were not the Boxers' assaults but rather the incessant scheming of the French. They insisted on being the undisputed patron of the Catholic Church, citing that every sister and priest in China should be under their control, and even Italian missionaries needed to obtain their approval before their every move.

The French also wanted to be the patrons of China and of all the Chinese people, working against our interests, even though we were allies. On a regular basis, the French troops, mainly Zouaves and Lancers, sprinted ahead of the other troops to raise their flags. One day, on seeing the same thing happen yet again, even our fellow Germans began to feel weary of their arrogance.

While we marched, one Frenchman shouted at us, "Ah, voilà, notre drapeau. Vive la France!"

One of our soldiers, a stout-looking trooper, came out of the column and hit the Frenchman flat in the face. a powerful jab which sent him sprawling on the ground. Other Frenchmen surged forward to attack our soldier and as an officer, I felt compelled to step forward, ending the brawl. I spoke sternly to our soldier, pretending to scold him for what he had done.

He gave me his name, which I noted ceremoniously on my notebook. Diego Sainaghi, a twenty-year-old peasant from Turbigo, a hamlet twenty-five miles from Milan. The French soldiers, seeing me speak so harshly to the man, thought I was ordering his arrest, and, grumbling, went away, carrying their half-dead comrade with them.

That same evening, we threw a small party in honor of Private Sainaghi who - even though sternly warned not to do it again – was congratulated for putting a stop to that insufferable Gallic cockiness. Even our German comrades sent tins of sausages for him. Many years later, I learned, from Sainaghi's commanding officer, that he had a difficult journey home. He was on the ship *Montenegro* when they had an epidemic of typhus. Several soldiers died, but he survived because of a strong constitution and disembarked at Singapore where he recovered for a couple of months.

He was then discharged from the army on medical grounds and left there penniless. He enrolled as a cook on a ship bound to Peru, where he remained for a couple of years and set up an ice cream shop but then, feeling homesick, returned to his small village, not having mailed even a postcard to his family.

On arrival, he discovered they were saying Mass for his soul in the church. However, in the end he proved lucky; his fiancée rejected all suitors, and the two finally got married and lived happily thereafter with their five children.

Just outside Ausung we met Father Scipioni, an Italian missionary, hiding and being taken care of by his faithful. It goes without saying that he was happy to see us. He had been declared dead two months earlier, but there he was, quite alive!

On Friday October 19, we formed a column and pushed forward. When we were about ten miles from our destination, we saw a railroad already functioning. It had been built by a Franco-Belgian consortium to connect Beijing to Hankow. The tracks had been pulled up but some French Zouaves were quickly putting them back in place.

On the way back, marching nonstop, we met two or three Chinese. Being suspicious of the time and place of our encounter, we took their lives without hesitation. . . these horrendous words, written in my comrade, Rodolfo Borghese' memoirs, published several years later, titled, *In China Against the Boxers*.

I was a witness to that cold-blooded murder, which was

sanctioned by Colonel Garioni, being anxious to emulate the steely Germans. Those executed were just young boys; I still remember their eyes full of terror and innocence when we lined them up against a wall to be shot. I have since concluded that justice does not belong to our world. Perhaps we'll find some in the next one, even if no one can be sure about it.

VI

Snow began to fall and marching forward became harder. We saw the massive walls of Pao Tin Fu emerging in the distance among the frost-covered vegetation. They reminded us - being literate, educated, young officers - of Dite, the infernal city described by poet Dante Alighieri. We approached from the north gate, and through the haze we found Mandarins waiting for us, offering fresh food and gifts.

No enemies were in sight, and once more, we saw French flags flying on top of the pennons. This time they were side by side with the imperial Chinese banners. Soldiers who belonged to the Chinese regular army were spotted patrolling the walls alongside the French. We knocked at the gate but incredibly, the French refused to open. When their commander, General Bailloud, was called onto the ramparts, he refused us entry declaring the city to be a French protectorate.

Cursing them, we had to find shelter from the falling snow among the pigsties outside the walls. The next day, General Gazalee arrived and when informed of the incident, threatened to shell the walls. Finally, convinced through arguments and as a precursor of their *entente cordiale*, the French opened the gates of the city, conceding that each of its corners could have a different flag hoisted on it.

We marched to the south gate, where we raised our flag to the accompaniment of cheers and singing.

On October 23, the largest part of our column went back to Beijing. Colonel Salsa also departed, but I had to stay. On that same evening, we received some credible intelligence that a division of 5,000 regular Chinese soldiers were marching twenty miles from our positions with every indication that their intentions were hostile. They made us walk for two days looking for them, but nothing was found.

On October 27, we witnessed the executions, a thrilling diversion for our bored soldiers, like watching the lions eating Christians at the Colosseum. I am not going to describe all the gory details because they were illustrated by Luigi Barzini in his famed pictorial style and published in his articles.

Further ahead, on reaching Pao Tin Fu, we discovered the only white people to have lost their lives were eight Americans and one Italian sister. On October 29, we burnt down a village after receiving intelligence from Catholic priests that it had been a Boxers' nest, although we found it uninhabited.

That last day of October is consecrated to the blessed Mary de Requeses by the Roman Catholic Church; a Catalan ancestor of my mother's, from the fourteenth-century. On her anniversary when I was a child, the lovely saint never failed to drop down from heaven some almond sweets for me. For that reason, it has always been a special day, even if in the middle of China, I thought I could not expect the sweets I was craving to fall from the sky. But I was wrong. That day I received an unforgettable gift, making it a day which will be forever carved into my memory.

We had decamped before sunrise with our commander, Colonel Vincenzo Garioni. Basing his assumptions on a faulty map, he thought we were not far from Pa Chau, which is on the main road connecting Tianjin to Beijing, but we had drifted during the march and at around ten in the morning found ourselves outside Hsing Cheng, on the left side of the Pai Kau Ho Canal. We crossed it using a lovely gray bridge built with granite slabs and on the other bank we spotted some chickens, a sign that no foreign soldiers had preceded us. The birds, unsuspecting of their impending fate, were quickly dispatched by our men and sent to the regimental kitchen.

The weather that day was magnificent after the ugly cold

and the rain we experienced before. While our soldiers were pitching tents, I strolled with four other officers inside the walls of Hsing Cheng. The local citizens appeared calm and friendly. We could see people napping in the sun with their backs against the brick walls. I was close to Vito Modugno when we noted a great temple at the base of a hill. In front, there was a pool full of dead and muddied lotus flowers.

"Gino, let's go inside," suggested my companion. Curious as we were, we entered.

That eerie edifice was apparently used as a sort of tribunal because inside we saw statues of angry-looking deities made of wood and plaster. Long scrolls hanging on the walls showed disgusting scenes. Images of tortured figures hung from the walls, portraying blood splatter, dismemberment, beatings with sticks, rolls crushing the unfortunate victims' bones, and, most gruesome, old men devoured by serpents coming out of the ground.

"These may have been evil women, but I would like to have one or two of them here in the flesh," said Vito, jokingly, while pointing his finger at the painting of female adulterers being punished in a brutal fashion. Their breasts were torn with iron pincers while flesh was cut from their buttocks and bellies with a knife. Every image was painted to frighten the accused and provoke them into confessing their crimes. We moved around this deserted place half-cast in shadow and we saw a throne on a pedestal where the magistrate would have listened to the confessions.

"Let's get out of here," I said, having had enough of it.

We surfaced through a massive door at the back of the building, opening on well-greased hinges and leading again into the sunlight. We found ourselves facing another artificial pool, and we walked along a portico of columns that led around to the back of the hill. In front of us was a lofty villa that had been hidden from our eyes. The semi-circular door was ajar. As we stepped inside, we stood in a room glowing in a crepuscular light.

"What's that rustling and whispering? Did you hear it, Vito?"

My comrade nodded, and we gingerly stepped forward.

That house had not been plundered yet, even though it was clearly the home of a wealthy Mandarin. One wall contained hardwood shelves with Chinese books lying flat on their covers of engraved bamboo. Paintings of brownish silk on scrolls were hanging, depicting serene mountain scenes. On the other side were ornate porcelain vases and black rocks of twisted shapes. We removed our side-arms from the holsters and crossed the room while trying, somewhat unsuccessfully, to minimize the clacking sounds of our feet against the warped teak floorboards.

"Let's go," whispered Vito, gesturing towards a room on the far side.

"Etci!"

We heard a sneeze followed by the sound of a girl's voice and approached, quietly opening the doors. There, hiding among rails of embroidered robes, we found two pretty girls - not the fierce Boxers we'd been expecting. The girls stared at us, eyes wide with fear. They wore their long black hair loose, parted in the middle and combed straight at the back.

"Pray, don't kill us!" said one of the girls, speaking in French.

Once we overcame our surprise, we put away our revolvers and reached out our hands. Reassured, they emerged, just as tall as us, and although not usual among Chinese females, they had ample bosoms like our Italian girls.

"We've been hiding for a month in this house from the Boxers." cried one of them in French and trembling like a leaf in the wind.

It was then I noticed lust in my comrade's eyes. In those days, no one would have objected if we had raped the girls.

Perhaps some German or Japanese soldiers would have done so. We saw many similar girls and children that, after being possessed by whole army units, chose to cut their own throats or hang themselves, rather than suffer the shame of that debasement. I lightly touched my companion's elbow and hinted with my eyes to calm down.

"Who lives here?" I demanded.

"Only us now. The Boxers killed our uncle. We arrived three months ago from Urga and now we're stuck."

"Urga, where's that?" asked Vito, who was slowly regaining control of his senses.

"Mongolia. We are Mongols."

"And your uncle's family?"

"Gone. The imperial troops dragged them away. We couldn't save them from these *mantzu*." I learned later this was a derogative term used to describe the southern Chinese.

"Please don't harm us. We'll give you a box of gold!" cried one of the girls.

These words rekindled the lust in my comrade's eyes but that time it was not of erotic desire.

VII

"Where is the box?" demanded Vito, grabbing her arm and shaking her violently. "Where? Tell us!" he screamed. The girl pointed at the staircase. We climbed to the floor above where one of the Mongol girls removed paneling from the wall to reveal a zinc box measuring about a meter on each side.

Vito opened it and we examined the contents of small and glowing bars of pure gold. They most likely were stored there to be used, once beaten into a thin leaf, to decorate the statues of Buddha. There were roughly ten kilograms in total, which could be exchanged for an enormous amount of money.

I saw Vito's neck flush red as he began to sweat. His mind raced, like a horse galloping at a furious speed. How could I know that? It is simple, I was also sweating and thinking the same things. The temptation was too strong for both of us and when we looked into each other's eyes, my plan began to take shape.

Vito pre-empted me, his face twisted with avarice saying, "Let's kill them and bury the treasure in a safe place. We'll be back later to pick it up, when the war is over."

"We can't kill them. We're officers of the Royal Italian Army and gentlemen," I answered, thinking how quick and easy it would be to throw away years of honest work and good intentions transforming ourselves into assassins. Then I added, "And besides, how can we be sure we'll be able to find the box when we return? Perhaps we'll find another of their uncles instead, and he'll chop off our heads in that temple."

"That's true, Gino. That's true, my brother. But we cannot leave this heavenly gift behind. . ."

One girl said, "We're cousins. French missionaries taught

us their language in Urga. My father is a very powerful man in our country. Our relatives will cover you in gold for saving our lives. My father is a prince. Are you French?"

"No, we're Italians," I answered, trying to take charge of my emotions.

Then I spoke again to Vito because we needed to hatch a plan fast.

"We probably have until tomorrow morning. After that they'll start looking for us," and then I said words I thought I would have never uttered, especially in such circumstances. It was as if a spirit took hold of my tongue.

"You. . . do you want to marry us?"

Yes, that is what I asked and I still cannot explain how it came to my mind. Was it the gold, their beauty, or perhaps, just the extraordinary circumstances we were experiencing? After so many years I still don't have an answer and I cannot explain it.

"Are you crazy, Gino?" Vito looked incredulous, "Is this a joke? I'm already married. My wife and daughter are waiting for me in Italy!"

"Yes, we want to marry you," and I cut him off, repeating my demand with more conviction adding, "There is no need to feel threatened by us, we won't harm you, even if you say "no", but we demand, through the right of war, to have you as our brides."

Without knowing, I invoked an ancient Mongol tradition. Later I learned that even the father of Genghis Khan, a warrior called Yesugei, while hunting with his brother, had kidnapped Hoelun from the arms of her betrothed, Chiledu, and having captured her they were married.

I repeated my proposal once more, and I should add I did so in a rather rhetorical poise, "Here, two warriors demand that you become their lawful brides."

My bride, on whom I already set my sights, was the more attractive of the two - or so it seemed to me - and a daughter of the prince. She was called Sarangerel, meaning *moonlight* in Mongol. Her cousin's name was Gazoos, *gazelle*. The two girls looked at us with eyes full of amazement. They exchanged a few words in Mongol then threw themselves down, hugging our legs. They brought their faces to our knees and squeezed them firmly. Sarangerel was clearly smelling me. At the time, I was not aware that Mongols considered bodily scent an important factor when distinguishing attraction from revulsion. From the sweet look both girls gave us, it seemed we passed their olfactory test, even though we had not washed in a week.

The marriage proposal was accepted. The two women were ours, and having demanded them as brides, they became our property, and we, theirs.

"Do you promise to feed us and to honor us, even when we are toothless and our bosoms fall below our belts?" demanded Sarangerel, with the flirtatious charm most women in the world instinctively possess. Their fear was gone.

"We swear it. Sure, sure. . ." answered Vito. He hadn't yet guessed what I had in mind, but because of the gold, decided to follow me down the path, thinking it was just a trick we were playing on them.

"Do you promise a gift of 100 horses to our families?" further pressed Gazoos in a tone between serious and facetious. I looked at Vito and he agreed with comical eagerness. With so much gold, 200 horses wouldn't be a problem.

Our brides grasped our hands and took us to a room on the upper floor. There they took two cups and a bottle of liquor from the shelf, and having poured it, placed them above their heads and recited something in Mongol. They offered the cups to drink, and we happily toasted. We repeated the same ritual over and over, possibly ten times, swearing eternal fidelity and getting quite drunk in the process. The girls then led us into a bedroom, and after washing and refreshing us with their hands, we climbed onto two large beds, and pulled the curtains.

Vito and I were men of the world, so to speak, but that night we experienced carnal delights beyond what two young officers from provincial Italian towns would ever imagine in a thousand years. Our brides later claimed to be taught such arts at thirteen by some old Chinese courtesans employed by their mothers for that very purpose, even though their mothers had warned them to reserve such deep knowledge only for their husband's enjoyment.

We were devoured by a lustful frenzy and hours later, just before dawn, we managed to fall asleep while a violent storm of clapping thunder and lightning was upon us.

Waking up in the morning, we asked our brides to fetch a camphor wood trunk we had seen in the bedroom and fill it with the gold and some silver coins. The two girls proved trustworthy, bringing to our attention two splendid porcelain vases known as moon-flasks. They told us they were their dead uncle's greatest treasure, worth more than their weight in gold. At the base, the square mark of the Qing emperor Yongzhen. Vito and I took them with us, picking up one each. We wrapped them in shawls of silk and put them in a bag as a posthumous wedding gift from our uncle-in-law.

We told the girls the house was a risky place to hide as it could be plundered at any time. Then we lowered the trunk into a cellar at the bottom of a well behind the house. On the way out, we seized a cart drawn by two horses, asking the driver to take us to the railroad we had seen the day before, which was partially operational.

We waited there an hour for a train going in the direction of Beijing. As the steam engine approached in the distance, we stepped on the ballast to stop it in good time, the common way of taking a train in China at the time. Then, we tossed two Mexican silver dollars to the conductor, managing to place our two newly wedded brides in a first-class coach that would carry them ten miles short of the capital where they would find a gig to take them inside the walls. They left, well-endowed with silver coins and a few small bars of gold and a pass we had written and signed.

"We'll meet again at the Temple of Heaven. We will be there every day at five in the evening," Sarangerel said, climbing into the empty coach.

They blew us kisses from the window, and shaking a red handkerchief in the air, Sarangerel shouted, "Au revoir, a Peking, mon amour!"

As soon as the train departed, we rushed back to the camp, where it seemed everyone was seized by a frenzy. They were preparing to launch a search for us, and as a precaution, a dozen local hostages had been arrested.

Luckily, we were career officers, not soldiers. As officers, if they ever learned of our sexual escapades we might receive a dressing-down from our captain, whereas privates would face the firing squad.

Vito and I devised a story to tell to our commander. We would claim to have lost our way while following the trail of some Boxers but were ambushed and forced to hide all night long. Then, waiting for sunrise, we had taken shelter in a flimsy shack.

We were escorted to the tent of Colonel Vincenzo Garioni who, to our great surprise, seemed to pay little attention to the silly story we concocted. Clearly he had more important things on his mind and readily believed us, or perhaps seeing us in such bad shape, thought it plausible we had not slept all night, chased by bands of howling Boxers. He even congratulated us for our lucky escape, telling us he would put us forward for a decoration. He then invited us outside, where a corporal of the Carabinieri, our military police, was being stripped of his grade. The night before he had caused great alarm by shooting a pig. The crack of his gun provoked a general call to arms lasting until the wee hours of the morning, and the camp feared a full-scale attack from the Boxers. This welcome distraction helped us immensely, so we were extremely grateful to that unlucky chap.

"Seems we did it," Vito told me once we were alone. "You're a genius. Good work, Gino!"

Reunited with our men, little time to be congratulated for heroism; we departed soon after, stopping only for a few hours when crossing some empty thatched huts. We were ready for sleep but were again foiled by a group of German soldiers - the usual band of bloody fanatics led by a captain - who informed us that in a nearby city they spotted a great number of Chinese soldiers together with Boxers. By that time, we began to think they were playing jokes on us, but Colonel Garioni heeded their advice and headed in that direction. We marched under a magnificent full moon, trying not to make too much noise.

Vito was close to me and as he looked up to the moon said with a sigh, "Ah, who knows, perhaps my beautiful Gazoos is also looking at it!"

That's love, I thought.

My own marriage ceremony with Sarangerel, up to that point, had only been an exciting erotic experience. I could not imagine then that my fascination would later transform into the greatest love story of my life, and because of her, my life would take a turn for the better, while Vito's would result in utter destruction.

The road was smooth and under the moonlight we could distinguish silver fields, glistening with ice. The only sounds reaching our ears were the faraway haunting barks of hungry dogs. We marched together with some sailors and pushed on for hours until we saw the fog lifting over the city of Ku Nan Hsien.

The Germans marched to the south gate while we were ordered to turn and position ourselves at the north gate in such a way that no enemy could escape. We moved as quietly as possible, clasping shut the mouths of the few horses we had. Suddenly, we heard the sound of a drum coming from inside the citadel, then a second and a third. Finally, the drumming became deafening. Major Agliardi ordered to his Bersaglieri to mount a charge. We were royal engineers, so we halted there and waited together with the sailors.

We saw a stream of people screaming loudly, racing out toward the open countryside from the east gate. They were mostly soldiers tasked with the defense of the city but there were civilians mixed with them, and, in spite of the civilians, Colonel Garioni ordered the troops to open fire. They obeyed, killing many Chinese indiscriminately, only a few returned fire, their bullets whizzing far above our heads. We discovered women and children were among those we had killed. In that war, civilian casualties were just an insignificant detail.

It was then that the gate in front of us opened, and from it emerged a group of tall and fierce-looking soldiers, perhaps Manchu. They were coming for parley, but Garioni seized the opportunity to order an attack and we hurled forward, swords and bayonets ready; a breach of war customs, respected even by savages, but no one cared and on we charged, killing those unlucky ambassadors of peace.

My friend Vito sliced at one of them with a swipe of his sword over the face and theatrically licked the blood remaining on his blade. Was it perhaps the full moon drawing out his true nature, or just the mark of a sadistic character? Lycanthropy was out of the question but the unleashing of emotions, the physical exhaustion, and the lack of sleep from the previous night may have been important factors to explain his behavior.

After the massacre, we entered the gate and went up to the ramparts. They were about five meters tall and still manned by Chinese soldiers, who were so frightened on seeing us coming that they threw themselves over the parapet. Some broke their legs and arms but others who managed to get up and flee for shelter in the forest outside the city were hit by our bullets while they ran.

It appeared to be a form of amusement for our Bersaglieri to shoot at them, like quail-hunting. We had orders to capture all the Chinese soldiers who surrendered, but Vito speared a couple of them with his sword in cold blood, as if they were chickens on a skewer. It was a disgusting sight. I tried to restrain him, warning he would ruin us by acting in such a senseless manner and would expose himself to punishment if found out.

"Do you want to throw away all we have gained? Take it easy, man!" I yelled at him, grabbing his arm. It did not help much, as even our soldiers were working with their bayonets, slashing randomly from right to left, without mercy.

We might have been outnumbered by the Chinese but the fact that we had attacked so suddenly in the dark and with such vicious violence left them no time to assess the situation and respond appropriately. We did not spare many, not even the young boys who threw themselves on their knees, begging for mercy. It was just horrible, far worse than the war we fought in Africa and it was there I made up my mind to get rid of my uniform as soon as possible.

We seized a great number of shotguns, mostly brand new Mauser rifles produced in Germany. Then we began a tour to inspect the city, with caution, as we were still hearing the discharge of musketry in the distance and were afraid that, having realized how few we were, our enemies might mount a counter-attack.

During that night Vito continued to look as if possessed by a demon and in a frenzy, he ordered to his men to attack a house he thought was filled with Boxers. When they arrived, they found one of our sailors locked inside, a man named

Calandrino whom we had taken for dead a few days earlier. He was unharmed.

When dawn broke, we disarmed the Chinese soldiers left standing and turned around the walls for inspection. We found many dead bodies, and many injured who dragged themselves in front of us, showing us their bleeding wounds and asking for mercy, water, and medical assistance. I still remember their faces, twisted in dreadful pain and fear. I felt great pity for them and finally some among us, seeing them in the light of the day, felt moved once they realized they were human beings, like us, not animals.

On November 4, 1900, after loading several carriages with spoils, we hit the road to Beijing. By then, Colonel Garioni was radiating pride because of his victory; I guessed he felt like Caesar after Alesia.

The next day we encountered the column of Colonel Salsa, also returning to the capital. His scouts knew the shortest way, and we followed them into the city. That time, they put us in the Duca degli Abruzzi barracks, right in the middle of a grove which, in better times, had been the private park of a rich Mandarin.

Two days later, washed and trimmed, we attended a great banquet thrown for all the officers of allied nations. At that banquet I again met Luigi Barzini, who presented two French writers to me. One was Major Jean Baptiste Marchand, the explorer, famous for the *Fashoda Affair* in Africa. The other, a plump and small man going by the name of Pierre Loti, was a French naval officer who had arrived in China a month before, when things were already settled; he was a decadent writer, like Gabriele D'Annunzio. Years later Loti collected his newspaper reports in a book entitled *Les Derniers Jours de Péking* which, for reasons I cannot fathom, was destined to be a great success. I read it, but did not like it a bit. I found it full of tiresome rhetoric and historically, it was way off the mark.

Because of my linguistic skills, I developed a strong bond of friendship with a British army officer writing for the *Daily Telegraph*. His name was Vernon Kell. He spoke six languages fluently, but I refined his Italian and in exchange he perfected my English. He later rose to become a general and the director of the British secret service. Our friendship was cemented by our common love for the historical works of Edward Gibbon, and in my library, I still display a photograph he sent to me, showing him surrounded by his happy family. We exchanged some correspondence until 1942, the year he died.

Another remarkable character I met in Beijing was a truly extraordinary American by the name of Homer Lea. Later, he would become the special military advisor to the founder of the Chinese Republic, Sun Yatsen, who held him in such high esteem that he considered giving him the grade of commander-in-chief of the Chinese Republican Army.

The Homer Lea I knew was a boastful character, as short men often are, and an adventurer but in spite of that, he was a man capable of keeping his word, who possessed an iron will despite being handicapped with a serious bodily deficiency, much like our King Vittorio Emanuele III, whom he physically resembled. He was obsessed by the myth of Napoleon. He had a powerful analytical memory but unfortunately, he died at thirty-five, failing to leave a deeper mark on our world. Yet he managed to write two extraordinary books, which I have read three times.

The first was *The Valor of Ignorance* published in 1909 where he correctly forecast a great conflict between the United States and Japan. A translation of this book became a bestseller in Japan like no other, to the point where someone claimed that since it was so widely read and studied, it influenced events rather than simply state the facts. It may not be a completely empty claim that the 1941-1945 war in the Pacific may have been prompted by the lingering effects of that particular book. His second book was *The Day of the Saxon* published in 1912, only a few months after he passed away. In it he predicted the end of the British Empire, its collapse resulting from, in his opinion, the surge of German and Russian expansionism.

Let us end here my literary and historical digressions, otherwise I might go on forever. Books have always been my passion as well as my weakness, as you may have noticed, but in this case, I am surely not alone.

I once met a man who was considerably worse than me in this respect. In Macau, lives a Chinese collector of European incunables named Pedro. A merchant by profession, he counted all his pennies and dressed shoddily, but one day he came to consult me on the expensive acquisition of a fifteenth-century Latin Bible printed in Venice which he was planning to buy through one of his agents in London. I would have never expected that, and I concluded that it is really difficult to judge a man by the way he looks or by what he does. We can never know for sure what goes on in another person's mind.

VIII

Beijing was getting back on its feet and seemed to be as rich and prosperous as it had before that useless war we waged. All the markets were reopening and the vendors' carts were stacked high with goods and provisions. The roads were swept, the rubble cleared, the houses restored, and the Chinese children again played happily in the streets. Vito and I went back to the Temple of Heaven in search of our brides but were unable to find them.

In the meantime, news came that Germans and Austrians were organizing another punitive raid, directed this time at Kalgan, beyond the Great Wall on the borders of the Gobi Desert. Italians were called out to help but luckily Vito and I were not selected. Even our comrade Rodolfo Borghese managed to dodge it with a medical dispensation he received because of his aristocratic connections. His place was taken by Lieutenant Colli di Felizzano. The commander of the Italian column would once more be Colonel Salsa, with the supreme command falling on Marshal Count Alfred von Waldersee.

While our soldiers were away, we enjoyed some rest in the Chinese capital, visiting monuments and dining in the small restaurants which had reopened as if no war had been fought, a clear demonstration of the resilience of the Chinese people.

The column of soldiers coming back from the punitive expedition to Kalgan, made an unremarkable return to Beijing on December 4. They were exhausted after twenty-five days of marching in icy weather.

The only skirmish worth mentioning, happened at Huai Lai, where our Lieutenants Ruspoli, Bichi, and Forteguerri distinguished themselves. Bichi survived a close call with death during an attack: his right thumb was sliced off by a

Boxer armed with a scimitar. The only dead person of note was the German Colonel Count York von Wartemburg, who died from carbon monoxide poisoning. He had fallen asleep, leaving a small stove lit all night. That was the official version. The gossip mill had it instead that a young Chinese girl he took to bed gave him a stroke.

"Dead like Attila, the king of the Huns!" remarked Vito, sarcastically.

We knew that Count Alfred von Waldersee, despite his age of sixty-eight, had taken a Chinese girl as his lover. She was a famous courtesan called Sai Chin-hua. A book in Chinese about their liaison circulated in 1935; it was translated much later into English as *That Woman: The Prussian and the Singing Girl*, but such liaisons were common among many officers and soldiers. We were left free to philander, provided the matter was kept confidential. Venereal diseases often gave the truth away.

Finally, the day came when we found our Mongol wives. The date was December 6, 1900, and we saw them on a gig close to the Temple of Heaven, right where they promised to be. We greeted them from afar but approached cautiously. They told us they had encountered serious problems getting back to the capital and had hidden in a village outside the city walls to avoid being harassed by Russian soldiers. When their horses moved forward, we stood aside, in order not to give any hint of scandal. They slowly returned home, and we followed. Our plan worked well. We followed them as they entered a large villa behind a brick wall while the gig was taken in by two servants.

On the following Sunday morning, we dashed together with our wives to their uncle's villa to recover our hidden treasure, but the beautiful house had been burnt down and all of its exquisite furniture destroyed. Vito ran his hands through his hair in disbelief. However, the Russian Cossacks had not found the well and we were able to load the trunk onto our gig and head back to Beijing, where we arrived late at night.

On December 22, 1900, the peace treaty was ready to be signed. The Chinese were impatient to sign it and watch us leave the way we'd come. They could not bear to suffer any longer the offensive mob of soldiers, often drunkenly roaming through the streets of their beautiful capital. As an interpreter, I was allowed to join a great hunt in the countryside reserved for all the top officers of the foreign nations. It was a crisp, sunny day, and the sight of the officers resplendent with their best uniforms and mounts was unforgettable. That was the last occasion when all the officers were reunited, and it marked the imminent departure of most of us.

Vito and I were able to stay on a little longer since as royal engineers we were charged with the task of building the new Italian legation as well as a garrison for our sailors. We were busy managing the project with hundreds of masons and construction workers.

I remember well that in the month of January 1901 we had almost half a meter of snow, much more than usual. It covered the capitol's roofs, changing its color from muddy and dusty into brilliant white.

It was then the news of Queen Victoria's death reached us by telegraph. I came across an English captain in tears. I tried to console him but he told me, "This is the end of an era, our era."

That turned out true when the Austrian contingent departed during the early days of April 1901 and sailed back to Trieste, which at that time was still part of the Austro-Hungarian Empire.

As for the elusive Boxers, a few more punitive raids were mounted but Vito and I could dodge all of them. By the month of May, the punitive Germans left on a new mission, directed again at Kalgan in Mongolia, and it proved to be the last.

In September, we offered our condolences to the officers of the American contingent after an anarchist gunned down their president, William McKinley. Apparently, the Chinese business was bringing bad luck to all the Western chiefs!

Russia, meanwhile, plotted to annex Mongolia and Tibet, but all the other powers were encouraging China to resist the Tsar's incessant bullying. A war of nerves between Japan and Russia was in full swing over control of Manchuria. A great tension spread among the allies, at times escalating to armed confrontation. We indeed offered a poor show of unity to our Chinese hosts. Then, almost overnight, the Japanese shifted sides, changing their behavior towards the Chinese. From their initial ferocity, they became more than happy to embrace them as Asian brothers, trying to conquer their hearts by opening the doors of their military hospitals, distributing gifts and food to the local citizens, and apparently asking for nothing in return. This was a clear sign they were planning to stay.

On August 26, a few more of my friends left: Lieutenants Manusardi, Bellegarde, and Calvino. They sailed back to Italy on two ships, the *Montenegro* and the *Singapore*, but Vito and I were happy to remain behind, because after all, we were leading a privileged life; so privileged that in Italy it would have been unthinkable. We rebuilt the Italian legation from the ashes, larger than before and strategically set between the French and the Japanese legations, right at the back of the Imperial City. On one side flowed the waters of the Jade Canal and in front was a wide road we had named Avenue of Italy.

The Club of Beijing was within walking distance and we went there every morning for breakfast, having excellent French brioches stuffed with jam and large steaming pots of quality black coffee.

In Tianjin, we took possession of a swampy plot of land

adjacent to the Austro-Hungarian concession, which the Chinese were using as burial ground and where hundreds of rotten coffins poked up from the mud, revealing their contents. It remained Italian until the end of the Second World War and we invested great sums of money to drain and improve it.

There we built roads dedicated to King Vittorio Emanuele III, to Marco Polo, and to Vettor Pisani, as well as majestic villas. In the great square named after Queen Elena we built the first public fountain in all of China.

Our concession was tiny, only half a million square meters in size, which proved useful in raising our profile but failed to promote our business interests. I saw it as a monument to our imperial dreams, though perhaps in hindsight, we should have invested that money in building better schools and hospitals in Italy. But what should I say? That was the spirit of the times and the product of our twisted minds, because with few exceptions, we all were convinced that to lift a nation from poverty, colonies abroad should be established. But I do clearly remember Colonel Salsa saying casually one day that people and entire nations always do things for no better reason than that they see other people and other nations doing it. He was absolutely right!

Vito and I volunteered to stay behind in China but for Vito it did not work out well. Grudgingly and with a broken heart, he packed his belongings and departed, leaving with 38 other officers and 1,138 enlisted soldiers. He took a part of the gold bars with him, and the other we deposited in a bank account at the Hong Kong and Shanghai banking corporation.

Vito reached Italy after a hard trip at the end of 1901 and as soon as he got there discovered why he had been recalled. His wife and father-in-law petitioned the Ministry of War to have him back. Knowing this, he became furious and even more determined to split from her.

Colonel Garioni and Vito left on the same ship and the command of Italian operations in China fell on Colonel Salsa's shoulders, and with his well-tested diplomatic skills everything went better. I had no wife in Italy and my relationship with Sarangerel, who I was by then calling Sara, was still being kept secret.

Vito wrote that he could not find a reasonable pretext to repudiate his wife, but his firm intention was to quit the army altogether, to leave Italy and his Italian wife, and then to return to Beijing to begin a new career as a Mongol trader.

IX

On January 7, 1902, the Empress Dowager Cixi returned to the capital, a signal China was getting back to normality.

Because of my friendship with Lieutenant Borghese, a prince with high connections, I could remain in Beijing until the middle of that year. I went hunting, dined, played polo, and spent precious days with my beloved Sara.

She still dressed her hair long, falling behind her and divided in the middle, contrary to the Chinese fashion of the day which called for braiding. We went out of the Tartar City separately, crossing the Hatamen Gate, both wearing Chinese clothes so as not to be easily spotted. I remember the moment I realized how much I had grown to love her. She was late one day and an inexplicable anguish seized me, thinking something bad might have happened, and when I saw her coming towards me, down the road, my heart jumped with joy. We were living the dream of a butterfly, to use a poetic expression common in China. It was pure bliss and happiness.

She was a great beauty, tall, with long and slender legs, black eyes, and a winning smile, and she used to wear jewels set in enameled silver. I could go on for many pages describing that period in Beijing, because it was the happiest time of my life, with all the small restaurants, the wine houses, and the painters, singers, and poets we befriended, but I feel this diary is not the right place to speak about romance and so I'll go on with my main story.

Knowing full well I could not remain in Beijing forever, I prepared my cards in advance. When my turn came to leave, having exhausted all possible excuses or reasons to stay behind, I was ordered to board one of our cruisers with the greatest part of Italy's remaining contingent still under the command of Colonel Tommaso Salsa, who was departing with us. Only 300 Italian soldiers were left behind in Beijing and Tianjin.

The day of departure dawned and we embarked from Taku on a small boat that carried us to a larger ship anchored a few miles off the coast. Sara was there on shore, waving and blowing kisses. We both cried as a German military band played the Italian royal march to bid us farewell and all the soldiers remaining on shore shouted three times, "Hooray!"

Once aboard the warship *Elba* we sailed slowly alongside the *Puglia* and the *Lombardia*, the other Italian ships anchored in the harbor. We set course for Shanghai and then Hong Kong, where we cast anchor before sunset on October 31,1902, once again on the propitious day of the anniversary of my mother's beloved ancestor, the blessed Mary de Requeses.

We moored in front of the district of Wan Chai and were at once surrounded by the nutshell-shaped boats of the Tangka, the people of the sea who wanted to sell us fresh fruits, delicate embroideries, and salted fish.

That evening the British crown colony of Hong Kong was like an oil painting framed against a golden sky, a very warm day with a red sun setting into the South China Sea. The city looked like the Garden of Eden, full of hope for people fortunate enough to live there, and I was determined to be one of them.

I prepared my luggage, and whatever possessions I left behind with Sara, who would follow shortly. My army service terminated that day, the papers filed and accepted. My father accelerated my release from the army, a relatively simple task because there was a strong mood of general demobilization and my indefinite, unpaid leave had been approved by our young new king, Vittorio Emanuele III.

Unknown to me at that time, some bitter debates were taking place in the Italian parliament, stirred by Socialists who questioned why so much money had been spent on the Chinese expedition - the considerable sum of thirteen million lire - without any practical returns, save for the meager territorial concessions of Tianjin, requiring further expenditures and a concession to station troops in Shanghai. An indemnity to be paid by China was agreed upon in the peace treaty, but few of our representatives were really counting on the debt being honored.

As I was preparing to disembark, having had my passport stamped by a British port officer who came on board, Colonel Salsa surprised me with an order for all officers to line up on the bridge and stand to attention in their best uniforms. He called me forward, gave me my discharge chart, and pinned a silver medal to my chest, while two trumpets and a drum played a happy march. It was called the *flik-flok*, a famous tune among the Bersaglieri. Then, breaking the protocol, he warmly embraced me, saying I reminded him of his son. It was a sad story; he committed suicide for having failed admission to the military academy. Salsa had tears in his eyes as he wished me good luck. I was more moved than he was by what he said and then, from his breast pocket he removed a fountain pen, a red lacquered Waterman with a gold nib.

"This is for you," he said as he handed it to me. "A small gift after all the years we have spent together in Africa and in China. Hold high the good name of Italy, and one day, write down your memoirs using this pen!"

A launch was waiting at starboard, ready to take me to dry land. I boarded it with a sack on my shoulders while the music kept playing the Savoy's royal march and all my comrades shouted with joy. I saluted them, deeply moved by their warm farewell, as I was closing a long chapter in my past life and opening a new one in a foreign land.

We landed by the Taoist temple of Hung Shin on Queen's Road. I gave a tip to the boys who had rowed with so much energy and took my first steps as a civilian on the island of

Hong Kong.

As night fell, there was a small party outside the temple. Some Chinese men and women were burning sticks of red incense, and as soon as the gods abiding there appeared, they lit strings of noisy firecrackers. They bowed their heads, and I followed them out of respect, putting my palms together as they did to pray for good luck. All the gods, including the blessed Mary of Requeses, must have listened, because I have truly enjoyed good luck during my long life.

X

After a couple of weeks spent as a guest in the house of Giulio Badolo, a merchant who founded the Italian Far East Trading Company, I moved into a flat with a large veranda on Old Peak Road where Sara came to join me. We were married at the Cathedral of the Immaculate Conception on Caine Road, just after her baptism and in the presence of only twenty people, half of them Chinese and half Italian.

Sara looked magnificent that day in a long, splendid white satin dress adorned with pearls and small rubies. When she entered the church, glistening in the sun filtering from the windows and escorted by her younger brother who had come down from Mongolia, I heard gasps of surprise. Initially, all the people fell silent, and then they erupted in applause, a thing rather uncommon in a church in those days. It drew some disapproving looks from our good priest.

The celebrating priest was a missionary of the Pime, Father Simeone Volonteri, and our Consul, Eugenio Zanoni Volpicelli, was my best man. Luigi Barzini gave a letter of introduction in which he warmly recommended me to our diplomatic representative.

Zanoni Volpicelli was a great sinologist and a scholar with a vast knowledge of culture and languages. We struck up a friendship almost immediately, and in the following months he gave me several tips on how to set up my business. I remember at that time he was busy translating Cesare Beccaria's *On Crimes and Punishments* into Chinese. He gave to me as a personal gift, a thick volume he published in London in 1898, using the pseudonym of Vladimir, entitled *The Expansion of Russia towards the Pacific*.

After retiring from the diplomatic service in 1919, he became a wandering scholar, spending years in Buddhist monasteries, looking for the gate which leads to the afterlife.

I don't know if he found that gate, even though we kept in contact until his death in Nagasaki in 1936. His grave was shattered by the atomic explosion of 1945, but on visiting Japan in 1950 with my son, I left some money to have it restored.

After one year spent in Hong Kong, Sara thought it better to move to Macau. The city was a colony of Portugal, a distance of only two hours by boat from Hong Kong, and it was better suited for a young couple made up of an Italian citizen and Mongol wife. Macau had a long tradition of racial tolerance and mixed marriages, which on the other hand were quite uncommon and discouraged in the British colony of Hong Kong. I could quote here an example of what happened in Macau during the Seventeenth Century, when lacking white women for the Portuguese garrison, a shipload of Christian girls was imported from Japan to serve as wives.

Using part of our capital, or more accurately, our war booty, we managed to live comfortably in that city, which at that time was a charming and laid-back place, a sort of Naples in miniature, with its Praia Grande shaped like a half moon. There was an Italian convent and a school. On the eastern side was the San Francisco Fort and the public gardens while on the western side was the Bomparto Fortress.

I refrained from dealing with opium as some people were advising me to do. It would have guaranteed large profits and in those years, it was perfectly legal. In Macau, there was a large factory where the narcotic was boiled and refined to be exported to America and Australia to be used as an anesthetic. However, I abstained, having seen the despicable effects it had on certain individuals and following the advice of Catholic priests, who were all strong abolitionists.

Instead of opium, we specialized in worsted fabrics imported from India, mostly light cloth used for Western suits. The British established magnificent mills over there; I traveled to Bombay twice a year and after hard bargaining with payments in cash, was getting large discounts. That was the only way for me to beat the competition. The next step was to buy Chinese silk and have it exported to Germany and France.

Sara and I decided to set up a small silk factory and imported some state-of-the-art shuttle looms from Manchester which we paid for in silver. I remember we were using sacks of Empress Maria Theresa's silver thalers minted in Thailand and Mexican dollars. Using these weaving looms moved by leather belts and connected to a steam boiler, we were able to compete with both the Chinese weavers of Suzhou and the Japanese of Yokohama, who were still working with handlooms. Our machines could reach close to 150-picks per minute and were running day and night. Later, we added a Jacquard system to create magnificent brocade we were selling to Western ladies who could afford our prices.

But it was not always smooth sailing. The first trouble to hit us was the great typhoon of 1906, which caused enormous damage to Hong Kong and Macau. The roof of our warehouse was torn off, and we lost a large quantity of fabric packed and ready for export. On September 18, at eight in the morning, the sky turned black in a matter of minutes and without warning. Nobody could have foreseen the furious winds which broke upon us, lifting and sinking several boats. The Anglican bishop Joseph Hoare and some of his priests were at sea fishing, and their bodies were never found. A French destroyer anchored in Hong Kong, the *Fronde*, was lifted and flung by a tsunami above the port.

I offered some money to raise a monument to the memory of those unlucky sailors. It is impossible to know the total number of dead, but it was certainly more than ten thousand. My workers and I lent a hand in the search for the bodies, countless children among them. I learned a hard lesson from that tragedy since we had no insurance and had to start again from scratch.

The turning point for us was again marked by a book - an illustrated book containing serigraphic reproductions of the clothes used at the court of the Medici in Florence during the Renaissance. Sara suggested transferring those beautiful designs, possessing a mysterious Oriental flavor, on to our fabrics. We did it, and they sold well against our competition. That proved to be a memorable success, giving us a large return on our investment.

I often visited Hong Kong for business because it was an important city, with 13,000 Europeans and 50,000 Chinese residents. There, it was easier to trade goods and raise money. We opened our own office as a branch of our Macau headquarters but I let everyone know my real home was in Macau, so as not to be troubled with lunch invitations and social gatherings, things which were *de rigueur* in those years.

Hong Kong was a stratified society, shaped around guidelines set by the British communities in India, where castes were observed and accepted even among Europeans. The colony of Hong Kong was a place obsessed by one's social status. It was of fundamental importance to have the right bench at church, the right chair at the racecourse, the right seat at the club. The wives of the expatriate residents lived shut in their homes - etiquette forbade them to wear light dresses. They had a miserable life during the sweltering summers and were dying like flies from drinking water that was not boiled and eating uncooked vegetables; but they wanted to see their husbands promoted and respected.

It is hard to understand today, but all the local policemen - Indian and Chinese - were supposed to stand to attention when a white man or woman walked close by, and white people would not pay cash at shops and restaurants - instead, bills were sent to their homes at the end of each month. What bothered me most was the European fixation for sports which boiled down to a strange mixture of Darwinism and Imperialism; cricket, tennis, golf, regattas, exclusive clubs, and Masonic lodges filled with white people. Because of my wife's positive influence, I was never involved in these groups, which seemed to have been conceived only to make a few people feel better and most others feel worse.

XI

After returning to Italy, my comrade Vito Modugno developed a strong dislike for his wife and kept me informed of everything, because he was a compulsive letter writer who wrote about everything going on in his life.

Vito was born in 1870 and was a native of Bitonto, in Apulia, in the south of the Italian peninsula. And like me, he was sent to Turin to study at the military academy. It was there we met. I remember him as a young man, very much taken by women, and he did nothing to hide it, in true south Italian style.

Vito managed to seduce a pretty girl in Turin, an elementary school teacher, during our last year at the academy. She was from Milano and her name was Elettra Barbieri. He made her pregnant and ran away from an unwanted marriage by volunteering for the war in Eritrea. She followed him, but the baby died of an infection soon after their return from Africa. He dumped Elettra and started to look for a better party, a wife of means with whom to settle down.

While in Bari, he spotted an attractive girl called Cenzina di Cagno, ten years younger than him and with a wealthy banker for an uncle. He proposed to her family first, still not having spoken to her. They checked on Vito's background and substance and agreed on the match. The marriage was arranged and the newlywed couple went to live in Pavia, a city close to Milano, where Vito was posted. It was then the first symptoms of the terrible disease of his wife emerged. She had syphilis, which at that time had no cure.

I am sure his wife's relatives knew about it and this may have played a part in their decision to give her away as a bride to an officer with little money. All of us would agree - I do believe - that having a syphilitic wife in bed is not the best dream of any husband. This is the main reason why

Vito volunteered for China. When he returned, decorated by our country and proposed for the German Black Eagle medal, he was reunited with his wife and saw for the first time their daughter, Maria, whom his wife had borne four months after his departure.

Vito and his wife had exchanged hundreds of letters and he was well informed about the family's affairs. Since he was in need of money for his house, he went to Bari to sell most of the objects he carried from Beijing and was able to make a hefty profit, especially from the porcelain moon flask, which was purchased by a famous industrialist of Varese, a collector of Oriental ceramics. Vito boasted to his fellow-officers about what he had done and achieved in China.

Soon after, a swirl of anonymous letters went around. They contained mostly false information, accusing him of having pillaged houses and stolen precious things. That forced a magistrate to launch an investigation and inform the military authorities. The army demanded his resignation, and he duly complied, filing a request which was accepted on October 22, 1902.

What made Vito famous - for all the wrong reasons - happened one year after his return, on December 29, 1902. I sent him a letter stating I was in the process of establishing a company in Macau and our gold was deposited at the Hong Kong and Shanghai Bank Corporation. Together with Gazoos, we were waiting for his return.

When he received it he decided to break the news to his wife while she was sick in bed. His intention was to separate on good terms since a divorce was not legally possible in Italy at that time. Then, he informed her that he wanted to relocate to Hong Kong or Shanghai, but without her and their daughter. He did not mention his Mongol wife, but said he would provide handsomely for her and for their daughter for the rest of their lives. The house in which they had been living would be under their daughter's name.

A furious row erupted. She refused to let him leave and vehemently accused him of being a bad husband and a bad father. Vito, to repudiate these accusations, questioned her faithfulness, calling her a harlot and thundering against her snakes of relatives who had lied to him from the beginning hiding any knowledge of her disease from him. The shouting match went on for at least an hour and then, exhausted, he went to sleep in another room.

The next morning, the maid and the gardener picking persimmons from a tree heard a shot. They ran to the master's bedroom to find their ladyship in bed with her head splattered with blood and cerebral matter. She had her husband's revolver in the right hand, a Mauser mod.1891. The maid, gardener, and Vito discovered that Cenzina was still breathing, but she died the following day after a harrowing agony. Underneath her cushion a farewell letter was found in which she demanded forgiveness from her beloved husband and from her relatives. She said she still loved Vito and asked his pardon for what she had done, as she was taking her life because "she was consumed by an unbearable remorse."

Perhaps she had betrayed him by having an affair with a fellow officer while he was away on his mission to China, as he had suspected, but was her death truly a case of suicide?

The police were skeptical that a woman, sick and weak like Cenzina, could be capable of firing a heavy gun and they doubted the farewell letter. They suspected that after he shot his wife, Vito went out of the window - their bedchamber being on the ground floor - and escaped over the garden, then returned inside, following his servants. Anonymous letters reached the police and two weeks after Cenzina's death, on January 13, 1903, Vito was arrested with a warrant issued by the magistrate Luigi Fata and charged with having murdered his wife.

The incriminating evidence was that the bullet entered

her left temple and went out by the upper part of her cranial cap, blowing a wide hole; she was not left-handed, and the pistol was in her right hand, so the magistrate suspected it was fired by Vito. However, the autopsy proved that the small hole on the left of her cranium marked the exit of the bullet and not the entrance, as they had initially thought, and no trace of gunpowder was found in proximity of the small hole on the left temple. In addition, the magistrate had wrongly opined that Cenzina did not know how to handle a pistol, but during the trial and despite all contrary claims by her relatives, it emerged that she had been sleeping with a gun under her cushion for a certain period of her life, fearing an attack by one of her cousins. Vito Modugno was kept in isolation, consistently claiming to be innocent and rejecting all charges with indignation.

The trial was held in a packed room in front of the press at the tribunal of Perugia on March 18, 1905. Two-hundred-fifty-five witnesses were called to testify and thirty-five experts provided their scholarly opinions. Fifteen lawyers debated the case; the head of the prosecution was Carlo Stuart, a famous attorney. The correspondents of sixteen daily newspapers were present during the debates. The case was national news from the beginning. Among the witnesses called by the prosecution to testify was Luigi Barzini of the Corriere della Sera who had met Vito Modugno with me in Beijing.

All Italians were mesmerized. Every morning they ran to get a copy of a newspaper just to know what had been debated in Perugia the day before. In the taverns and coffee houses people's opinions were split on this subject, very much polarized but not entirely tied to the facts. Generally, the people believing that Vito was guilty were socialists, opposed to the army and to the colonial expansion of Italy. They saw in Vito the essence of what they loathed, a well-to-do man, a professional officer, a violent warmonger, and a bloodthirsty monster.

On the other side were the patriots, who would not believe a decorated officer like Vito could stain his honor with such a ghastly crime. The army and the conservative part of the country thought him a hero unjustly accused of a crime he didn't commit.

The case was even discussed in the Italian parliament by Bissolati and Dal Verme, and some of Vito's soldiers testified at the trial, giving damaging reports of his violent behavior. Because of this, Vito was referred to the military tribunal where he risked, if convicted, a firing squad. Three of his soldiers, Viscillo, Mirelli, and Bontempi, testified to have seen his violent crimes. Mirelli, in particular, complained that he had been assaulted by Vito with a lash, and unbuttoning his shirt, showed the jury the scars on his back, adding that a German soldier present at his beating actually cried upon seeing how badly he was mistreated. An infantryman mentioned the episode of the licking of the bloody sword, to which I had myself been a witness. That, of course, made an awful impression on the jury.

All were basically true facts and were indeed actions which contravened the rules, but unfortunately, in most of the armies of the world, sergeants and petty officers behaved in a similar violent manner. The basic point being that a soldier should be more scared by his superior than by the gunshots fired by the enemy. Without condoning unlawfulness, I say they should have seen how the Japanese officers brutalized their soldiers!

Vito Modugno was forced to admit a part of the truth to the jury. He opened his arms and said, "What would you have done in my place? Just try to step into my shoes. . ."

The prosecution then turned to the matter of the farewell letter left by his wife. If they could prove it to be false, then Vito was bagged. This letter was found inside an envelope with his wife's name on it and was dated December 28,

1902. The greatest graphologists of Italy were summoned. Professors Vismara, Castelli, and Thevenet debated for long hours about compression of the characters, of feminine and masculine strokes, slopes, accents and friezes, but in the end, the only point on which they could agree was that the date on the envelope could have been added later. Some among those luminaries, nominated by the prosecution, concluded the letter might be a fake; others, appointed by the defense team, said it was genuine.

The final blow delivered by the team of defense lawyers was that they could not find a true motive for the murder and challenged the prosecution to find one.

We should remember that no one had listened to their argument the night before, because the servants were away and Vito's lawyers were able to convince the popular jury that Vito's project of resettlement in China, which he mentioned to a few friends, was not a serious and viable one. My name never came up. Well before his arrest, all the letters I sent to him had been burned out of fear that his wife would find them.

Just after the death of his wife, Vito wrote a short note telling me what had happened and asking me not to write anything until further notice. They did not discover any hint of our gold stash or anything about his Mongol wife because if they had found it, innocent or guilty, that would have made a very negative impact on the jury.

Before the sentence was passed, his character was described in the press following the fashion used by Cesare Lombroso, a Darwinist of the worst kind who was popular in those days. I still keep some press cuttings in my library. They argued that, looking at his actions and facial features, one could only conclude that Vito was a violent moron, a criminal without a moral conscience, a vulgar individual capable of committing a crime, including willingly passing syphilis to his wife, an illness he must have contracted through fornication in Africa, as was common among soldiers. They did not even consider that his wife and several members of her family were syphilitics well before they met.

The jury sided with those considering Vito a bad subject. Had he not returned from China with eighteen crates containing booty of war looted there?

The final verdict was announced six months and six days after the first session of the trial, at the end of ninety-three court hearings. Vito Modugno was judged innocent and his wife's death was ruled a suicide.

Released from prison and after having settled all the pending matters with the Italian justice system and defeated an appeal presented by the family of his late wife, Vito Modugno sold his house to pay for his defense team, which demanded a small fortune from him. Other troublesome legal matters tying him down in Italy had been cleared, such as the request for further compensation by one of his lawyers and the trial mounted by the army about his violent behavior in China, where he was also acquitted. Maria, his daughter, was in the hands of his in-laws and they were holding on to her using all possible excuses, and besides, the poor girl refused to see him. To her, he was the ogre who murdered her mother.

Vito sent me a letter saying he finally obtained a passport and wanted to leave without further ado. In the spring of 1909, he departed, bound for Hong Kong on a ship sailing from Naples, but I did not hear anything from him for several months.

Finally, I received a letter from his sister announcing his death, which had occurred in Singapore, probably caused by cholera. Vito's mortal remains were repatriated by the Italian embassy in Singapore with his few possessions. Among these his sister found some letters I had written to him and for this reason she wrote to me.

She wondered if I could help her financially since she

had spent a considerable sum to have his mortal remains repatriated. She was enclosing a copy of the court order of the tribunal of Bari, nominating her as the sole heir of Vito Modugno's estate. I sent off a considerable amount of money in several installments, his part of our nine-year-old raid. Among his papers she found what appeared to be his last letter directed to me with a Singapore stamp on it. He had written a date on the back with a shaky hand - the day of his death.

I keep this letter inside an old Latin Bible, still unopened after so many years. Every so often I take it out of the Good Book and turn it with my fingers, wondering whether I should open it or not, but I always come to the same conclusion, "Not on this day!" and I put it back. I think I am afraid of what I may read inside and I don't want to know.

I have often asked myself if my friend Vito murdered his wife that morning, or if she indeed committed suicide to take a revenge on him for wanting to leave her behind. Had she any intuition about the Mongol wife who was waiting for him? I haven't reached a clear verdict in my heart and I suspect the final solution to this enigma lies in that letter written by Vito in *articulo mortis* at the end of his life. Since then I have read all that was published on this subject in newspapers, books, and magazines that an agent of mine in Italy mailed to me whenever he could. With the passage of time this case was forgotten, buried under worse tragedies.

I told Gazoos that, even though she was still young, she had been widowed; she took the news badly and wore mourning clothes for three years, during which she often offered paper gifts and fruit to the soul of her deceased husband, following the Oriental custom. She eventually resettled back in Mongolia and a few years later married a local nobleman and had two children, a son she named Vito and a daughter she named Maria.

We have lost all trace of them since 1929, and we fear the

worst, as they were possibly murdered by Bolshevik thugs, a fate shared by many Mongols belonging to the upper classes.

XII

All the tensions I noticed during our expedition to Beijing reached an explosive level in Europe in 1914. The mistrust, misunderstandings, and excesses of nationalism stirred up by a press gone awry threw the old continent into a useless and monstrous war - and then, in 1915, during a black day in May, Italy joined the fray.

I duly presented myself to Consul Eugenio Zanoni Volpicelli, telling him if necessary I was ready to volunteer, even if I was beyond conscription age. Zanoni Volpicelli advised caution and said I could be much more useful to our country by taking care of the supply of raw materials, which were in great demand by the war industry. He gave me a list of minerals badly needed - ferrous minerals, coal, tungsten, aluminum - as well as chemicals needed to manufacture explosives. I promised to do all that I could to source them in Asia, even though prices were going up by the day with the acceleration of hostilities and their scarcity was greatly felt after the first year of war.

I believe I did my part for my country's war efforts, and although the payments were always late, I managed to break even without profiting or losing too much on those transactions. The British governor of Hong Kong thanked me after we joined their side but the Austrian and German residents in Hong Kong - some of them my business partners - were arrested. Every week I sent them gifts of cheese and fresh fruits for their children, letting them know nothing had changed for me. I had been through the utter stupidity of war and knew this was no different than all the others. I knew one day it would end and the living would eventually forget the reason they had fought.

Sara became pregnant in 1913, but she suffered a miscarriage and the doctors told us she would never be able to have another baby. That was a devastating blow for us, but my wife was not a woman to give up easily. She consulted several Australian and Japanese doctors as well as a sorceress. She had a special devotion for Guanyin, the Chinese goddess of mercy, whom she compared to the Holy Mary. She kept two statues close by - on the left, Mary and on the right, Guanyin. Every morning she prayed to them to grant us a son. With the passing of the years it grew into an obsession and I began to fear for her mental health.

One day she asked me to accompany her to Mongolia because she wanted to go to see the brother of the regent of the Mongol State. She said he would be able to perform a miracle for us if she could speak to him. It was not the first time she had been back to Mongolia, but that was to be a special occasion and she insisted on having me at her side. It was the month of August of 1923 and Sara was forty-one-years-old. We bought two first-class tickets on a deluxe Japanese ship, which stopped at Hong Kong every month and went up to Shanghai.

After two nights spent at the Hotel Palace of Shanghai, we boarded another ship which took us to Tianjin. I had visited Shanghai several times on business trips but since the time of my participation in the Boxer uprising I had not been back to North China. I was thrilled to see again the spot where the Taku Forts once stood, but on reaching that place I remembered that they had been pulled down as part of the peace treaty.

We visited the city of Tianjin, stopping for a night at the small Italian concession, which appeared to us tidy and well kept. About 5,000 Chinese lived there with 110 Italian nationals. There was even a small hospital directed by Doctor Maurizio De Giovanni from Vercelli and a barrack for the soldiers of the San Marco battalion.

The Chinese policemen of our concession were fairly well-known. Some of them spoke Italian and were skilled athletes. I can say, without fear of being contradicted, that we were the first to have roads paved and to treat Chinese nationals the same as Europeans, allowing them access to our small public park. Small things, indeed, but significant in a period when racism was rampant.

We met there a strange character with a journalistic past who invited us to his home and introduced his family. His name was Amleto Vespa. We discovered later, because of a book he published in England and the United States titled *Secret Agent of Japan*, that he was a spy in the service of the Japanese first, and of the Chinese later. He was apparently shot in 1941 in Shanghai by the Japanese who did not appreciate his going public with their scheming.

Travelling from Tianjin to Beijing station under a bright sun, we spotted the place where many years before, Vito and I stopped the train to put our ladies on it. Sara and I cried with joy, expressing our deepest emotions, kissing each other and remembering the beautiful days full of bliss and love we had experienced since that moment.

We went to see our friend Sir Edmund Backhouse - by then second baronet after the death of his father - but we found him completely Sinicized and even more detached than before from the community of expatriates. He was dressing like a Chinese Mandarin and sporting a long white beard. It was well known to most Beijing residents that Backhouse was not interested in women, but rather in grown-up boys. During the Boxer insurrection, he had found shelter within the legations but he always refused to join in the defense because he loathed all kinds of violence, even defensive.

We then went to greet our ambassador, Vittorio Cerruti, who invited us to his home for dinner, where we spent a wonderful evening together with his charming wife, a former actress.

After visiting some of our old friends living in Beijing,

too many to mention each by name, we rented a Fiat car with an experienced driver, and moving in relative comfort, we traveled up to the borders of Mongolia until the roads became too rough. Seeing it was impossible to proceed in the car, we were unhappily forced to send the car back, then we entered the Gobi Desert on horses with a small escort.

We encountered a camp or a Buddhist temple from time to time where we could stop and rest. There we would often sip *arc*, a drink made of mare's milk, or fresh milk, which was always offered free of charge, due to an old Mongol tradition in force since the times of Genghis Khan. There was a prohibition on selling fresh milk, because in the desert nothing more precious could be found, even if travelers were willing to pay with gold - thus it had to be given free (a truly skewed logic).

Our first real stop was the lamasery of Khamaryn Khiid, famous all over the East for having been the seat of the Danzan Ravjaa, the fifth reincarnation of the Noyon, a great mystic and poet who died in 1853. We rested there for three days because for me, that trip was very hard, though not for Sara, who was born on a horse and was a splendid Amazon. Unfortunately, that lamasery was destroyed in the following years by the iconoclastic Bolsheviks. All their treasures disappeared, but who knows? Perhaps one day they might re-emerge from the sands.

Departing from Khamaryn Khiid, we met an old lady collecting dry animal dung to be used as fuel in winter. She was clearly suffering from arthritis and was covered with black dust. She carried a dingy bag on her back where she was putting that precious organic material which they call *argol*.

Feeling sorry for her, I tossed a few coins. She proudly refused and then, thoroughly squaring me up, she addressed me with these words, "Foreigner, was your travel peaceful?" This is their standard greeting, like good day or good evening for us. She added, "I feel sorry for you, because you were not born Mongol, and yet here you come, with one of our women. You are lucky because she will show you all our happiness before you die."

I was astonished that she was sorry for me when at the time I had been sorry for her. I have remembered her words as tangible proof of the relativity of our standing in life.

At that time Mongolia was still a country of nomads and lamas, and the tradition in force was that the firstborn in every family would enter a lamasery. This, in a country with a low birth rate, influenced their demographic expansion. It should be noted, however, that the supposed celibacy of most of the lamas was not strictly enforced and was often the target of jokes, as Mongols have a very strong sense of humor.

I discovered that the lama' training consisted mainly of memorizing long prayers in Tibetan, a tongue most of them did not understand - one of the wives of Kublai Khan introduced Tibetan Buddhism among the Mongols - which they then recited like mantras when paid to do so. A difficult concept to follow for all lovers of logic, but this was the tradition. They call it *bhakti*, a word which can be translated as devotion or faith. The basic concept is that to think or to know is not important because, in reality, nothing exists; no truth nor lie, no Buddha, no doctrine, nothing. It all depends on the inner state of our minds.

Lamas were much in demand for funerals. When a Mongol dies, they first wash his body and then call the lamas from the closest temple. They recite some Tibetan prayers and one lama among them who specializes in necromancy chooses a suitable spot to lay the body. We observed one instance of this ceremony. The lamas put the body nude on the ground, covering it with a white sheet. They withdrew into a *yurta* where they reveled to their heart's content for three days, after which time they went to see if the dogs and vultures had consumed the flesh, an event which is believed to be favorable. Then the lamas collected the bones, washed them, and used them to produce beads and cups. With the femurs, they produced Tantric trumpets, believed to possess the power to dispel evil spirits.

We then crossed the lands of the Ordos, one of the great Mongol tribes, and finally reached Urga, the capital. During that voyage, I was able to better understand the Mongols, their cheerfulness and their resistance to hunger and pain. At that time, there were no prisons at all in the country, except in Urga, where the number of people in prison never went over twenty and cases of theft and murder were rare. They had few buildings made of stone and brick in that city, but large tents were everywhere to be seen, some even mounted on wheels.

Because of Sara - the daughter of Prince Lob-Tsen Yen Tseng - I was granted the title of duke in a solemn ceremony. I started to wear clothing made with long shanks of skin like them, useful when sitting on horseback and, on my head, I wore one of their cone-shaped hats. With Sara close to me all doors opened, and in certain places, she was worshipped as a living goddess.

The aristocrats of Mongolia were called Darkhad to distinguish them from both the lamas who had their heads shaved and the blue Mongols, the ordinary people. Mongol women had always been considered the most liberated in Asia, far more so than the Chinese, as Marco Polo already noted - Mongol women never bound their feet, unlike the Chinese, who deformed them to make their walking appear more attractive. I came to know that up to three days after a Mongol wedding, if the bride was not satisfied with her husband's performance, she was free to leave and return to her parents. Or, in cases where an unmarried girl became pregnant, if the man responsible did not step forward, then her family celebrated a marriage at home without the groom, considering him to be an accessory of no great importance.

Using Sara's connections, we were introduced to the Bogd Khan, known as the Living Buddha. The Bogd Khan was born in Tibet, and since childhood had been recognized as a reincarnation of his predecessors. He was very kind and hospitable to us. I saw in him nothing of the pedophile and licentious poisoner painted by Bolshevik propaganda. Nor did he look anything like the sinister and scheming man described by Ferdinand Ossendowsky in his bestseller, *Animals, Men, and Gods*, which, as far as I could see, was mostly a work of fiction created by that fake adventurer from Poland.

The position of the Bogd Khan in Mongolia was like that of the Catholic Pope in Medieval Europe. He was placed on the throne in the year 1911 when the Mongols wrested their independence from China. The Chinese were not willing to accept such a large territorial loss and in 1919 sent a small army, commanded by a Chinese general known as Little Hsu.

They were chased out again in February 1921 by the notorious Bloody Baron, a former tsarist officer who killed hundreds of Chinese and took possession of Urga. Ethnically he was an Austrian and his name was Unger von Sternberg. They say that he brought electricity to Urga and repaired roads and bridges. That might well have been true, but nonetheless he was a murderous lunatic, and he was ultimately defeated and shot by the Russians one year later.

The Bolsheviks granted solemn guarantees of independence to Mongolia, promising to respect the Kiakhta's Agreement they had signed, but almost immediately began to put up obstacles between the Living Buddha and his loyal subjects.

To us the Bogd Khan looked wearied by the weight of his reincarnations and he was greatly worried by what the future had in store for his people. In 1924, the year following our meeting, his life ended abruptly when he was only fifty. A few months before his death his beloved wife, Tsendiin, considered by all a reincarnation of the white Tara, a Tibetan goddess, also died. The air blowing there, at a political and social level, was indeed awful, and even a foreigner like me could sense it. People were saying openly after the death of the Bogd Khan that the Bolsheviks would block the enthronement of a new reincarnation which in fact they did; but no one could have imagined the level of homicidal fury which the Bolsheviks would unleash on their fellow countrymen.

Sara and I stood briefly in front of the Bogd Khan, who was sitting on his throne, explaining the true motives of our journey. Sara asked him for a baby boy. From his high golden throne, the Bogd Khan looked down at us, even though he was nearly blind. He sipped a little of his tea, thick with salted yak butter, and advised us to go and see his brother, the State Oracle, at the Choijin temple.

He ratified my appointment as a duke of Mongolia and Sara, already a princess, was declared a duchess. Then he added that he was sending out a messenger to his brother to announce our arrival. I left a Swiss-made alarm clock as a gift for him and we said farewell with a bow. Sara told him, out of courtesy, that she hoped to see him again during our next trip to Mongolia. The Bogd Khan answered he was certain it was our last meeting, and added in an enigmatic fashion, as we were stepping out of the large tent where our meeting had taken place, that his brother was going to make us very happy and very sad.

XIII

The Bogd Khan's brother, the Choijin Lama, had his seat in a temple not far away from that of his brother and we reached it walking. It looked rather new and was divided into four pavilions, one of which was built to look like a Mongol tent.

At the entrance stood two gigantic statues of wood representing the muscular king guardians, the two Dvarapala. The one on the right was Garbhavira, holding a stick with a *vajra* at the end with his mouth half open, pronouncing the sound of *Aaaa*, signifying the beginning of life. On the other side stood the second giant, Vajravira, and his mouth was half closed in the sound of *Umm* - the end of life.

It was dark inside, with piles of Tibetan books on the shelves and discolored *tangka* hanging on the walls. A strong smell of yak's butter came from the lamps. They let us sit in the main pavilion of the *Yidam*, which was usually taboo for secular visitors, especially female, and used only for the prayer of the lamas. Tantric temples have rooms where women cannot enter because they fear they may be pregnant. A pregnant woman, according to them, has two hearts, two minds, and two souls, thus they fear the fetus can monitor events invisible to us and can even break into the future and change it.

Gilded sculptures of bronze were placed in the center of the pavilion, increasing the sense of uneasiness we were feeling, with representations of the ugliest and frightening-looking Tibetan gods: Kalachakra dancing together with his bride, who was offering him a human skull full of blood to drink; Palden Lhamo, the patron of Tibet, traveling on a horse saddled with the skin of her son; then Vajradhara, the master of the lightning bolt.

The gods were exhibiting their characteristic ruthless

compassion but their terrific nature is direct against the enemies of human mercy; I later learned that the images were put there with the intent of shattering the ego of the beholders.

We waited for about twenty minutes for the arrival of the Choijin Lama, who finally entered with a group of young lamas as his assistants. He was wearing a robe of silk brocade with a yellow hat on his head. We reverently bowed before him and he invited us to sit, exchanging some cheerful words with Sara. The lamas arranged in front of us a glowing copper brazier with burning coal in it. The Choijin took some bones - sheep's scapulas, in fact - and deposited them carefully in the fire. He took them out a few minutes later with a pair of bronze tongs and studied the cracks produced on their surface. He said something gentle to Sara, who suddenly, full of happiness, raised her arms. She told me we would have a son but on condition that we would have him consecrated to the Sangha, the monastic community.

"Do you mean that our son will be a lama?" I worriedly asked.

"Not a lama with a shaved head, but a lama living in the world," she told me. The idea of consecrating my son to the monastic community did not please me greatly, but at that time I thought it was just pretense to make Sara happy, and so I did not give much weight to that promise. I was unaware at the time that Sara was already pregnant and about eight months later our son would be born.

They burnt incense on the brazier and the young lamas intoned some monotonous hymns. The Choijin settled on his head a heavy crown made of silver and decorated with coral and turquoise and began singing in a guttural tone. What happened later impressed me greatly and I will never forget that half hour spent there, sitting in front of the Choijin Lama.

He was clearly falling into a trance and his eyes were

turning inside their orbits in a manner which I had never seen before, not even among some of our epileptic soldiers. Foamy saliva appeared on the sides of his mouth and was wiped with a cloth by one of the assistants. He breathed deeply, his eyes turning completely white. By then he was looking like a deity of the tantric hell.

We could not put direct questions to him, but only listen to the words he was mumbling, which were diligently noted on a parchment by one of the young lamas.

The Choijin's voice suddenly changed tone, becoming more powerful and deep, very distinct in every syllable he was articulating. Even though I understood nothing of what was said, I noted the expressions of fear appearing on the faces of everybody present there, even Sara's. I thought something terrible was being said. The panic on their faces was evident as if the devil in person was addressing us.

They lowered their eyes and Sara whispered she would explain to me later in detail, saying only, "Mongolia is finished, the monastic order will end, and countless lamas will be killed like mice. Justice and mercy will be forgotten."

That was a truly apocalyptic vision; but then the Choijin added, "We should not despair, because Mongolia will revive after three generations." He also said that he had an important task for us and, because of that task, had saved our lives from the scheming of a false friend.

Then the oracle revealed the name of the spirit that had seized him: Borjigin Temujin, Genghis Khan. When he pronounced that name, I saw the lamas falling on the floor, touching the ground with their brows. He spoke again, and later it was explained to me that he expressed happiness about my union with Sarangerel and blessings for our son. To this new descendant he wanted to entrust his soul, to avoid its loss and destruction. The sweat began to flow from the Choijin's head onto his cheeks and he awoke from his state of trance, shaking violently. His eyes returned to their normal position, but he looked exhausted, nearly collapsing over his throne.

He asked to see a report of what he had said, and when they passed the parchment to him he also looked horrified and distressed, then wanted Sara to come close to him. Speaking with great sweetness, he caressed her like a good daughter. Sara lowered her head and shed some tears when he told her the great conqueror's soul would be entrusted to us, and we should pass it to our son.

"We will protect it with our lives!" Sara, very emotionally, promised.

The Choijin smiled down at us full of benevolence and asked the young lamas and me to get closer. "Now I want to tell you an old tale I heard a long time ago from the lips of my master, when I was a young novice studying at Sera's monastery, in Lhasa:

A very powerful demon called Virtra drank all the waters of the world, provoking a drought which lasted nine thousand years. Indra, the king of the immortal gods, had an idea - he took one of his lightning bolts and hurled it against Virtra, destroying him. The waters flowed again, and the land blossomed with flowers and trees. Indra was proud of himself for having defeated the demon so swiftly. He ascended in procession to Mount Meru, the seat of the immortal gods, and realized the divine palace needed urgent repairs. He called Visvakarman, the divine mason, and ordered him to build a new palace with loftier towers. Every time Indra returned to follow the progress of the construction he ordered additional alterations. Visvakarman, knowing that Indra was immortal, feared that the building site would never be completed. Tired and with little hope left, he went to lodge a protest to Brahma, the creator of the material world. He found him sitting over a lotus flower and told him why he was unhappy. Brahma promised to solve his problem.

After their meeting, they found an attractive child sitting right before the palace of Indra. The courtesans let him enter and took him to Indra, who demanded to know who he was and what he wanted. The child replied with a thundering voice that he had been told that this palace was the most majestic ever built by the Indras, and that now that he had contemplated it, he could admit that it was true. Indra was very pleased but asked why the child used the plural, the Indras. . . Perhaps other Indras had existed before him? The child replied that indeed many had existed and added that Visnu sleeps on the endless snake of the cosmos, and from his navel grows a lotus flower; on that lotus sits Brahma; and when Brahma opens his eyes a new universe appears, with an Indra ruling it. When Brahma closes his eyes, a universe with an Indra vanishes, then another reappears with another Indra, then another one, and another, and still another.

That child was Brahma himself. After he had said all this, he added, almost in jest, that all the Indras in the past had killed Virtra, and proud of their valor, had ascended to Mount Meru, where they built their wonderful palaces in turn."

The lamas looked up at him, charmed by the tale, and understood what it meant. Then the Choijin said with a smile, "Yes, the universe is an illusion, a divine joke, like Mongolia, like Genghis Khan, like all of us, and Brahma will someday shut his eyes."

XIV

Still shaken by those revelations, in spite of the Choijin's exquisite sense of humor, Sara and I moved to the camp of her father, Prince Lob-Tsen Yet-Tsen. He was living in five great tents about ten miles from Urga. He was a very important man, respected and rich due to his great herds of horses. Mongols do not keep their money in banks, which are unknown there, but invest it in herds of animals.

In his childhood, the Prince was sent to a lamasery where he passed all the examinations and received a high monastic degree, but he abandoned his religious career, let his hair grow, and married an attractive girl, the mother of Sara, who unfortunately had died a few years earlier. He worked in a high position for the Mongol government, both as Prime Minister and as the head of the Darkhad, the five hundred families chosen by Genghis Khan to conduct sacred ceremonies. He was an extraordinary hunter and took us to hunt foxes and wolves. Unfortunately, he died two years later of natural causes. In a way, he was lucky because death spared him the horrors of the Bolsheviks' madness, which would have meant torture and violent death for him. We could communicate in Mongol, which I had learned from Sara. He loved to talk of his ancestor, Genghis Khan, being immensely proud, like all Mongols, of his exploits and invincible armies.

We did not tell Sara's father that we were going to get the Sulde out of Mongolia, afraid he would have talked about it out of happiness for the honor bestowed on his daughter. After a few days, we bid farewell to him, thanking him for his hospitality, and left with an escort of a group of knights.

We were heading to visit the lamasery of Erdene Zuu, in the Ovorkhangai Aimag region, near the ancient capital of Karakorum, in the direction of Tibet, carrying with us a written order from the Living Buddha to collect the Sulde and take it to a secure location. Originally kept in the small lamasery of Shankh, it had been moved to Erdene Zuu for safety reasons.

Erdene Zuu had the shape of a Mongol camp, with five pavilions shaped like a *ger* and 108 stupas arranged around the Blue Temple. Some large, scattered stones were visible, all that remained of the old buildings of their ancient capital. Erdene Zuu was built in 1585 by Avtai Sain Khan, with the help of lamas belonging to the Tibetan sect of the *Gelug*, or yellow hats.

That place, like Shankh, is indelibly tied to the name of Zanabazaar, a great mystic, artist, and descendant of Genghis Khan venerated by all Mongols. He was born in 1635, and he was a poet, a painter, a sculptor, and a spiritual master. At the age of Five he was recognized as the reincarnation of the saint Jhavan Taranata. He died in 1723 in Beijing, perhaps murdered by the Chinese emperor, Yongzhen, who had hegemonic aims towards Mongolia and disapproved of his frantic search of the relics of Genghis Khan.

Zanabazaar, in an effort to preserve the sacred symbols of the past, drew a figure which is today part of the Mongol flag - the *Soiombo*. He found the Sulde of Genghis Khan and placed it first in the small wheeled lamasery of Shankh and then on the main altar of the Blue Temple, the Khökh Süm of Erdene Zuu, surrounded by dozens of gods cast in bronze and covered by sheets of gold which he had modeled with his own hands. Though great works of art, they were melted down during the great purges launched by the Bolsheviks as if they were useless metal scraps.

It was thanks to the great Zanabazaar that the Sulde was preserved for centuries under the watchful eyes of thousands of lamas. They did it because it had a religious as well as a spiritual value, being a symbol of the god Shiva, dear to Hindus and Buddhists alike. Its three points represented the past, the present, and the future; destruction, maintenance, and creation; the physical, the historical, and the mental worlds.

I later collected some ancient sculptural representations of Lord Buddha, which in certain cases had that type of trident in hand, even if its points were often closed. The special case of this trident represents the Triratna, that is, the Buddha, the Dharma - his teachings - and the Sangha - the monastic community. All this might explain why Zanabazaar and his successors preserved it: not just for nationalist motives, but for religious ones.

When we reached the lamasery of Erdene Zuu, we asked to see the abbot who appeared after a couple of hours. He was an old man with a face shriveled by the sun and the wind. He listened intently to what we wanted and our escort gave him the parchment with the wax seal of the Bogd Khan, which commanded him to deliver the Sulde of Genghis Khan to us.

Seeing from whom it came he bowed deeply three times, then reread it and called one of his assistants to read it aloud again. He rolled up the document and delivered it to another lama, perhaps the keeper of their archive. We entered a great room in the Blue Temple and turned behind a great bronze statue of Kalachakra placed on the main altar. We went through an iron fence and another lama approached us to open the big padlock with a key he was carrying on his belt. Squeaking, the heavy grating moved on its hinges, and we stepped inside the large Mongol tent.

On the walls hung old weapons, bows, shields, and a saddle. On a shelf stood some gilded statues of Tibetan deities and a couple of silver goblets. That seemed to be the treasury of the lamasery. On a stand was a long spear of wood about two meters high, on which they had placed a trident head with a lock of old black horsehair attached to it. The old lama took it with his hands, unlocking it from the top. The disk with the tied hairs came off. With great reverence, he folded it and carefully deposited the whole set into a rigid box covered with yellow silk. The fabric was a Chinese-woven brocade with threads of gold representing dragons with three claws. Before adding the lid, he covered the piece with a yellow velvet cloth, and without saying a word, delivered it into Sara's hands. It was heavy, and she thought that perhaps the box had an iron frame; only later did we discover it was made of gold.

"Does the wooden shaft remain here?" Sara asked.

"That has nothing to do with the Sulde. We added it about thirty years ago," he answered.

"Thank you, great Abbot. We are traveling to Shanghai. . ." Sara imprudently said.

"I don't want to know," he said. "I am just following my instructions," and, bowing his head, he withdrew into the shadows.

One week later we were back in Shanghai, going through Beijing. We were never separated from our box, not even for a second. In our room, we found it difficult to fall asleep when the box was opened; I felt my heartbeat increase and was seized by waves of fresh energy. I felt an impression of awesome power radiating from the object close to us.

During the night, immersed in darkness, we felt like we were running through the prairies of the world, entering the yurta of Genghis under an immense lapis lazuli-colored sky while the Sulde, caressed by a sacred wind, was standing outside. We dreamt of colored images which had never visited us before but from then on remained imprinted in our memories for a long time.

When the Sulde was exposed to open air, the wind came to caress it, lifted by magic. The wind has great importance for all the Mongols. They fear and worship it. They forbid their children to whistle, believing that by doing so the wind will be summoned.

From Shanghai, we were to board a ship bound for Hong Kong, but since we had three days to wait for its arrival, I visited some of my compatriots with whom I had business relations, mostly from Como and the Brianza region. They were among the first Europeans to set up modern silk factories over there. First, we went to see Giuseppe Ros, a famous collector of ancient Chinese coins, then I met Perotta, Gatti, Carpani, and Beretta, all names which are forgotten today but were well-known and respected at the time.

Back with Sara in our room I wanted to study the Sulde, even if by then I had to admit it clearly has a strong hypnotic effect on the beholder. It is a trident made with a damask-patterned steel, the type used for the best Japanese swords. We had to keep it well, putting a veil of linseed oil on it every month and never letting it get dry. We could not touch it with our hands directly but instead used a special type of Japanese paper. The horsehairs taken from the mane of Genghis Khan's war horse were dipped into protective seize liquid made with rice starch which preserved them, even after eight centuries. The dry air of the desert must have also greatly contributed. The hairs were carefully interwoven and bound to a plate of silver with eighty-one holes.

Seven months after our return from Mongolia, our house was blessed by the birth of a splendid boy. Sara was convinced he was a gift of the sky and I tend to think she was just right. The night before her delivery, she dreamt of a white elephant visiting our residence, like the one for Queen Maya when she gave birth to the Lord Buddha. We named our son Ferdinand, because he saw the light on May 30, the date of the birth of Genghis Khan and of the death of Saint Ferdinand III of Castile, who married Elisabeth of Hohenstaufen, cousin and patron of Frederick II of Hohenstaufen, all distant ancestors of my mother.

The decision to entrust to us that precious relic of

Genghis Khan was indeed farsighted, looking at what later happened to all the lamaseries of Mongolia. Everything was destroyed and the monastic community dispersed and murdered. Tens of thousands of lamas succumbed to the Bolshevik's paranoia in the space of a few years and the world Sara had known - Mongolia, unchanged since the times of Genghis Khan - disappeared in a frenzy of madness and violence. Her close relatives were murdered.

We offered shelter to some refugees and to others we offered financial support. Many more we helped to resettle with their families in Tibet, Bhutan, and Sikkim. Sara was never seized by anguish or depression, because at least a small particle of her world was surviving, hidden inside a bright piece of metal in our possession and acting like a catalyst, capable of recreating a new Mongolia. The Sulde, according to her, had the capacity to regenerate everything out of the void. It contained the past and future, like a new Indra appearing after Brahma opened his eyes.

XV

We took great care of the Sulde, devoting our entire life to its protection and preservation and as soon as we could do so, we opened the windows of our house to let the light of the sun enter, and magically the wind, without fail, came to caress the horsehairs. We commissioned an old Japanese swordsmith living in Kyoto to make a faithful copy of it based on my drawings and instructions. It took several trials, but in the end the old man did a good job. As soon as our son, Ferdinand, grew up, he was told of our secret and of the risks its knowledge involved. We told him never to speak about it with anybody, because if the truth came out, our lives would be in grave danger.

Every year on the birthday of Genghis Khan, we granted a free day to our servants and dressed in the traditional costumes of ancient Mongolia. We placed the Sulde on a rack under the sky, making offerings of *Airak*, fermented milk, cheese, and salted yoghurt to his great soul. Then we burnt paper gifts in his honor and summoned lamas to chant *sutra* in our garden. All these ceremonies are also performed during the Chinese festivals on a smaller scale, on the days when the souls of the dead exit hell and wander freely on the roads.

We kept our word and Ferdinand was taught by an old Tibetan lama whom we employed as a part-time tutor. The two forged a strong bond of friendship, like grandnephew and granduncle. The old lama told us he was certain Ferdinand was the reincarnation of a Tibetan teacher because he knew too many things by instinct, but we never pursued this matter further.

We were lucky to live in Macau when Italy, on June 10, 1940, entered the war on the losing side. The British would have interned us in one of their camps in India as was the case with some of our Italian friends. Things changed only when our Japanese allies invaded Hong Kong some days after the attack on Pearl Harbor. The colony of Hong Kong surrendered on Christmas Day of the year 1941. The British thought they could hold out against them because of their blind sense of racial superiority - I remember them boasting that a white soldier was worth more than ten yellow soldiers and the belts of their pants were good enough to defeat the Japanese! I correctly estimated they wouldn't invade the Portuguese colony of Macau, respecting the neutrality of Portugal. Some Japanese friends told us later, to my great surprise, that the territorial integrity of Macau was maintained because of a personal intervention by Adolf Hitler with the Japanese ambassador in Berlin. Hitler feared that if Portugal went to the Allies, he would lose Portuguese deliveries of tungsten, a metal in great demand for the war industry, and Portugal would allow the landings of British and American bombers on its territories. The Japanese postponed their invasion plans but extorted from the Macanese governor the power to station troops, and since they were in control of the Chinese hinterland, they could control the supply of rice.

The population of Macau had risen in a few months from two hundred thousand to a million. Thousands of people slept in the streets. The governor of Macau, Gabriel Teixeira, proved to be a capable and generous man who opened the gates of his city to hundreds of thousands of refugees. None of the people who experienced Macanese hospitality in those years of death and destruction would ever forget what he did for them. There were several cases of cannibalism, and during the worst periods up to 800 dead corpses would be collected every morning - all poor refugees who expired during the night because of starvation and disease.

Sara was my source of strength in those difficult years. She was strong and fearless yet full of love for our son and for me, and proved to be a worthy descendant of those warriors of the steppes, her ancestors. Our aim was simple, to defend the Sulde and our son Ferdinand at all costs. To preserve them and pass them forward to a next, and hopefully better, generation of men. Our task made us forget our daily problems, like the scarcity of food, even if for a couple of critical months, we were reduced to living only on wild bananas. To her and to our son Ferdinand that seemed a source of amusement, not of distress. I was welcomed home with the question, "Guess what we have for dinner? Bananas!" and they laughed, seeing my dismay.

I remember one evening at our home when Sara prepared a menu for our dinner based solely on wild bananas and water, but they were cooked in several ways. I must have been extremely hungry because I remember it as one of the best dinners I had ever tasted!

The Japanese never suspected the Sulde was in our hands, else they would not have missed the chance to seize it. They attacked Mongolia well before the beginning of the Second World War and we knew from our contacts that they had been also looking for the Sulde, yet had been beaten back by the Soviets.

Nevertheless, it was not all smooth sailing for us. Our greatest scare happened perhaps during the middle of 1942 when we received a very unwelcome visit. I arrived home one evening, after visiting some people in the local government, begging them for some food concessions. Sara told me with a worried look that we had a visitor.

"Who, one of our friends?"

"No, a German gentleman. He wants to speak with you."

I moved into the sitting room and saw Ferdinand talking to a man sitting on the sofa. I entered, bidding him good evening. The man stood up and gave me a stiff Nazi salute with a "Heil, Hitler!"

He was wearing cheap Bavarian clothes but I could

sense at once he was an evil and brutish creature, indeed a frightening man, coarse-faced with a bald head and ugly eyes.

"Gino Montecorvo?"

"Yes, I am. And who are you?"

"My name is Josef Albert Meisinger, an SS colonel in the German army."

There I was facing the "Butcher of Warsaw," as he was called, who was now soiling our home with his presence. Later, I learned he was known among his peers in the SS as an animal.

"Welcome to my house. Has my son offered you an aperitif?" I demanded.

"Thank you, a glass of water will do. I don't drink alcohol, like our Fuhrer," he answered in English.

"The water will be served soon. Can I ask the reason for your visit?"

"I'll get to the point. I have been living in Japan since last year, helping our Japanese allies, and I am on the way to Shanghai, where we are planning to set up some camps to help them assist the starving Jewish population. Passing through Macau I was informed about your presence here, and since you are an Italian officer, I thought it a good mark of camaraderie to call on you. But I have to confess my curiosity was further aroused on learning that your wife is the daughter of the late head of the Mongol Darkhad."

"Yes, Prince Lob was a fine man."

He sat down, shifted on the sofa, then fired a straightforward question. "Have you ever heard of Genghis Khan's Sulde?"

XVI

I turned to Sara, who was carrying a glass of water, and I asked her with all the ingenuity I could muster, "Sara, do you know what the Sulde is?"

"Ah, the spear of Genghis, it was stolen and destroyed by the Bolsheviks!"

"That's what everybody says, but we have a bit of intelligence in Japan, discovered by a man working in our embassy by the name of Richard Sorge, who reported that it disappeared before the arrival of the Bolsheviks. My boss, Heinrich Himmler, heard about the powers of the Sulde from one of the Fuhrer's friends, the Swedish explorer Sven Hedin. You may know Hedin - he traveled to Mongolia and Tibet and claimed to have seen the Sulde before its disappearance and this has been confirmed by Paul Pelliot and Henri Maspero, two eminent French historians who are under our watch."

"I have heard about it from my father," said Sara. "But I personally think it was destroyed or it was shipped to Moscow."

After staring at Sara for a couple of seconds he said with a laugh which distorted his mouth, "That confirms our worst fears, even if we are planning to get to Moscow and have a look there!"

"I was not aware of Hitler's interest in Genghis Khan. . ." I said.

"A Russian historian, Michael Charol, using the name of Michael Prawdin, published in 1934, if I am not mistaken, a book having the title of *Tschingis-Chan: der Sturm aus Asian* and the following year another one: *Tschingis-Chan und seine Erben*. These books were read and greatly appreciated by our Führer, also by Heinrich Himmler who, in 1938, commissioned a new edition in a single volume by the *SS*

Schulungsamt. All SS officers, including me, own a copy. It is compulsory reading for us."

Then, without waiting for our comments, he picked up his hat and ordered, "If you hear anything about the whereabouts of that relic, you should inform me at once, because my boss is willing to pay a large amount of money to secure it. He intends to put it in his historical collection at the castle of Wewelsburg, close to the Spear of Destiny and other important treasures in our possession. If you get any information, you should talk to Manfred Müller, our representative in Macau." Then he adopted a threatening tone. "I would be grateful to you if you do not speak about my visit to our Japanese comrades!"

Walking through the door he asked me about Jews in Macau, whether we knew about their presence and how many they might be. I told him we could not distinguish a Jew from any other foreigner so we could not help. On hearing that, he gave me a wry smile, and left together with the devils he was carrying inside. He ended his life being hanged in Warsaw in 1947.

Our position as Italian nationals became critical after September 8, 1943, when Italy switched side and declared war on Japan. But again, because of our personal friendship with Governor Teixeira, we managed to survive. In the month of August 1945, after those useless and cruel atomic bombs dropped on Hiroshima and Nagasaki, Japan surrendered. These catastrophes filled us with horror and pity. I call them useless because they did not quicken the end of the war, not even by a single day, contrary to what it is generally believed. The Japanese surrendered because of the declaration of war issued by the Soviet Union. The Japanese, being defeated and massacred in Mongolia, conceived a sacred terror of the Soviets. They would have surrendered even earlier if the United States had guaranteed to leave their emperor on the throne as they finally did. I wonder how we can still speak about the cruelty of Genghis Khan today after what has happened during our century, which unfortunately, is not yet over as I write.

After a happy trip to Sicily, where I showed Sara the places of my youth, she suddenly died. The great love of my life was still young at seventy-one, full of energy and life, but it is not up to us to decide when it is time to leave. She had a stroke and died a few days later. On her deathbed, she entrusted the Sulde to me and to Ferdinand, then departed life peacefully. My life since her death has lost more than one dimension, becoming flat and white, like this paper on which I am writing. I lost my best companion and my best friend, not only my loving wife. I keep her ashes in our house, and when I'm cremated, our ashes will be spread on a certain spot in Sicily, on the island of Pantelleria.

While I write, I cannot see any hope for Mongolia, no change in the bloody regime enslaving that noble nation, nor any sign of withdrawal by the Russian army. I don't believe Communism will fall without a awful third world war; it will still be here with us well beyond the new millennium.

Without Sara, we made several mistakes because of our bad judgment, the worst, I am afraid, being the employment of Frankie Bayartsog in our house. He was the grandchild of a Mongol friend living in New York, and came to stay with us in 1959, the same year in which the fourteenth Dalai Lama fled from Tibet to India. Ferdinand and I dreaded that, after Tibet, the Maoists would soon take Taiwan, then Hong Kong and Macau. Because of this we prepared to evacuate our precious relic to the United States. We bought a house at Cupertino near San Francisco and furnished it. In case of danger we would take a plane or a ship and get over there.

From the very beginning, Ferdinand and I recognized that Frankie always had a hostile look on his face and seemed consumed by negative thoughts. One day we found him examining the copy of the Sulde we were keeping hidden in our house. He was studying it carefully, but he excused himself by saying he was only doing some dusting.

A few weeks later two strange characters from New York appeared. They presented themselves at the door of the house without an invitation, wanting to speak with me and Ferdinand. At a certain point, instead of using their American slang, they spoke to me using the Palermo dialect, which even I could not decipher completely. They told us they knew we owned something very precious and were willing to help us sell it. We suspected Frankie not only had connections with the Mafia but that he was also a Communist informant. We asked Zorig to keep an eye on him, and we followed his every move; during the following months, we experienced two serious incidents and I do believe they were somehow related.

First, thieves visited our house after poisoning our dogs. When Ferdinand heard the noise, he went to see what was happening, and the thieves fled. The next case was much more serious. They tried to kidnap Ferdinand right under the Monha's Hill in Macau, a densely populated area. Luckily Ferdinand was with Zorig, who jumped on the assailants, apprehending one of them. The man refused to say who sent him and was sentenced to ten years of jail for attempted kidnapping. Yet, after only three months in the gutter, he was released back to China because of the weakness of the Macanese colonial government. He was exchanged for a couple of Portuguese tourists arrested on trumped-up charges of espionage. That proved he was not a common criminal, but we could not figure out why he and his accomplice had attempted to take Ferdinand. Perhaps they wanted to frighten us or were planning to ask for the Sulde as a ransom. By then, we were very suspicious about Frankie and decided to talk about him with a captain of the Hong Kong police, John Montgomerie, the son of an officer I met in China during the Boxer war. I asked Frankie to deliver a bank check to one of my clients in Hong Kong as he had done before then I phoned Montgomerie, telling him Frankie was on a boat bound to Hong Kong. Our check was posted back to us a couple of weeks later and we never found out what happened to Frankie. One day I asked Captain Montgomerie about him and his answer was, "You don't want to know, he was in it up to his neck."

At that time the Hong Kong police resorted to brutal means to defend the colony from the hostile forces surrounding it. Ghastly to say, but they were using illegal methods of execution, like those used in Venice in the Sixteenth Century, when men were drowned at sea at night, hands and feet tied. If that is what happened to Frankie, then I feel sorry for him.

I put down the pen here because this is the story I wanted to recount. I wanted to explain why we received the Sulde. I'll carry on writing only if there is something very important to add on this subject.

If nothing new comes up or if I am called to meet our Maker, I salute you and I wish you a good life, full of love and the pursuit of a noble mission, like the one I was so fortunate to live.

Macau, December 3, 1962.

PART III

Now faster than ever Hong Kong is swept towards its next incarnation. We are too soon for epilogue - I can only offer interim - but I have to say it is not at all unlike contemplating the mysteries of death.

Jan Morris

I

Lantau Island, Hong Kong:
Sunday, January 11, 2015, 1:00 p.m.

Marco and Blanchefleur boarded a green taxi at Discovery Bay, on Lantau Island. Their small son, Gino, was at home in the care of a domestic helper. In twenty minutes, they reached the Tian Tan Monastery, a Buddhist complex of pavilions built during different periods of time. The oldest one was a type of barn, dated 1906. It was raised by three monks fleeing China who settled in the remote, or so it was at that time, corner of the British colony of Hong Kong, and intended to live and meditate in a humble hermitage.

Things had changed drastically since their arrival, and now the large courtyard facing the pavilions was full of colorful groups of chattering Chinese visitors, happily flashing their cameras at themselves and at a giant statue of Buddha, shown as a dispenser of peace and towering over the sprawling complex of edifices. Hundreds of those tourists were lining up in front of a large portico to get a cheap vegetarian meal, served by the monastery's kitchen, before getting back to the city.

On the hidden side of the structure, facing the mountains and secluded in a quiet cell, Mogul had lived for the last four years and it was there he had died the previous week.

Marco's mother, Elisa, had arrived two days before from Italy for the funeral and she reached the monastery together with Cathy, Mogul's wife, Aldo and his wife, Sarangerel.

Two years before, Blanchefleur and Marco sent Mogul a picture of their son after his birth. Mogul replied with a card on which he had written that he was well, content and extremely busy, but that unfortunately, he could not see the three of them, not even for a minute. He asked for their forgiveness, saying that "having wasted so many years in mundane pursuits I cannot be distracted any further."

They understood and respected his wishes.

As soon as they stepped out of the taxi they were met by a young monk waiting to escort them to the abbot. They crossed the main temple hall, where three statues of Lord Buddha representing the past, the present, and the future were visible. Their guide bowed in front of them and then went on into the monastery's library, and, passing through a narrow corridor, reached the abbot's studio.

It was a bright and white cell, simple, with little furniture besides a desk, two armchairs, and a sofa made with bamboo canes. A few photos were framed and hanging on the walls. One of them portrayed a very young abbot close to Pope Paul VI during the Roman Pontiff's short visit to Hong Kong in 1970. In another he stood side by side with the former president of China, Jiang Zemin, and the first Hong Kong Chief Executive, Tung Chee Wah, at the time of the handover to China in 1997.

The abbot entered and humbly welcomed them. He was a short man, over eighty years of age with a solemn and peaceful expression stamped on his face. He was wearing a long saffron robe of the type normally used for funerals.

"Welcome to our monastery," he said, adding "may I offer you some tea?" Then he invited them to sit down. Two young monks prepared tea, pouring hot water into a rough teapot of reddish clay.

"We are very sorry for your loss. Mogul died a week ago at sunset, as he had forecast, and everybody here is talking about his sanctity," said the abbot, smiling. "He passed away peacefully while immersed in deep meditation. Our young monks who were closer to him say he switched off intentionally when he felt ready to depart. He warmly saluted them, saying farewell and giving his blessings. He was a very determined man, very determined to achieve enlightenment."

"Thank you, your excellency. Where is Mogul's body?" Marco asked.

"Oh, you will see him now. He is in a chilled room close by, right where we'll celebrate his funeral. He left a letter to be read with his last will and we were waiting for you to begin our ceremony and open his testament."

After sipping some tea, they moved into a room where the temperature was very cold, placed only fifty meters away from the abbot's studio. On the chairs about 30 people were sitting, wearing down jackets to protect themselves from the chilling cold and waiting for the ceremony to begin. Mogul's body was arranged on a table surrounded by white lotus flowers, with only his peaceful face visible. Some of the Buddhist monks of Tian Tan were standing there and mumbling prayers while moving their Rosary beads with their hands.

Three Tibetan lamas had flown in from Bhutan and were intoning sutra with their low and guttural voices. Then bells rang and holy water was sprinkled on Mogul's body.

Marco and Blanchefleur sat down close to Aldo and Sarangerel in the front row of chairs. A strong scent of violets and roses was in the air. After twenty minutes of singing in Tibetan and aspersions of holy water, the sound of two tantric trumpets closed the somber ceremony. A notary from Macau was let in and in front of all the people broke the seals on Mogul's testament, and with his quavering and monotonous voice proceeded to read it out. Mogul was leaving a large amount of money for charity; the cup which Empress Cixi gave to his father, he left to the monastery's museum; and he provided to fund a biography in honor of his friend Fatty Ng, to be written in Chinese, containing an anthology of all his articles, complete with all the necessary biographical notes.

Then the notary added, clearing his voice:

"Dear Marco and Aldo, dear friends and family members. I can now reveal to you that I was in fact a reincarnation of Mongolia's Bogd Khan and I always knew it. I have been aware throughout my life of the fact he was me and I, him. When my mother and my father met him, I was only a month-old fetus but I communicated with the holy man and I still have a vivid recollection of those fleeting moments, even of several things which happened before my birth while I was in my mother's womb. With the Bogd Khan's death, which happened a few days before my birth, he was reincarnated in me. Why had he chosen me? I don't know and I cannot fathom it, but this is the revelation of a secret that no one ever knew, not even my parents, and that I am now revealing to you.

I always thought I was myself a living Sulde, and this foreknowledge of being what I am, had always been my pole star guiding me throughout the highs and lows of my existence. I had to follow my father's business and protect the precious relic entrusted to us, but this task took away precious time from me, especially the grievous business of running the Mongol State, which was, in my previous reincarnation, indeed a great limitation. For this reason, I had to make haste to recover the lost time. I was very fortunate to have had the last four years of my life free from mundane worries and was able to regain a part of my lost spirit, but in spite of that, I failed to reach Nirvana. Now, after this statement, which to some will seem boisterous and immodest, I would like to counter it with the humble disposition of my mortal remains.

I here claim a proper sky burial. The best place would be the sacred mountain of Kailas, which we Tibetan Buddhists consider the center of the universe. However, the earthly power which controls Tibet is obstructing these ceremonies, and knowing who I am, it certainly will not compromise.

Now that the Sulde has been delivered to Mongolia, I am asking you to take my body there. I leave to you the choice of the place from where I shall ascend to the sky, but Sakya remains the best place for me to return.

Now, having said what was left to say, I embrace and bless you all. Your Mogul."

II

Hong Kong. Lantau Island:
Sunday, January 11, 2015, 3:00 p.m.

The session ended and everybody left the room. Marco and Aldo, with tears in their eyes and together with Blanchefleur and Sarangerel, withdrew to the abbot's cell to discuss how to organize the transport of Mogul's body to Mongolia.

"Aldo, with the contacts you and Sarangerel have, you should be able to find the way to do it, right?" Marco asked.

"Yes, I reckon there will be no insurmountable problems. I will call them this afternoon and we may leave tomorrow. I'll ask the people I know within the Mongol government to arrange our trip and send a plane," Sarangerel answered.

"Do you know anything about sky burial, Aldo?" Blanchefleur asked.

"Just a little, but Sarangerel knows better," Aldo said. "Her uncle died two years ago and his body was disposed of in that fashion."

"Yes," confirmed Sarangerel, "but we should keep Mogul's body frozen, and before leaving, we should ask a surgeon to break his back. Better do it here than on the mountains."

"Break his back? What do you mean?" Blanchefleur asked, with a worried expression.

"Dead corpses are moved with their backs broken, this is our tradition. It is easier to load them on the shoulders when they have become like knapsacks."

"Fine, then we should ask a surgeon at the Queen Mary Hospital to perform the operation. In the meantime, let's call a truck capable of freezing the body. I am afraid the temperature here is not cold enough. As soon as everything is ready, we will fly back to Ulaanbaatar."

"May I ask about the letter from Vito Modugno Mogul

gave you? Have you opened it?" asked Blanchefleur, remembering it. Aldo and Marco looked into each other's eyes and nodded.

"Yes, we did it, yesterday."

"Can you tell us what was in it? No secret between us. . . right?"

"Will you tell them, Marco?" demanded Aldo, hesitantly.

"If you really want to know, then it is fine with me," said Marco. Leaning forward he said, "It contains a short note written in Italian in a very shaky hand, the hand of a sick man, and it was not easy to decipher all the words. Vito wrote that, yes, he murdered his wife and that he would have done it anyway, even with no prospect of getting back to China. After her disease became manifest, he had been planning it, even if he had hoped she would die from it naturally, but when he returned to Italy, a doctor told him she had several years to live. It was then he decided to act."

"Is that all?" pressed Sarangerel.

"No. That's was not even the worst part of it," Aldo said. "Marco, please, carry on with it."

"Vito was writing while in Singapore where he lay sick in bed with typhus. A British doctor visited him that very morning and told him his chances of living to the next day were very slim. Vito was left with the prospect of facing God Almighty stained by all his sins. No priest had been found to listen to his confession, and for this reason he was making that confession in his letter to Gino."

"The smart move of a wife-killer! If he recovered, then I am sure he would have ripped it up, but if he died that night, he could be free of all his sins," Sarangerel said.

"Yes, the sort of twisted reasoning of a criminal mind. Perhaps he was seeing that letter as a sort of insurance against the flames of hell. He was also confessing to Gino his future murders, which he had already planned, and asking for Gino's forgiveness."

"Which murders?" Blanchefleur demanded.

"It was a scheme he devised while he was in prison for his next three murders… he was giving away the names of his victims rather candidly: Sara, Gazoos, and Gino himself. He would have killed the three of them by staging a freak accident, taken sole possession of the treasure, and grandly settle down in China."

"Ah, and Gino thought him a good friend throughout all his life!" Blanchefleur exclaimed.

"Anything else?" Sarangerel asked.

"No, not much, but Gino had been right not to open it; he was spared a dive into a cesspit…" concluded Marco.

"And by doing it he let Vito's soul sink to hell." Blanchefleur added. "What a hypocrite! Will your God pardon him?"

"I believe only a great doctor in theology could answer that question, but what is certain is that if Vito had reached his destination in good shape, Aldo and I would not be here with you tonight. So, perhaps, we can see a sort of backward planning by the Sulde. That also could explain why the spirit of Genghis Khan spoke of having saved their lives from the threat of a false friend. The oracle told this to Sara and Gino, remember?"

"This could well have been the case. In our tradition, there are several examples of backward planning made by our gods. We might call it Genghis Khan's gift, like dew falling from the sky," Sarangerel concluded.

III

Mongolia, Ulaanbaatar:
Wednesday, January 14, 2015. 1:00 p.m.

Once they landed in Ulaanbaatar, Mongol government officials and the head lama took Marco, Aldo, Blanchefleur, and Sarangerel aside, wanting to express their deep condolences for the passing of Mogul. The head lama gave assurances that a proper sky burial had been organized and expressed his intention of having a bronze statue of Mogul casted as a reincarnation of their beloved Bogd Khan. They asked permission to copy the outlines of his face using a sheet of gold, in the traditional manner, to get his features right.

"Yes, please do. We'll certainly not oppose that," Aldo and Marco agreed, granting their demands. The special coffin containing Mogul's body was opened and his smiling face appeared under the ice. An artisan, working with a thin foil of gold and brushes, quickly took the impression of his death mask.

The lama asked if they could help him by giving any hint as to where Mogul might be reincarnated and added, "Departing holy men who have not reached Nirvana, like him, leave behind clues on where they intend to reincarnate and where we should look after their passing." Aldo shook his head, but Marco remembered the last sentence in Mogul's farewell letter and said, "Sakya, he was talking about descending in Sakya."

"Sakya, in Tibet!" remarked the lama, brightening and after a few seconds in meditation he cheerfully told them, "Sakya is an ancient lamasery, very dear to all Mongols. Kongchok Gyalpo was based there, and the lamasery flourished under Sakya Pandit, who was called to the court of Ogotai Khan as his spiritual advisor. Phakpa, his nephew, then became the spiritual leader of Kublai Khan."

"China will not like your search," Blanchefleur said.

"Well, we have special connections there. With great discretion and without letting the Chinese know, we'll keep an eye on all the newly born babies. Who knows, perhaps in a few years we'll have our Mogul back!" the lama concluded with a broad smile.

"If King Herod doesn't get there first. . ." quipped Sarangerel.

The Ministry of Defense arranged a small plane for their travel, a propeller-driven twin-engine type made in Russia, to take them to the National Park of Altai Tavan Bogd, a magnificent and unspoiled area bordering Tibet and Kazakhstan, where 4,000 square miles of lakes, glaciers, and forests lay in the shadow of high snow-covered peaks.

Their plane landed at the military airfield of Olgii after five hours of quiet flight and they moved forward in two jeeps. The temperature was below zero and the roads were in an awful state. It was already late at night when they reached their destination, so they slept in a small draughty chalet built for people going on trekking expeditions. From the windows of their rooms they could see a very bright moon illuminating the majestic peaks, which rose in a dark blue sky dotted with stars. Those mountains were the *Five Holy Men*, a part of the Mongol Altai chain.

"Are we going to have some food before going to sleep?" Marco asked.

They were tired and hungry but quickly agreed and from their bags took out some soup which they heated in the kitchen as well as some dried codfish with rice.

They sat around the fireplace which Aldo rekindled, with the flames lighting up the darkness in which the main room was immersed - the electricity supply, provided by a diesel generator, was cut at midnight.

Then Blanchefleur said, as if talking to the flames, "Do you know why Mogul read the book to Richard and Fatty? Why not simply book a flight to Mongolia and deliver the Sulde?"

After a few seconds in silence Marco tried to answer, "It is a difficult question which we have all asked ourselves, I am sure of it. The first answer that comes to my mind is this: the fact that we are here all together tonight is a result of what he did. Perhaps he saw it as the only way forward but the truth remains unfathomable . . . . All these things had to happen and by doing it, he could hide the fact the real and only Sulde was him, not those blades of steel," answered Marco.

Aldo nodded, "I agree with Marco. Our union is a gift from Heaven, not only a gift from Mogul. . .but now let's go to sleep. We need to wake up after a few hours."

IV

Altai Tavan Bogd, Mongolia:
Thursday, January 15, 2015. 5:00 a.m.

Well before sunrise, six lamas reached their place. With them was a young novice, about fourteen years old. They were lamas known as *rogyapa*, specialists in the dissection and disposal of human corpses. They spoke freely with Sarangerel, mentioning they had traveled twelve hours - starting from their lamasery at Hovd - following orders received from Mongolia's highest religious authority. Since that place had been transformed into a national park, the kind of ceremony they were going to perform was banned; for Mogul, an exception had been made. The place where they were heading was not far, and the lamas assured them that over there, vultures were abundant.

The lamas loaded Mogul's body, reduced to a large rucksack, on their shoulders and departed, taking a narrow path in the icy forest still immersed in the dark shadows of the night. After an hour's walk, they reached a rocky plateau that looked like a large natural altar. The head lama politely asked Marco and Aldo not to shoot any photographs or film and to sit quietly over a rocky spike one hundred meters further up on the mountain. While exchanging funny jokes and stories, they brewed some tea, lighting a fire with juniper wood under a copper pan. When the water reached boiling point, they threw inside some fermented tea, yak's butter, and salt.

High above their heads they saw the first vultures circling. Two of them came down, landing on trees and emitting piercing cries.

All over Asia vultures are considered sacred animals, just as in Egypt at the time of the Pharaohs they were considered the goddess Isis' messengers. Mongols believe when a vulture dies he ascends towards the sun until the heat and strong winds destroy his body; convinced of the vulture's gentleness because, contrary to hawks' and eagles' habits, they do not kill living creatures, rather dispose of the mortal remains of animals which died a natural death. While they are flying at high altitude, they can spot an animal approaching his final hour with their sharp eyes. They glide down and wait patiently until it passes away. One legend has it that before devouring a dead body, the vulture beats on it with its beak three times, as a kind of blessing and to make sure the animal is indeed dead.

At around eight o'clock the sun fully illuminated the rocky altar. That was the signal they were awaiting. The eldest lama wore a white apron and headgear, similar to a surgeon's hat. With a long curved knife - like the one we see in the hand of the goddess Kali - he cut the ropes that bound the body of Mogul, then he stretched him face down, straightening the backbone while pushing down with his feet. He cut the garments and sank the blade into the hardened flesh, carving out the center of his back. He started from the left scapula then slit pieces of skin and flesh. Shreds were elaborately cut following a swastika-shaped pattern, a favorable Buddhist symbol signifying eternity. They continued to exchange jokes and laugh while working, like some jolly woodcutters up in the mountains on a logging expedition. This is something which should not be seen as a lack of respect for the deceased but rather as a sign of their belief in reincarnation.

Everything was done speedily and with a cheerful mood. They severed Mogul's left arm and threw it among other shreds they had already prepared. They threw the left foot to the boy who by not catching it made everybody laugh, while the chief lama was busy breaking all the bones into small fragments with a hammer, then mixing them with *tsampa*, barley flour, adding tea leaves and yak butter to make them tastier. They also made some meatballs using the flesh hiding inside the splinters of the bones and tendons as if they were dumplings. Everyone was entrusted with his own task and was carrying it out with great diligence. Two lamas concentrated on the large bones, breaking them with heavy hammers. They were working quickly and efficiently, like a well-trained team. They began with the right side of Mogul's back and in little time with great efficiency, Mogul's body was taken apart. Meanwhile vultures were taking off from the trees and circling, in a rather excited fashion, above their heads. Some blows with a scalpel and hammer were clearly heard when they separated the ribs and opened the chest cavity.

Mogul's heart was torn out by the chief lama who held it high towards the sky for a few seconds and then threw it to the boy who this time caught it and cut it into tiny slices. The lamas removed the stomach and the intestines and put them aside. Those were the best parts, but the birds had to earn them by eating the hard bits first. Finally, with a clean blow, they detached Mogul's head.

A crying Blanchefleur braced Marco, turning away not to see. Again, his head was held high and passed to another lama, an image reminiscent of a painting of Salomé and Saint John the Baptist. They picked up a large stone and with that split Mogul's skull apart. The brain was removed and put together with the intestines while the hammering to crumble the bony parts continued until the hard work was completed. Then they again prepared some tea and removed their filthy aprons. All the lamas sat down to drink, still looking very cheerful. A flock of vultures, probably made up of elders, glided down like a reconnaissance mission and landed on the edge of the small plateau. Once on the ground, their size and shape could be measured. They were magnificent birds in their splendid livery, their necks and legs covered by white feathers. A pair of them, the most daring, tried to steal some slices from the hands of the boy but were chased away.

When all was ready, the head lama gave the signal, almost as if he was speaking the language of the birds. He screamed at the top of his voice, *triu, soi, triu*!

On hearing that, several vultures took off from the trees and flew above them, gliding majestically on the rocks and hurling themselves at their food. The lamas stayed aside and left the birds to complete their meal of dumplings containing the hard parts. The place was by then covered with vultures, and after about twenty minutes, the sack containing the soft parts was also opened and the contents thrown to the birds, who devoured them rapidly. At the very end a couple of eagles joined the party and finally some ravens and sparrows, which consumed the tiniest fragments.

Marco looked at his watch, eleven o'clock. The last wish of Mogul was fulfilled and his mortal remains returned to nature according to Mongol tradition.

Marco, Aldo, and Blanchefleur had their eyes full of tears, but not Sarangerel, who was used to these acts of extreme mercy. She stood up with a solemn air, wanting to intone an ancient farewell song she learned from her mother and thought capable of easing the soul's path in death. An icy wind blew, rushing down from the snow-covered peaks and carrying with it a fragrant scent of incense from the pine trees. A stronger rush of air moved her long black hair, like the mane of a galloping horse. She began to sing in the traditional Mongol way, the *hoomii*, keeping her voice inside the chest, with her diaphragm vibrating like a musical instrument:

Your breath has ceased.
You skin is cold.
Don't be afraid,
All before you have died.
Leave behind all that you possess and love,
You cannot remain.
You will go where the winds do not blow.
Like a baby getting out of the mother's bosom,
Leave behind pain and suffering.
This is death.

THE END

About the Author

Angelo Paratico is an Italian writer, novelist and historian. He studied Chemistry, Classic History and Literature in Milan, then in 1983 moved in Hong Kong, where he is currently living with his wife, Donatella, while taking an active role in the local community. Angelo freelances for several newspapers, blogs and magazines in Italy and Hong Kong. He is a frequent guest speaker at the radio program *Morning Brew* hosted by Phil Whelan, airing weekdays on RTHK3.